THE BOAT HOUSE

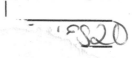

Recent Titles by Pamela Oldfield from Severn House

The Heron Saga
BETROTHED
THE GILDED LAND
LOWERING SKIES
THE BRIGHT DAWNING

ALL OUR TOMORROWS
EARLY ONE MORNING
RIDING THE STORM

CHANGING FORTUNES
NEW BEGINNINGS
MATTERS OF TRUST

DANGEROUS SECRETS
INTRICATE LIAISONS
TURNING LEAVES

HENRY'S WOMEN
SUMMER LIGHTNING
JACK'S SHADOW
FULL CIRCLE
LOVING AND LOSING
FATEFUL VOYAGE
THE LONGEST ROAD
THE FAIRFAX LEGACY
TRUTH WILL OUT
THE BIRTHDAY PRESENT
THE BOAT HOUSE

THE BOAT HOUSE

Pamela Oldfield

severn House

This first world edition published 2010
in Great Britain and in the USA by
SEVERN HOUSE PUBLISHERS LTD of
9–15 High Street, Sutton, Surrey, England, SM1 1DF.
Trade paperback edition first published
in Great Britain and the USA 2011 by
SEVERN HOUSE PUBLISHERS LTD.

British Library Cataloguing in Publication Data

Oldfield, Pamela.
  The Boat House.
  1. Governesses–England–Henley-on-Thames–Fiction.
  2. Family secrets–Fiction. 3. Detective and mystery
  stories.
  I. Title
  823.9'14-dc22

ISBN-13: 978-0-7278-6914-2   (cased)
ISBN-13: 978-1-84751-261-1   (trade paper)

Except where actual historical events and characters are being
described for the storyline of this novel, all situations in this
publication are fictitious and any resemblance to living persons
is purely coincidental.

All Severn House titles are printed on acid-free paper.

Severn House Publishers support The Forest Stewardship Council [FSC],
the leading international forest certification organisation. All our titles that
are printed on Greenpeace-approved FSC-certified paper carry the FSC logo.

ONE

' I t's the man,' said Emmie. 'The man in the garden.'

Marianne frowned at the girl's picture, carefully drawn in pencil and coloured in with crayons. 'Which man in the garden? Do you mean Mr Blunt who does the gardening?'

'No! The man last night. The ghost.'

Her twin, Edie, nodded and held up her own picture. 'We saw him in the garden. I didn't want to look at him so I shut my eyes.'

Marianne, their governess, stared from one picture to the other. They were eerily similar but that, she knew, was because Edie copied her sister whenever possible. Marianne had learned from the children's grandmother that eight-year-old Emmeline had been born six minutes before Edith and had taken the lead ever since.

She studied the pictures, which showed a tall thin man walking past a low building. There were tufts of grass, trees, four rose bushes complete with thorns and a large circle in the sky which she took to be the sun.

'What is this?' she asked, pointing to the building. 'Is this the house where we live?' It hardly seemed likely as the Matlowes lived in some splendour in The Poplars – a six-bedroomed, three-storey house near Henley, on the Buckinghamshire bank of the Thames.

'No. It's the boat house,' said Emmie patiently, in a tone which suggested that it was surely obvious. 'We don't have a boat any more, though, because Grandmother doesn't like them.'

Edie added, 'And that's the moon.'

'I thought it was the sun.'

Two small heads shook blonde curls and Emmie explained. 'It was night-time.'

'But you are both asleep when the moon comes up.'

'Last night I woke up with a tummy ache,' said Emmie, 'and then we looked out of the window and saw him. I think it was the ghost.'

Edie shuddered. 'Don't say that! It wasn't the ghost. I don't like ghosts. Cook said there aren't any ghosts.'

'Grandmama says there are, so there!'

Marianne held up both hands. 'Now wait a moment, girls. If your grandmother says there are ghosts . . . I expect she was joking.'

She met two withering stares. Emmie said, 'There's a ghost in the boat house and that's why we mustn't go down there – ever! Nobody must go down there. Because it's haunted.'

Edie nodded, her expression solemn. 'And that's why we don't want to play in the garden – because he might see us and come out of the boat house.'

As a newly employed governess, Marianne felt unable to argue the point any longer but she made up her mind to speak with her employer at the first opportunity. Better still, she thought on reflection, she would ask the kitchen staff if they knew anything about a ghost. In her short six weeks in the household she had quickly learned that very little that happened was missed by the staff. Maybe Mrs Matlowe had invented the story of the ghost to prevent the children from venturing too close to the end of the garden which ended where the Thames flowed past, deep and fast, past Henley on its way to the sea.

The Poplars was an elegant house with a large garden. At the end of it there was an old structure which Marianne had assumed was a summer house, but since her time with the children was mostly taken in the schoolroom, she had had no chance to explore further.

Now she glanced at the clock and saw that only ten minutes remained before they would stop for the midday meal. Changing the subject, she said, 'We have just time for some spelling.' Ignoring the groans, she went on. 'Please put your pictures away – no, you do not need your notebooks. You will spell the words aloud . . .'

Could there have been an intruder in the garden, she wondered, still faintly disturbed by the children's insistence that they had seen a man in the moonlit garden. The so-called 'nursery' where the girls slept looked out on to the lower part of the grounds where in summer, apparently, a makeshift tennis court had once been laid out.

'But that was when the young Mrs Matlowe was visiting,' Cook had told her. 'Neil's wife. She was very athletic, so we're told, although we never actually met her. The gardener says that the young Mrs Matlowe – that is, the twin's mother – thought croquet much too slow and preferred rushing about. They used to have friends round for tennis but not, of course, since . . . she left.'

The information had abruptly dried up at that moment, Marianne recalled with a slight frown. Odd, she thought. She was intrigued by the entire household, which she felt had a mournful air about it, but she had so far been told very little and had not been encouraged to ask any questions. The twins' widowed grandmother, Georgina Matlowe, appeared to have sole custody of the girls and had never referred to their parents in Marianne's hearing.

Now, pushing her thoughts aside, she started her impromptu spelling bee. 'All the words will be animals. Emmie, I want you to spell "horse" . . .'

Outside the nursery-cum-schoolroom, Georgina Matlowe stood with her ear close to the door. She was dressed all in black, which improved her somewhat dumpy figure – a choice which had been influenced by the recently deceased Queen Victoria. Her shoes were sensibly laced and she wore her hair severely drawn back into a bun at the nape of her neck. Her features had settled into grim lines, which hid the fact that she had once been quite handsome.

Now she was frowning. The governess's probationary period was over and Georgina had decided to extend her stay. Marianne Lefevre, twenty-four years old, seemed eminently suitable. She had a pleasant face and a good complexion but was not exactly a beauty, and Georgina understood that there was no admirer on the horizon – her occasional letters came from a friend by the name of Alice. The brother in India never bothered to write. Georgina had learned at the interview that Marianne had never been married and had recently nursed both parents through their last illnesses.

The governess, patient but firm with the twins, was half French and Georgina had recently decided that Marianne should teach the girls a little French. That would impress her own small circle of friends, Georgina reflected with satisfaction. Living near Henley meant that social standing was important and the chance to 'score points' must never be missed. That frightful woman Marjory Broughton rarely missed the chance to mention her son who was at Eton, or a nephew who had just been accepted at Oxford, *but* had either of these young paragons been taught French at the age of eight? Georgina did not think so!

Nodding to herself, she pressed her ear closer to the door.

'Now it's your turn, Edie,' she heard the governess say. 'Your word is "gorilla".'

There was a pause, then Emmie prompted her sister. 'G, o . . .'

Marianne said quickly, 'Don't help her, Emmie. Edie can do it without help.'

'G, o, r, i, l, a.' There was a note of triumph in Edie's voice and her grandmother frowned.

'Nearly right,' Marianne told her. 'Gorilla has two "l"s in it but it was a good try.'

Georgina frowned. Not good enough, she thought, but she acknowledged that Edie would never be as clever as her twin. Emmeline took after Neil, Georgina's son. After her firstborn arrived, she had considered childbirth entirely too hazardous and Neil grew up as an only child. But he was clever and had once had a great future ahead of him – a future that had been snatched away from him. Her expression hardened abruptly as a host of unwelcome memories flooded in. Forcing them aside she concentrated on Neil's young twins. Emmeline, bright and forthcoming, took after him. Poor little Edie, so like her twin physically, had obviously taken after her ghastly mother, Leonora, in the intelligence department. 'All froth and no substance' was the damning phrase Georgina had used to sum up her daughter-in-law.

Georgina shook her head and moved on along the passage. If only Neil had never met the woman – how different all their lives would have been. He could have married anyone, she reflected bitterly. The women were available and willing, but in a sudden rush of blood to the brain Neil had fallen for an American adventuress. A terrible mistake. Leonora was beautiful, of course, and no doubt exciting, in a frivolous way, but totally wrong for an Englishman of Neil's calibre. Not that he would ever have admitted it, not even after she had apparently abandoned husband and family.

Georgina sighed. Her son was convinced that Leonora had returned to her family in Virginia in America and had wanted to rush after her but Georgina, afraid to lose her son, had tried to persuade him to stay with the twins ... But enough of those dreadful memories. She must not torment herself.

Georgina moved on along the passage and ended up in her bedroom. Sinking into a chair, she put a hand to her aching head. Nothing unusual there. She suffered from frequent headaches and the doctors could not help. Not that she expected them to. They were unaware of the particular strains and stresses of her life and, *had* they been aware, they would still have been helpless to improve her condition. The past was unalterable and Georgina knew she had no choice but to live through her remaining years without relief.

Next morning dawned cloudy and cool but Marianne came to a sudden decision – she would take the children down into the garden, warmly dressed, and, if challenged by her employer, would pretend innocence of the 'ban' and insist that they were studying nature. She would, hopefully, put an end to the nonsense about ghosts. She hustled the children into suitable clothes and set off downstairs and through the kitchen.

It was a large semi-basement room with large deep

windows and whitewashed walls. The latter were home to various kitchen utensils – copper pans of different sizes hung from hooks, pottery ware resided on wooden shelves, a large stove kept the kettle on the boil and crockery and cutlery lived in a vast dresser. A small ice house was visible through the rear window and a variety of aprons and outdoor coats hung behind the door. But the feature that most amused Marianne was the row of bells relating to each room in the house, which were used to summon Lorna, the maid.

Cook was sitting at the large scrubbed table, preparing a shopping list, and Lorna was up to her elbows in soapy water, washing up the breakfast things. They glanced up as Marianne entered after a polite knock at the kitchen door.

Marianne smiled. 'So sorry to interrupt you but I thought the twins would like to enjoy the garden for half an hour.' She moved towards the door that led into the garden but not before she caught a quick glance that passed between cook and maid.

'That'll be nice,' Lorna said dubiously.

The cook looked up from her list. 'Does Madam know you're taking them outside?'

Marianne regarded her innocently. 'Does she need to know?'

Before there was time for an answer Emmie said eagerly, 'We're going to find some leaves and stick them in a book . . .'

'And write down the names – like oak leaf or rose bush.'

'It's called nature study,' Emmie continued. 'We're going to learn about the life around us, birds and butterflies and flowers and things.'

Lorna said, 'You'd best keep away from the boat house then, because that's haunted. Leastways that's what Madam would have us believe and we—'

'Hold your tongue, you silly girl!' Cook told her. 'It's none of our business what they do.'

'Sorry I'm sure!' Lorna tossed her head. 'I was only saying . . .'

'Then don't! Get on with your work.' Turning to the twins, Cook smiled. 'You go on out with Marianne and look for your leaves. The sun'll do you good.'

Emmie said, 'If we see the ghost, Miss Lefevre will take good care of us. She's going to shoo him away!'

The two girls giggled at this idea.

Cook said, 'I'm sure she will, Emmie.'

Edie said, 'We saw him and he looked very sad, didn't he, Emmie?'

Turning from the sink, Lorna said, 'That's because ghosts can't find any rest and they . . .'

'Lorna! What did I tell you!'

Cook glared at her and Marianne decided it was time to go. She hurried the girls through the doorway and watched them scamper off in the direction of the lawn. 'I had no idea I should ask permission,' she said.

Cook looked uncomfortable. 'It's nothing really, just something that happened in the past. When the girls were babies. We're not supposed to discuss it. Not that we know much, because we weren't here then.'

'Then I won't ask you about it.' With a smile Marianne followed the twins out on to the lawn and together they headed for the shrubbery and then to the ancient oak tree in search of leaves.

While the girls selected the best specimens Marianne took stock of the larger garden – lawn surrounded by shrubs, a small rose garden, a few fruit trees and a vegetable garden. At the far end of the garden the boat house stood neglected and apparently unloved. It resembled a large summer house and was built entirely of wood with carved decorations over the door and windows. One of the glass windows was cracked and, even from a distance, it had obviously suffered from the weather, for the wood was warped in places and the steps up to the door looked rotten.

Marianne imagined the boat inside the little house. Presumably that, too, was no longer in use. Beyond it, hidden by hedges, the river flowed past.

Henley Regatta! That must take place not far from here, she thought, her interest quickening. Former inhabitants of the house must surely have joined the hundreds of boats that were punted or rowed up and down the river during the annual regatta. How could anyone live so near to one of England's most glorious summer events and not take part? Not that she could imagine her employer enjoying herself. So far Mrs Matlowe had proved dour and tight-laced – rather forbidding in fact – but in her younger days she might well have shared in the excitement.

Marianne wandered through the garden, keeping a close eye on her two young charges, but her thoughts remained with her employer. Georgina Matlowe might have been an attractive woman, she reflected, although her looks were spoiled now by her severe expression. Her face, though lacking any artificial colour, was healthy looking and she had no need for spectacles. So how old was she? Marianne wondered. Old enough to have grandchildren, obviously. Maybe forty-five.

'Excuse me! Miss Lefevre!'

Glancing up, she saw that their next-door neighbour was waving from the other side of the hedge, and that the twins were rushing towards her with cries of delight.

Emmie turned to Marianne. 'It's Mrs Brannigan. She makes lovely fudge and she gives us a box every Christmas.'

Mrs Brannigan was surprisingly thin for a woman who made fudge but she was smiling at Marianne. 'It's our little secret,' she said. 'Now and then I give the girls a piece of fudge.'

Both girls cast anxious looks in Marianne's direction and then studied the house with narrowed eyes.

Having checked the windows, Emmie said, 'No one's watching!'

'May I?' Mrs Brannigan held out a plate with three generous cubes of fudge. 'Orange with walnuts!' she whispered.

'Of course. How kind of you.'

Marianne took one and the girls helped themselves and thanked Mrs Brannigan.

'You're welcome, my dears.' She turned to Marianne. 'Such polite children. Beautiful manners.'

The twins hurried away to sit together on one of the garden seats.

The neighbour smiled. 'They always do that. They sit there

nibbling away like two little mice, to make it last.' She rolled her eyes. 'Their grandmother doesn't like them to eat too many sweets and I do understand but one piece each now and then won't harm them.'

'Your secret is safe with me. It's delicious.'

They both laughed.

'To be honest,' Mrs Brannigan confessed, 'I thought it a good excuse to get to know you. My husband thought it rather forward of me but there . . .'

'Not at all.'

'The twins are charming and I'm sure you will enjoy working with them. And we do miss the children who used to come into our sweet shop before we retired, clutching their pennies in hot little hands, wide-eyed with excitement.' She gave a slight shrug. 'We never did have any children of our own. It wasn't God's will, apparently.'

'A sweet shop!' Marianne smiled. 'Isn't that every child's dream? I remember wanting to own a sweet shop. My brother wanted to be an engine-driver, of course. Not that he did. He worked for the railway as an inspector – visiting various towns and making checks on the administration. Hardly exciting work but some years ago he was sent out to India as some kind of supervisor.'

It seemed that her words were falling on deaf ears, however, as her neighbour, a wistful look on her face, continued. 'We bought in some of the sweets – the barley sugar and the pear drops, the gobstoppers, sugar mice and liquorice strips, but we made toffee apples and coconut ice and . . .' She tucked back a lock of grey hair and sighed. 'Now it's no more than a hobby.'

Suddenly Marianne saw a chance and took it. 'The twins insist there is a ghost in the garden – a male ghost that lives in the boat house. I expect they've told you about it.'

Surprised by the change of direction, the older woman frowned. 'Yes, they do mention it from time to time . . . It's odd, though, you know, because once I thought I glimpsed someone down there but I wasn't sure. My husband says I must be psychic! I hope I'm not, I told him. I'd rather think it was a prowler.'

'A prowler? Oh dear!'

'Oh, it's nothing to worry about, my dear. People climb up the bank from the river, you see. We do occasionally have a small robbery but not recently. We've all got very secure locks on all the doors, as you can imagine. A prowler – that's what they saw, I expect. A would-be burglar! Flesh and blood. Nothing eerie.'

'Do they ever use the boat house – the Matlowes, I mean? Do they have a boat? I'm thinking that, being Henley and so near the site of the Royal Regatta . . .'

'I'm told by your gardener that in the old days, when Mrs Matlowe's husband was alive, they had a punt and he used to take part, but they never have since we moved in. And their neighbours on the other side, the Barneses, who've been here much longer than we have . . .'

'I haven't met them.'

'He's a photographer. Anyway, his wife said that Mrs Matlowe is scared of water so she was never involved. And her son's no longer around, of course. Such a tragedy. And we don't really know Mrs Matlowe.' She leaned forward confidingly. 'I think she thinks of us as "trade" because of the shop we owned.' Her tone had changed slightly. 'Our house here was left to my husband by his parents six years ago and we do rather rattle around in it. Still, you can't look a gift horse in the mouth, can you?'

'Certainly not.' Marianne hesitated, wondering whether she dare ask further questions or whether she had gone far enough already. There would no doubt be other occasions when they would talk, and there were the kitchen staff. Marianne had not questioned them yet.

Excusing herself from the conversation, she went across to the girls who had finished their fudge and were now awaiting instructions.

'Choose three leaves each,' Marianne told them, 'and we'll take them inside and look them up in a book and then we'll know the names of the trees.'

They nodded dutifully but Emmie said, 'May we go down to the end of the garden? There are some lovely big trees down there – right next to the boat house.'

Edie added, 'But only if you come with us in case we see the ghost man.'

'Yes, of course I'll come with you.'

Edie promptly took hold of her hand but Emmie strolled ahead, trying to appear nonchalant. The sun shone, a blackbird foraged among last year's leaves in search of food, and to Marianne's discerning eyes there was not the slightest hint of danger.

While Emmie and Edie searched out their leaves Marianne went carefully up the decaying steps of the boat house and tried to look inside through a panel of glass in the door. The years, however, had greened the glass and she could see very little of the interior. It was just possible to make out the dim outline of what she assumed was an old punt, which rested upon the water, tilted slightly to one side. Or was it shadows and a trick of the light? Perhaps her imagination was working overtime. Beyond it Marianne saw the outer gates. Presumably the gates would have opened to allow the punt access to the river itself.

'Please, Marianne, I've found three leaves.'

'So have I!'

'That was quick!' Marianne stepped back feeling rather guilty. 'I was looking into the boat house,' she said unnecessarily. 'But it's dark and empty. Your grandmother is right – there's nothing to see so it's best that you stay away.'

'Empty?' Emmie challenged. 'But there must be a boat because it's a boat house.'

'Too dark to see anything,' Marianne lied, feeling even more guilty. 'And there was no ghost! Now let me see the time . . .' She consulted the small pendant watch which she wore round her neck. 'We have half an hour before Hattie comes, so let's hurry back to the schoolroom.'

Hattie, a fifteen-year-old girl who lived nearby, came in three afternoons each week to take the twins for a long walk – somewhere between an hour and an hour and a half, depending on which route she chose. Mrs Matlowe had explained that, since Marianne was not a nanny but a governess, she was entitled to an afternoon break. 'And a whole day is too long for the twins to be studying. It also gives you time to yourself.'

Marianne was grateful for her employer's consideration and, as they returned to the house, she put aside any doubts she might have and whispered, 'Be thankful for small mercies, Marianne!'

During the afternoon, while the twins were out with Hattie, Marianne was summoned to the study to be told that her probationary period of six weeks had now ended. She stood dutifully silent before the large desk as Mrs Matlowe reminded her of her duties, her revised salary, and her set hours of work.

'I should also be pleased if you could introduce a few French words into the twins' vocabulary,' she told Marianne. 'Nothing too complicated but enough to familiarize them to the idea of other languages.'

'That will be no problem, Mrs Matlowe.'

'Good. So, Marianne, do you understand everything? If not please say so now.'

Marianne hesitated but then decided that this was her chance to improve the children's lot. 'I am a very keen naturalist,' she said, 'and I would like to include a nature walk once a week as well as occasional forays into the garden. I do hope that is acceptable.'

Mrs Matlowe frowned. 'A nature walk to where, may I ask?'

'To the park, perhaps, or along the river bank.'

'The river bank? I don't know . . .' She looked alarmed, Marianne thought. 'I don't like the girls to get too close to water, Miss Lefevre. I associate it with danger. I always have. Drowning . . .' She shuddered. 'And especially so now, after what happened last month to the *Titanic*. Fifteen hundred souls lost! Too horrible for words.'

'It was terrible, I agree, but the riverside walk is quite safe. I will always keep my eye on them. And I swim.'

'You do?' Mrs Matlowe made no attempt to hide her surprise.

'My father was a great swimmer. He insisted that I learn

and taught me how to save someone who might be in difficulty. The twins would be quite safe with me, Mrs Matlowe.'
She crossed her fingers.

'We–ell . . . I daresay it would be possible. As long as
these are short walks so the children are not tired. The main
thrust of their education must be arithmetic and clear hand-
writing . . . and reading, naturally, and learning poetry by
heart. The latter is good for their memories. I still recall a
great many poems from my childhood.'

'I understand.'

'And bible study. I set great store by a familiarity with
the normal bible stories. They go to Sunday School, as you
know, with Hattie. And then there are the prayers they must
learn. I expect them to thrive in an atmosphere devoted to
the church and its teachings.'

'I understand.' Marianne glanced down at the large desk
behind which her employer was sitting. There was a large
leatherbound diary, a bible and a hymn book, an illustrated
book of prayers as well as a framed picture of Jesus on the
cross.

Seeing her glance, Mrs Matlowe said, 'I like to think of
this house as a place of reverence and to that end I have
been meaning to ask – to insist, in fact – that you should
wear less colourful clothes. As you may have observed, I
am always in black, and I would prefer you to wear black,
brown or dark grey.'

'Oh!' Marianne tried to hide her surprise.

Her employer stiffened. 'This is a God-fearing household. The twins have endured a very sad and tumultuous
start to their lives but thankfully that is all in the past. It
is my duty to ensure that from now on they lead sober,
respectful lives.' She gave Marianne a thin smile.

'I have very few dark clothes, Mrs Matlowe, but a suit
in mid blue . . .'

'Mid blue? Well, that will do for now. I shall give you
a small grant to buy something suitable.' She gathered up
a few papers. 'That is all.'

Marianne made her escape with mixed feelings. She
had secured a permanent post, which was a relief, but it

promised to be something of a mixed blessing. The accent on religion dismayed her and she had never felt at her best in sombre clothes, but, since her employer felt so strongly on the subject and would give her some money towards a new outfit, she decided she must make the best of it.

Feeling somewhat subdued by the interview, Marianne made her way to the kitchen, where she had been told by the cook that she was always welcome to a cup of tea. She found the cook at the back door, arguing with the butcher's boy over the recent delivery, while Lorna refilled the cruets with salt and pepper.

The latter looked up enquiringly. 'So are you staying on? The last one was sent on her way without a reference! Madam took against her. Lord knows why!'

While she talked she fetched cup and saucer and poured a cup of tea for Marianne. 'We've only got digestives left in the tin,' she apologized, pushing it across the table. 'Mr Blunt has eaten the rest. He reckons gardening gives him an appetite.'

Marianne nibbled obediently while she explained the main details of her interview. 'So I'm to have some darker clothes!'

'And did she go on about being God-fearing and all that? I feel for the twins. As if they haven't had enough bad luck with their mother running off like that . . .'

In the background Cook was saying firmly, 'So, Billy Brice, you can ride back and tell Mr Bray I want the sausages I ordered and I want them now. How am I supposed to make toad-in-the-hole without sausages? Now get along!' She turned back and sat down heavily at the table.

Lorna said, 'I could go out and catch you a few toads!'

Marianne smiled but the cook groaned. 'Is that your only joke, Lorna?'

'No! I know one about Rosemary Lane but it's a bit rude.' She winked at Marianne and poured a third cup of tea.

Marianne finished her biscuit. 'What exactly did happen to the twins' parents?'

Cook leaned forward and so did Lorna. 'That's the thing – nobody really knows. It was soon after they were born and we weren't here then but Mrs Brannigan next door says they were told by someone who *was* around at the time that the twins' father – that's Mrs Matlowe's son – came home from America with a beautiful bride – Leonora her name was – who was already in the family way and Mrs Matlowe was furious!'

Lorna nodded eagerly as the cook paused for breath. 'And they all quarrelled all the time and then the twins were born and soon after the wife ran away. Just disappeared!'

Cook, robbed of the most exciting part of the story said, 'You'd better get upstairs, Lorna, and air the beds. You're not paid to chatter!'

It was Lorna's turn to groan but she obeyed reluctantly, departing with a heavy sigh and rolling eyes.

'And didn't the wife come back?'

'No. Never set foot in the place again. They reckoned she'd gone back to America. Everyone expected her to sue for divorce – or for him to sue for divorce – or something. But then the son and Mrs Matlowe went on quarrelling and suddenly . . .' She glanced towards the door to the passage and lowered her voice. 'The police started to suspect foul play and came round to question the son and when he also went off . . .' She rolled her eyes. 'No one knew what to make of it.'

'And did they catch him – the son, I mean?'

'No. Everyone round here waited for news but nothing happened. The police gave up eventually.' She shrugged plump shoulders. 'It's what they call an unsolved case.'

Marianne stared at her, deep in thought, as she considered the ramifications of the story. 'So . . . what do the children think about their parents? What have they been told?'

'They've been told not to ask questions! You ask them – they don't know anything.'

'How dreadful for them.'

'In a way, yes, but then just as dreadful if they knew the truth – that their mother abandoned them and so did their father.' She glanced at the clock on the wall and tutted impatiently. 'Just wait 'til I get my hands on that butcher! It's not the first time he's messed me about with the order. If it happens again I shall speak to Madam about him.'

She heaved herself to her feet and went to the back door, but at that moment the twins appeared with Hattie who cried, 'Bye, twinnies!' and held out her hand for her payment. The cook took the money from a jar on the nearest shelf, thanked her and sent her off.

TWO

Marianne took the children upstairs where they hurled off coats and gloves and struggled with the buttons on their leggings, each child vying for Marianne's help.

'It was very windy,' Emmie told her. 'We were nearly blown away.'

'Hattie says we mustn't tell you something,' said Edie. 'But we could if you want us to.'

Emmie said, 'It's not something bad but nice. About a nice man who . . .'

The girls looked at each other, wondering if they dared.

To encourage them Marianne smiled. 'Something nice? You can tell me if you want to.'

Emmie said, 'He said it wasn't a secret. Not really and . . .'

'Hattie said we could and so she had one too.'

Then, as if it had been rehearsed, they said in chorus, 'The nice man bought us lollipops!'

Emmie said, 'Mine was raspberry and Edie's was . . .'

'I'll tell her mine!' Edie snapped. 'Mine was orange and Hattie's was lemon!'

Alarm bells rang in Marianne's mind even as she smiled. 'And this nice man – was he Hattie's friend? Was he Hattie's young man?'

The children giggled at her stupidity. 'Of course not,' said Edie. 'He was *old*!'

'He had a moustache . . .'

'And he asked us our names and where we lived and he winked at Hattie and made her laugh.'

Marianne was becoming rather concerned but told herself it was probably harmless. 'Perhaps he was Hattie's father,' she suggested.

Emmie shook her head. 'No, because he asked her what her name was.'

Marianne was trying to decide whether she should make Mrs Matlowe aware of the encounter but that would mean getting Hattie into trouble. But if she said nothing . . . She was well aware that unsavoury men were sometimes to be found in parks and playgrounds, preying on the vulnerable and unwary.

Edie said, 'I'm going to draw a picture of the three lollipops.' And she rushed for her sketchbook and coloured crayons.

Emmie said, 'He was waiting for his wife.'

'His wife? Ah!' Marianne felt much better. 'So he had a wife. Was she nice?'

'He didn't say but I expect so. I expect she was old, too.'

'Didn't you see her?'

'No. She didn't come. He said she was always late.' Emmie joined her sister at the table and Marianne decided she would speak to Hattie the next day and discover if there was anything to find out about the lollipop man.

The following morning Edward Barnes sat over his breakfast of eggs and bacon and toast while his wife Davina sipped a cup of Earl Grey tea and then cut up an apple into careful slices. She had recently discovered that indigestion was becoming a problem and had blamed the fried breakfast. Instead she now had fresh fruit and thin bread and butter and fancied that she felt *more comfortable on the inside*, as she chose to put it. Anything more graphic would be indelicate, she thought, having been carefully raised by a spinster aunt.

From their dining room they could see into Georgina Matlowe's garden where Lorna was hanging out three tea towels, pegging them on to the washing line in her usual unhurried way.

Davina said, 'I do think Mrs Matlowe should be told, Ted, about that chap the twins saw snooping around in the garden. Creeping around at night – he was obviously up to no good.'

Edward pushed the last triangle of toast around the plate to collect the last of the egg yolk. Waste not, want not – that was his excuse for his lower-class habits. He said, 'Don't look at me, dear. It's second- or third-hand information. The governess tells the Brannigans and Mrs B tells you and you tell me! Anyway, the last time I tried to tell that woman anything, she made it clear she considered me an interfering old fool.'

'Oh, Ted! She didn't say any such thing! You do exaggerate.'

'She may not have said it but she certainly implied as much.' He adopted Georgina's prim tone. '"Thank you, Mr Barnes, but we have everything under control."'

Davina shrugged, acknowledging the point he made. 'I suppose after the scandal the poor soul is desperate for privacy. The servants are forbidden to chat to anyone and she seems to have no real friends . . . and those poor twins! They must be lonely.'

'How can they be lonely – they have each other. They're *twins*, Davina.' He rolled his eyes. 'The new governess seems quite pleasant. Her six weeks must be up so we can presume she is being taken on permanently.'

Davina smiled. 'So you have noticed her. Attractive, isn't she? What my uncle used to call a "looker". I expect she has been told "No Followers"! I wonder what her status is – a childless widow, perhaps. Or a spinster who has been looking after an aged parent . . .'

'More to the point, what does she know about what happened? I can't imagine Mrs Matlowe being very frank about the children's history.'

Davina glanced at the rows of photographs on the piano. It was a very small sample of her husband's favourite images – Derby Day, Ascot, Cowes Regatta, and, of course, their own Henley Royal.

She smiled. Their own wedding photographs, taken by a local man, had long since been relegated to the back row but she let it pass. She knew how large a part professional photography played in her husband's life and she was immensely proud of him. However, one photograph in the front row, framed in ornate silver, and taken from a higher angle, was nothing to do with society events. It showed a vivacious young woman in what was obviously the Matlowes' garden. Slim, beautiful and fashionably dressed, she was holding two very young infants, one in each arm, and glancing up at her husband with a proud smile.

'I do wish that, wherever she is, the young Mrs Matlowe had a copy of that picture.' Davina sighed.

Edward sighed too. 'You never give up on that, do you?'

'I know I don't, but . . . wherever she is she must long for something to remember them by.'

He shrugged. 'I wasn't supposed to be taking photographs of them so how could I give her a copy? I couldn't explain it without admitting I was snooping! From a bedroom window. Not at all gentlemanly. We both know I made a mistake.'

'I know, dear, but Leonora Matlowe looked so wonderfully happy then – before it all turned sour.'

'She ran off, Davina, and left them, so I don't know why you persist in thinking she misses them.'

'She probably ran off because the children's grandmother hated her and made no secret of it. A beautiful woman and an American at that . . . Mrs Matlowe was jealous of her daughter-in-law.'

'She should have been pleased for her son.'

'Well, she wasn't. It was all a dreadful shock for her. Fancy missing your own son's wedding! A second cup of tea, dear?'

Edward shook his head, pushing his plate away. 'I could have made a mint of money out of that photograph if you hadn't made such a fuss. The police appealed for relevant images but there were none as good as that.'

'But then everyone would have known that you spied on them! What would our friends have thought?'

'It's what press photographers do, Davina,' he said irritably. 'It's what's known as a candid shot.' He pushed back his chair.

His wife jumped to her feet. 'Oh do stop, Ted. We've been over and over it. I just pray that the young couple found each other again somehow . . . somewhere.' She looked wistful. 'But then they would have come back for the twins, wouldn't they?'

'I know exactly what you want, Davina. You want the big reconciliation with the grandmother and the young people and beaming children . . . and all the trimmings! Probably an orchestra playing in the background! I'm afraid life isn't like that.' He shook his head. 'There can never be a happy ending, dear. The police suspected Neil of foul play – and him disappearing the way he did certainly makes him *look* guilty.'

'Poor Neil. He seemed such a nice young man. I can't imagine him doing anything bad. Certainly not killing the mother of his own children – a woman he obviously adored.'

'Mrs Matlowe probably drove him to it! You know my theory – that she drove a wedge between husband and wife. I blame her. Miserable old . . .'

'Ted! Watch your language, please!'

'Don't you start!' He gave her a peck on the cheek to show that it was meant in jest and headed for the door. 'I'll be in the dark room for twenty minutes or so.' At the door he glanced back. 'The regatta is going to be rather special this year, Davina, because of the royal visit. Do you want to come with me? I know you have rather lost interest over the years but it should be quite an event if the weather is decent.'

'I haven't lost interest but it's a bit lonely on my own. I know you have to be here, there and everywhere for your photographs but that leaves me with no one to talk to.'

He shrugged. 'Bring a friend with you.'

Davina brightened. 'What a good idea. I'll try and think of someone.'

'They are sure to put on a splendid show for the King and Queen.' He regarded her hopefully.

'I wonder if Princess Mary will come with them.'

'Anything's possible. Which day are they coming?'

'On the Saturday. I suppose they want to be there for the prizegiving and the end of regatta celebrations. Can we beat the opposition this year, do you think? First it was the Belgians and now the Australians!'

'We can try! So you'll come this year?'

'Probably. I'll ask Mary if she'll come with us. I'm sure she would if we could get tickets for the Enclosure – then we could watch from the Grandstand.' Davina crossed her fingers. This was a familiar argument.

He was already shaking his head. 'You know that's out of the question. The only people who get into either are the stewards, rowers, their families and invited guests. A very select group!'

'And photographers aren't select enough!' She grinned at him. 'Never mind, Ted. I'd still like to come with you. I might need a new hat, though!'

He laughed. 'I thought you'd say that!'

'And . . .?'

'A new hat? Why not!'

He had only been gone five minutes when someone rang the front door bell. The daily help was not due until ten o'clock so Davina hurried to answer it and found a man she vaguely recognized on the doorstep.

'Mrs Barnes?' He smiled. 'I wonder if you remember me?' He handed her a card.

Davina took it but she looked more closely at him and recognized him. One blue eye was slightly darker than the other. She tried to recall his name without referring to the card.

'Donald Watson!' she said and a smile of triumph spread over her face, lighting up her plain features.

'At your service!'

'Private Investigator *extraordinaire*!'

'Indeed.' He smiled at the compliment.

She had no idea what he could want but she opened the door to allow him to come in. 'My husband is in the dark room so I dare not interrupt him but we can have a cup of tea, if you'd like that, while we wait for him.'

He followed her into the lounge and Davina felt the first flutter of excitement. Was Mr Watson on another case? It was six or more years – maybe eight – since he had been involved with the Matlowes and although that had been a

harrowing business at the time, life had seemed rather tame
when it ended.

Without thinking, she asked, 'Have they found Mrs
Matlowe – Leonora, I mean? I still live in hope.'

'Not to my knowledge.' He opened the buttons of his
jacket and sat down.

Surely not the same grey suit, she thought, surprised. He
had become quite well-known at the time of the young
mother's disappearance and Davina would have expected
him to look a little more affluent by now.

As if reading her thoughts he grinned and at once looked
much younger. Not that she knew his age but she prided
herself on being able to make an informed guess and thought
thirty was quite likely.

He said, 'This is my "looking inconspicuous" suit. It doesn't
pay to look too upper class – no offence meant – when you
need to blend into the background. I look on this faithful old
suit as my private investigator's uniform!'

Flustered, she retreated and came back with a tray of
tea for one, explaining that they had only just finished
breakfast.

He glanced out of the French windows at the hedge that
separated the Barnes' garden from that of the Matlowes. 'It
doesn't seem long ago that we were all trying to make sense
of what happened next door.'

'And failing dismally!' Davina rolled her eyes. 'And here
you are again. I'm wondering why.' Receiving no reply,
she went on. 'So they really haven't found Leonora?'

'I do have news,' he said cautiously, 'but if you don't
mind I'll wait for your husband to join us and tell you both
at the same time. But how are things with you and the
neighbours? Everything peaceable?'

Needled that she was not going to learn anything before
Edward did, Davina smiled sweetly and took her time
pouring the tea. 'How many sugars? Two, isn't it?' She
handed him cup and saucer. 'Your mother keeping well? I
remember she had a nasty turn when you were last here.'

'I'm afraid she had another turn for the worse and she
died two years ago.'

'Oh, Mr Watson! I'm so sorry. A peaceful passing, I hope.'

He nodded. 'She died in her sleep without pain.'

'That's what we all hope for, Mr Watson.' Unable to wait any longer with her own news she said, 'We have a new governess next door. The previous one only lasted a few weeks. I'm hardly on speaking terms with Georgina Matlowe but that's just because she goes out of her way to avoid her neighbours.'

'So how did you hear about the governess?'

'I see Mrs Brannigan once a month at our sewing circle and she keeps me up to date. The children talk to her through the hedge.' She frowned. 'I must say that Georgina Matlowe has rather withdrawn from the rest of us. Dropped out of the ladies' luncheon group soon after it happened but still plays bridge . . . But the strangest thing is that she no longer attends church and she used to be a regular churchgoer, come rain or shine.'

He shrugged. 'Tragedy takes people in different ways,' he offered. 'I knew a young woman once who came home from work to find both her parents dead.'

'Good Lord! Had they been murdered?'

'No. The coroner's verdict was that the father collapsed and died of a heart attack and then the wife found him some time later and died of shock. But the daughter, poor soul, went into a convent for a few months and is still there years later.'

'Poor soul indeed. But I daresay she . . .' There were footsteps on the stairs. 'Ah, here comes Ted.'

As soon as Edward was seated, their visitor began. 'As you know I was engaged by Neil Matlowe's family when Leonora went missing, to try to discover her whereabouts, and this was during and after the police investigation. Neither of us found any clues. There was no sign of her in America, either, and at some stage everyone lost hope and the investigation was ended.'

Edward said, 'You all did your best. It was nearly three years before the police finally gave up on the case.'

Donald Watson nodded. 'No one is blaming anyone on

that score. But I have learned that something did come to light about eighteen months ago. The Prestons – that is Leonora's American family – discovered that Neil Matlowe had been found dead four years ago – killed in a car crash in Nebraska of all places.'

Husband and wife exchanged shocked glances.

She said, 'In a car crash? Oh, the poor man!' She turned to her husband. 'We liked Neil, didn't we, dear? Rather dominated by his mother, of course, but when he was offered the chance to go to America, he jumped at it – and met Leonora. He really wasn't the sort of person to die in a car crash!'

Her husband said, 'In Nebraska?'

Donald Watson nodded. 'It seemed he'd been living under an assumed name – with a woman named Bella Williams. She told the police that he had confessed to her that he was on the run because when he'd left England he was afraid he'd be framed for a murder he didn't commit . . .'

'Be framed?' Davina stared at him. 'By whom?'

Ignoring the interruption he went on. 'But Bella Williams didn't believe he was the sort to murder anyone and she never would believe it.'

There was a short silence.

Davina said, 'So he's dead! Has been for years. That's terrible!'

Her husband shook his head. 'We never thought there had been a murder. Never. This Bella woman was right. Neil Matlowe wasn't violent.'

'Quite the opposite!' said Davina. 'I thought him very nicely brought up. Good manners. Quietly spoken. A gentle soul. I think the vivacious Leonora must have been quite a tonic for him!'

Edward nodded. 'As you know, we understood that Leonora had run away after a series of rows with her mother-in-law. When he also left we didn't know what to think.'

Davina said, 'We supposed he had gone to find his wife who must have been quite distraught . . . But we told you all this at the time, Mr Watson. It must be in your reports.' She frowned. 'Do you think they'll ever find her?'

'I'm afraid not. I've been engaged to look again into what happened.'

'Look again? By whom?' Ted leaned forward in his chair.

'By Leonora's younger brother, Richard Preston. He was sixteen when it happened so now he must be about twenty-three.'

'Good Lord!' She looked at her husband. 'Did we know Leonora had a brother?'

'I don't think we did.'

Donald Watson continued. 'The Prestons never recovered from the loss of their daughter, apparently. The mother took to drink . . .'

Davina said, 'They often do!'

Edward turned to her. 'How would you know?'

Ignoring the reproof in his voice she said, 'I think I might do something like that. Desperate measures . . .'

'You don't know what you'd do!'

'I most assuredly wouldn't go into a convent!' she told him scathingly.

Hastily Donald Watson went on. 'The father, Arnold Preston, has developed a serious lung condition and the doctors aren't hopeful. The son wants to solve the mystery for his parents' sakes as well as for his own.'

After a thoughtful silence Edward said, 'So you're here in your official capacity as a private investigator to rake over the coals, so to speak, and hopefully turn up new clues.'

'Something like that.'

'I doubt if we can help you, Mr Watson, much as we'd like to.'

His wife nodded. 'The Brannigans might know something . . . or you could talk to the governess. Her name's Marianne something. French, I think. She looks French anyway – dark hair, brown eyes.'

'Lefevre,' said Edward. 'Marianne Lefevre. But she's new. She wouldn't know anything, would she? She probably doesn't even know what happened – although she must wonder where the twins' parents are.'

Donald Watson agreed, adding, 'I'd be grateful if you

would both keep your eyes and ears open for any bits of gossip or rumours. You know the drill from last time.' He glanced again at his watch.

Edward said slowly, 'So this time are we supposed to think there might have been foul play? A murder, even. Are the police involved again? Can we expect a visit from them?'

'Not at this early stage but if anything suspicious surfaces . . .'

Davina placed a hand over her heart and lowered her voice. 'You should talk to Mr Blunt, their gardener. He's been with the Matlowes for donkey's years. If anyone had to dig a grave, for instance . . .'

Her husband tutted. 'A grave? For heaven's sake, Davina! Your imagination is running away with you. All this poor brother wants is to find his sister – if she's still alive. Which no doubt she is . . . even though she might have remarried.'

'Which she can't because she's still Mrs Neil Matlowe!' Her tone was triumphant.

Donald Watson raised his eyebrows.

'Oh no! She isn't, is she!' she amended. 'Now that Neil has died in a car crash . . . She's a widow! If she knows he's dead, that is.' Seeing her husband's warning look she stumbled to a halt.

The private investigator stood up. 'It's all very confused, Mrs Barnes, but these are questions I hope to answer. My brief is not to solve a crime but to find Leonora Preston, wherever she is. I've warned young Mr Preston that after all this time I am not very hopeful. I don't want to give him false hope. I shall notify the police, naturally, before I start stomping all over their "patch", as they call it. Only courteous to let them know I'm snooping around again. But if I unearth anything suspicious I shall pass it on to them.'

Davina said, 'This younger brother – what is he like?'

Donald Watson shrugged. 'Very young and sounds somehow earnest. A slightly heroic cast, if you know what I mean. Determined to right a wrong. That sort of thing.'

Davina nodded. 'Riding to the rescue of his sister!'

'Exactly.'

They both got up to see him out.

Edward said, 'Let us know how things go, and if we can help, we will. Same telephone number, is it?'

'Yes.'

'No glamorous new office?'

'I fear not!'

Minutes later they stood together watching him walk away.

Davina's eyes had narrowed, her husband noted with a sinking heart. She said, 'Maybe it wasn't an accident – Neil's car crash, I mean. Maybe he killed his wife and the guilt drove him to suicide! He could have driven into something deliberately.'

'And pigs could fly, Davina!' He sighed loudly. 'Make us another pot of tea, dear – it will calm you down.'

Two days later, as Donald Watson waited at the reception desk in Henley's police station, Detective Sergeant Ackrow walked past, paused and turned back.

'Watson! Is that you?'

'It is indeed and I was just asking for you.'

The Detective Sergeant rolled his eyes. 'What have I done to deserve this unexpected pleasure?' Glancing at the clock on the wall he said, 'I'm due at a meeting in half an hour but I can spare you a few minutes if it's urgent.'

'It's urgent enough.'

'Come through here then.' He was a large man, large frame, large hands and feet and a large square face. His voice matched his size, and when he raised his voice, everyone sat up a little straighter. DS Ackrow led his visitor to a small room where they normally interrogated suspects. A gloomy room with sparse furniture and a single light bulb overhead from which dangled a sticky fly paper.

'It's about the Matlowe case,' Donald explained, as they sat down. 'And please spare me that look!'

'What look?'

'The one I recognize from seven years ago! There have been some new developments. I've had . . .'

'Why do I know I'm not going to be happy about

× mostly still gas lighting in 1912

whatever this is!' A look of resignation settled over the detective's face, making him look lugubrious.

'I've had contact with a young man named Richard Preston who is the—'

'Preston? That rings a bell!' He looked puzzled.

'The younger brother of Leonora Matlowe née Preston.' He watched the policeman's eyes light up with recognition. 'He's now twenty-three and wants to find his sister. He's been looking in America without any luck and now . . .'

DS Ackrow held up his hand imploringly. 'Haven't I got enough on my plate? There's a robbery, a suspected suicide beside Henley Bridge, a suspected arson at a timber mill on the other side of the town – a fireman died.'

'I heard. Poor blighter.'

'So if it's not important I'd rather not hear any more, Mr Watson.'

'He's not asking you to reopen the case. Richard Preston has engaged me to check out everything we did before and find anything new that might be significant.'

'What makes him so sure she's still alive? We began to suspect foul play, if you remember. Mrs Matlowe stirred up a can of worms but when we switched our attention to her son she changed her tune – and by then he'd taken off.'

'All I'm asking,' Donald said patiently, 'is to know whether or not there have been any developments or leads in the years between then and now that might warrant a follow up. He's coming to England – might even be here already for all I know – and will be hoping for something, if not much.'

The detective shrugged. 'When I have a moment I'll have a quick glance through the file and if I find anything worth passing on – which I doubt – you shall have it. Will that do?'

'Most certainly will. Thanks.'

'Just don't drag us into it unless it's something spectacular. We're pretty well up to here at the moment.' He held a hand up to his chin and stood up. 'You at the same address?'

'Yes.' He stood up also and reached for his hat.

The detective said, 'I'll send someone round tomorrow with anything I find.'

It wasn't much but Donald was satisfied. He'd worked with DS Ackrow and knew he was a man of his word. And so the search begins, he told himself with the familiar rush of adrenalin that he always experienced at the start of an investigation. The financial rewards of the work scarcely interested him, except as a way to pay the bills and keep the small business afloat. He loved his work and finding the solution to a problem was what he craved. The satisfaction of a job well done. As he stepped outside into the sunshine he was smiling.

The next morning Marianne was told she would have the day to herself.

'My sister telephoned late last night to invite the twins to a little party she is giving for the son of her housekeeper,' her employer explained with a trace of irritation in her voice. 'It seems the boy – Ivan or Ivor or some such name – has a birthday in a month's time but is likely to die before then.'

'Die?' Marianne gasped. 'How frightful!'

Mrs Matlowe shrugged. 'The child has gone downhill faster than expected, apparently . . . Oh it's nothing infectious or I wouldn't allow the girls to attend. Something he was born with – something unpronounceable to do with his brain.' She sighed. 'All a bit of a rush but Ida, my sister, is like that. Very impetuous. There will be two other children there – the son and daughter of a neighbour.'

'How very kind of your sister.'

Georgina rolled her eyes. 'She means well, I know, but she lives on her own in a ghastly service flat and expects me to trail over there to see her, which entails travelling by tram.' She sighed. 'I always come home with a severe headache.'

Marianne said, 'The twins will be thrilled. They don't mix with many children.'

'I hope that's not a criticism?'

'Certainly not. Just a comment.'

'I shall get away early by telling her the children have a strict routine and an early bedtime.'

'Shall I get the girls into their party frocks?'

'If you would – and tell them what's happening. We shall have to get off the tram somewhere and buy two gifts for the twins to give him.' She shook her head. 'I shall ask the shop assistant to wrap the presents. Oh dear! Everything at the last moment – that's my sister. Still . . .'

An hour later Marianne waved the three of them off as they set off for the tram stop. It was going to be quite an adventure for Emmie and Edie, she thought, pleased for them.

But what shall I do with *my* day? she wondered.

Lorna, however, had no such decisions to make. As soon as the front door had closed behind her mistress and the girls, she hurried from the kitchen in search of the governess, her eyes shining with excitement.

'Come on, Marianne,' she said. 'I've something to show you!' She held up a key.

'What is it?'

'You'll soon see! Follow me.' She led the way to the stairs and then rushed up them, leaving Marianne trailing a little behind her.

'You're like a mountain goat!' Marianne told her as they hurried along the first-floor landing and set off again up another flight of stairs. This was an area of the house Marianne had never had cause to explore as her own room was on the first floor next to the twins. 'More bedrooms?' she asked. 'Who uses them all? Does Mrs Matlowe ever entertain?'

'Almost never, although her sister came once or twice and Mrs Brannigan next door says they had quite a lot of visitors after her son married that American woman, Leonora.' She paused in the middle of the passage. 'Mrs Brannigan says that on Leonora's twenty-third birthday – when they'd only been here for about six weeks – they invited seven couples to a weekend house party but Mrs Matlowe disapproved and quarrelled with them over it. Neil insisted they go ahead – well, it was his wife's birthday after all – but his mother refused to stay. She would have nothing to do with it and went away to her sister's for the weekend!'

'You mean she left them to their own devices?'

'Yes! Left Leonora to plan it all, rearrange the bedrooms and everything. They even had to have caterers because Mrs Matlowe had given the cook and the maid the weekend off!' Her eyes were like saucers.

'That was rather a nasty snub!'

'A real snub!' They had reached a door. 'Here we are. Wait 'til you see this!' With a flourish Lorna turned the key in the lock. She flung open the door and ushered Marianne into the room.

'Good heavens!' Marianne stood aghast.

'We're not supposed to come in here – not ever. Not even to sweep or dust or anything but she doesn't know so how can it hurt?'

The room was in semi-darkness because the heavy black curtains were almost closed but as Marianne's eyes became accustomed to the gloom, she realized the room was some kind of shrine. Or else perhaps a private chapel.

Lorna threw her arms wide to embrace the entire room, as though she had personally created it. She eyed Marianne with triumph in her eyes. 'So – what do you make of it? Quite amazing! That's what me and Cook think.'

Lorna opened the curtains to give the room more light.

Marianne's shocked gaze took in the darkly striped wallpaper, the dark stained floorboards covered with dark rugs, and the chairs upholstered in black velvet.

Lorna pointed a dramatic finger. 'Look there. We think it's an altar. Cook says there's no two ways about it.'

It seemed to be made up of a rectangular table with a raised portion in the centre. A white cloth covered it entirely and hung down on all sides, and a glass vase of white silk roses stood at each end. In the middle, on the raised portion, there was a model of Jesus on the cross. It looked expensive, thought Marianne – carved wood, exquisitely painted and decorated with gold leaf. To the left and right of the statue was a black candle.

'But what is it in aid of?' she asked, puzzled.

'Her son Neil!' Lorna watched her expression with satisfaction. She crossed herself and said, 'God's honour and hope to die!'

'Good Lord!' Marianne felt a rush of pity for her employer. Mrs Matlowe, who seemed so confident, so *implacable*, was in fact vulnerable where her son was concerned.

'She started it as soon as he left the house and didn't come back. Then she heard that he was dead. Things started to be delivered and brought up here but she didn't allow us to see anything. And look at that!'

Marianne saw the hassock in front of the altar.

Lorna said, 'She embroidered that herself – it's got her son's initials on it. To kneel on.'

Marianne's shock was giving way to sympathy. She said, 'People deal with grief and loss in their own way. This must be hers. Losing your only child . . .' She shrugged. 'And in such dramatic circumstances. I don't know how I would deal with something like that. Poor woman.' She was struggling to reassess her opinion of Georgina Matlowe. Perhaps she had been too quick to judge her, she reflected guiltily. The claustrophobic room with its sombre undertones gave her pause for thought and she frowned. Was this room the early signs of paranoia? Had the events of Leonora's defection and her son's death turned her mind? She could imagine Mrs Matlowe on her knees before the altar, praying – her eyes closed, her hands clasped in prayer.

Lorna pointed again. 'Over there – all those photographs are of him – the son. Not one of Leonora and not one of the children. Cook thinks she's got a guilty conscience.'

'About what? She didn't send Leonora away, did she? Leonora walked out.'

'No, but Mrs Matlowe might have driven her away by hating her so much, thinking she was nothing but a gold-digger – as they call it in America. There were lots of quarrels. We think she was very jealous of her son. Maybe she hoped he would never marry but stay at home with her for ever.'

'Some men do, that's true.' Marianne tried to make sense of it all. Possibly the son had blamed his mother for Leonora's disappearance and could not forgive her. Then he went in search of his wife, assuming she may have gone to friends or even back home to America . . . but never did find her.

She sighed. 'All very sad. And the twins were orphaned . . . or were they? The father died, it's true, but where is their mother? It would be a shock if she suddenly turned up again to claim them.'

'I wish she would! Then they'd have a happier time than they do now.'

'But the girls aren't unhappy,' Marianne protested.

Lorna was staring at her. 'Would you want to live with a grandmother like Mrs Matlowe? Can't do this! Can't do that! Don't talk to the neighbours.' She dangled the key. 'We're not to stay up here too long, Cook says.'

Marianne nodded, giving the room a lingering look before preceding Lorna on to the landing. *Drew the curtains again?*

Halfway down the stairs Lorna said, 'The old nanny thought the children should go to school when they were five and mix with other children and she told Mrs Matlowe. She said it wasn't healthy for them to be shut away from other people. She was always on about what they did in America, so Mrs Brannigan says. She used to hear them arguing. Ivy something – that was her name. Ivy Busby! She may have been old but she wasn't afraid to speak her mind.'

'So did you ever meet her?'

'Yes. She came over with the family and was still looking after the twins when me and Cook were taken on. The story was that she'd been widowed three days after her wedding – Ivy Busby I mean, not Mrs Matlowe – and she became a nanny and never looked at another man. Isn't that romantic?'

'It's terribly sad,' said Marianne.

Lorna shrugged. 'Anyway she was nice enough, I suppose, but very outspoken. A bit doddery – Cook thought she must be nearing seventy – but then Mrs Matlowe gave her the sack for interfering and the poor old thing had nowhere to go.' She tossed her head indignantly.

'So no one knew what happened to her?'

Lorna nodded. 'Then eventually the first governess came and went and then you came.'

They stood at the foot of the stairs, finishing the conversation, until Cook called to ask if anyone wanted a cup of tea and a jam tart, and Lorna and Marianne hurried into the kitchen.

THREE

'Small but bijou' was how Donald Watson liked to describe his office, and to him and his secretary, Judith Jessop, it was a second home. They both spent more than half their lives among the crowded furniture, sagging shelves and overflowing filing cabinets. The frosted windows were rarely cleaned, the floor was hardly ever swept and the two desks were never tidied.

Judith Jessop told people that she and her employer saw to the cleaning of the office and that an office cleaner would muddle everything up and set back important investigations. Her maiden name was Judith Watson and she was, in fact, Donald's cousin. At twenty-four she was a few years his junior and recently married to Tom Jessop. The cousins were vaguely similar to look at – she had the same friendly open face and warm smile – but whereas Donald was what she called 'a plodder', she was full of nervous energy and inclined to be hasty.

'The stuff's arrived from the police station,' she called when he bowled into the office four days later, ten minutes after her own arrival. 'One of the lads brought it round first thing.' She tossed the slim package on to his desk and helped him off with his jacket. It was her philosophy that, simply because she was part of his family, it didn't mean she need not give him the kind of respect another secretary might give. It irked him a little to be fussed over but Judith insisted. 'I'm paid to be a secretary so I'll act like one,' was her frequent reply to his protests.

He picked up the package, tore it open and settled down in his chair to examine the contents. 'We have to come up with something new,' he told her for the third time. 'There has to be something we've overlooked. No one vanishes off the face of the earth without a good reason. Just one small clue, that's all I need . . .'

'You should have been born a bloodhound!'

'So you keep telling me!' He flicked through the pages which, hastily copied, had smeared in places but they were readable and he studied each sheet with concentration.

Judith set a cup of tea in front of him – strong and sweet the way he liked it. She teased him that that was the way he liked his women but, to her disappointment, he rarely seemed to last long with anyone, whatever they were like.

'Mrs Montini was in here yesterday, asking about her husband,' she told him.

'We have to tell her,' he said. 'Her husband's been dead these last eight weeks. She went to his funeral. How can we go on looking for him? She's mad as a hatter, that woman.'

'I know, but she likes to believe it's just a matter of time and maybe . . .' She shrugged. 'And the money's useful.'

'I don't deny that, Judith, but it's false pretences. Write to her today and ask her to settle the account – just a nominal sum because I haven't been looking for him. Run off a copy of the death certificate and send it with the letter.'

'I did that two weeks ago.'

'Send another one. Make it sound final. I'm going to be tied up with the Matlowe business again and I can't be sidetracked by Mrs Montini and her whims.' When he saw her expression he said, 'Do the letter!'

'Yes, Mr Watson!' She only called him this when she was piqued.

He sipped his tea, reading eagerly but without discovering anything worthwhile until two pages from the end of the police report.

'Judith, listen to this. Eight months after the disappearance, a body was found near here – close to the water's edge in an area near Phyllis Court and . . .'

'Phyllis Court? Should I know her?' Judith tossed her head so that her auburn hair fluttered in its newly cut bob. Her husband liked it but her cousin had so far failed to notice it.

'Don't be flippant!' He grinned across the desk at her. 'Near the area *where the Phyllis House stand is erected.*'

'Erected each year just for the regatta? Is that what we're talking about?'

'Exactly. The body of a young woman resembling Leonora Matlowe! Young, nice features and with blonde hair. The husband, Neil, had gone missing by then so they asked Georgina Matlowe if she would identify the body and she agreed.'

Judith stared at him, shocked. 'How is it we knew nothing about this?'

'I'm coming to that!' He read aloud from the notes. 'Mrs Matlowe immediately identified the body as that of her daughter-in-law and broke down in tears with the words: "Thank God this is over!"'

'So how did she die? And when?'

'Don't hurry me, Judith.'

'Sorry!' She rolled her eyes. 'Fools rush in! I know!'

He read on. *'The body was originally adjudged to be that of Leonora Matlowe until the post-mortem was undertaken by Mr Eric Spencer. His examination produced the following evidence. The woman had been strangled and then thrown into the Thames. She had been in the water for up to two days . . .'* He glanced up. 'So why did Georgina Matlowe identify her? The body wouldn't have changed much in a couple of days.' He read on in silence, then added, 'She was almost the same age, give or take a year, and had blonde hair . . . and was pretty.'

'Height, etc.?'

'Two inches shorter – but hard to tell that when a body is horizontal on a mortuary slab – and the same slim build.' He tapped his pencil on the desk while he considered the facts. 'I suppose Mrs Matlowe made a genuine mistake. It's possible she wanted it to be Leonora so the uncertainty would be at an end.'

'Ah! But if the police suspected her son, earlier on, of course, then the discovery of the body would bring the police nearer to finding the truth.' Judith narrowed her eyes thoughtfully. 'She wouldn't have wanted that, surely.'

'Unless it would help pinpoint the real killer. If Leonora

had gone to stay with friends one of those might have done it.'

'Fine friends they'd be!' Judith tossed her head again but her cousin still failed to notice the bob.

'Or she might,' he said slowly, 'have booked into a hotel under an assumed name and then fallen in with someone who eventually murdered her. Is that likely?'

Judith hesitated. 'Anything's possible.'

'But it wasn't Leonora! It was someone else. A woman called Eliza Broughton.' Donald began to pace the small room, still clutching the police reports. 'All we can do with this information is wonder why Georgina Matlowe was so quick to identify the wrong person. If, for instance, she suspected that Neil had killed his wife, surely her instincts would be to deny that the corpse resembled Leonora. To put them off discovering the truth.'

Judith nodded. 'And if she didn't suspect her son, she would be still thinking that Leonora might be with Neil . . . that they had found each other . . . and that they didn't want Georgina to know.'

'Maybe we're missing something.'

'Why don't you go for one of your walks, Donald? It often clears your head.'

'I think I will – and I'll try and have a word with the Matlowes' new governess. Someone on the inside would be invaluable.'

Minutes later he left the office, and she watched him from the window as he strode purposefully along, his mind no doubt filled with exciting possibilities. 'You'll get there in the end,' she muttered and turned her thoughts to the composition of poor Mrs Montini's final letter.

Georgina sat in the corner armchair of her sister's service flat and watched with barely disguised irritation as the twins and the two other children raced round a circle of chairs, waiting for the music to stop. Even as a child herself, Georgina had never liked games that involved pushing, shoving or screaming. When Ivan had suggested Musical Chairs, she had groaned aloud but her sister, always a bit

of a hoyden in Georgina's opinion, had clapped her hands
with delight, organized the chairs and rushed to seat herself
at the ancient but well-tuned piano.

Ivan, confined to a wheelchair, watched with excitement.
He was thin and pale with huge brown eyes and his head
was shaved. Sickly was the word for him, Georgina thought,
regarding him uneasily. She felt a frisson of compassion
but it was followed by one of satisfaction that her own
grandchildren were hale and hearty.

Screams erupted as 'John Brown's Body' came to an
abrupt stop and the excited children scrambled for the
remaining chairs. Ida turned from the piano, laughing, to
find Edie was without a seat.

'Never mind, dear,' Ida cried. 'You can come and stand
by me but first I must take away another chair! Oh, this is
getting so exciting!' She caught Georgina's eye and winked
then turned back to the piano. 'What shall I play next?' she
asked Edie.

'Pop Goes the Weasel.'

'Pop Goes the Weasel? Right you are! Your wish is my
command!'

Georgina did her best to ignore her surroundings and
thought instead about the cook's complaint regarding the
butcher, who apparently made too many mistakes with the
orders, and her suggestion they change to another butcher.
It sounded sensible but Georgina was reluctant to take
advice from one of the servants. She thought longingly
about the days when she was younger and she and her
husband entertained friends to dinner. Somehow everything had seemed to work like clockwork without all these
aggravating problems – unless it was a case of distance
lending enchantment to the view.

She watched Emmie rushing red-faced around the last
chair. It was a pity they took after their mother in looks
and not their father – it was a permanent reminder of something she preferred to forget – but hopefully they might
grow out of it. She took a surreptitious glance at the clock.
Not that it would help, to know the time, but a little of her
sister's company went a long way.

When the game ended Ida produced five small jigsaws and gave the children one each. 'Now we're going to have a little competition. The person who finishes the jigsaw first is the winner,' she told the children, who had settled obediently around the table while Ivan was wheeled close enough. 'Look on the box the jigsaws come in and you will see your picture – that's the way. Yours is a train, Edie, Emmie's is a bus. Let me see . . . Ivan, yours is a boat with white sails . . .'

'I like boats!' he said.

'That's good then, dear.' She patted his shoulder.

Emmie, flushed with victory from the Musical Chairs asked, 'Is there a prize?'

Georgina stiffened. 'You shouldn't ask, Emmie. It's not polite.' A little too forward, like her mother. She sighed.

'A nice red apple is the prize,' Ida told her, smiling. 'Now is everyone ready? Ready, steady, start!'

Ida then beckoned Georgina into the kitchen where Ivan's mother had provided a platter of paste sandwiches, a plate of butterfly cakes and a yellow jelly. 'She has a dentist's appointment, poor woman. She suffers with her teeth.'

Ida indicated a chair by the kitchen table and her sister sat down warily, aware that Ida was watching her with that concerned look on her face.

Ida said, 'You look very tired, Georgie. Is it all getting too much for you? Bringing up the girls, I mean.'

'I hate being called Georgie. You know I do.' She also hated being told she looked tired because immediately she *felt* tired.

'Sorry, sorry! But you do look a bit pasty. You're probably overdoing things. You should have kept Nanny. I did my best to persuade you.'

'It was none of your business . . . and anyway, it was for her own good. She was getting on in years, for heaven's sake!'

'But she was all they had left, with both parents gone.'

'They had me, didn't they? Really, Ida!' She pursed her lips. 'The last thing two lively children need is a faded old woman who spent her time talking about their vanished mother. She claimed it was to keep Leonora fresh in their minds but I know better. She did it to spite me; to encourage the girls to compare me with their mother!'

'Oh what nonsense! Why on earth should she try to disparage you?'

'You weren't there, Ida. You cannot possibly understand what went on.'

Ida held up her hands in mock surrender. 'Please yourself, dear, but the fact remains, you do look very tired. I'd hate you to have a heart attack or something. Then where would the twins be?' Swiftly changing the subject, she prattled on. 'I thought the jigsaws would keep them busy for a while, because I need to talk to you about this man who called last week. Has he been in touch with you? His name is Richard Preston.'

Georgina frowned. 'Richard? I don't think I know the name but . . . something at the back of my . . .' She blinked suddenly. 'Preston? That was Leonora's maiden name, but it can't . . . Are you sure it was Preston?' Her eyes widened fearfully. 'Leonora's father was quite ill last time I heard from them. The usual Christmas card. I don't know why they bother – I never send them one. Preston. It must be a coincidence.' *Please God let it be a coincidence*, she prayed silently.

'Oh no, Georgie, this wasn't the father. It was a young man.'

'I don't understand.' She stared at her sister. Keep calm, she told herself. Count to ten. Do not let her see that you are upset.

But Ida, tying a ribbon around the birthday cake, wasn't looking at her. 'It was Leonora's brother. Her younger brother. In fact her only brother.'

Georgina felt her heart beat faster. 'Leonora's brother called on you? Here? He's in England?' Her voice faltered as the shock set in.

'No, no, not here in person,' Ida explained, arranging seven small candles on Ivan's birthday cake. 'Poor little lad. Just to think that he will die before his . . .'

'Ida! For heaven's sake, don't tell me this is all starting again. The trouble about Leonora. This younger brother . . .'

'He's only in his early twenties and sounded very nice. Polite. Respectful. No, he's not here yet but he explained what he wanted. I thought he would have called you already. He'll get in touch, I'm sure, so you'll meet him.'

'What . . . what does he want with us?' Georgina leaned forward, one hand on her heart.

Ida stood back and admired the cake. 'I made it for Ivan specially. It's a lemon sponge because he doesn't like fruit cake. His mother said this is his favourite. My little present to him.' She tilted it towards Georgina. 'See – his name and "Happy Birthday". And I made a lucky dip for them. Just a few sweeties. Sugar mice and lollipops. Blue wrapping paper for the boys and pink for the girls.'

Georgina was taking deep breaths and now she forced herself to sit a little straighter. 'So . . . young Richard Preston. You were telling me, Ida?'

'He telephoned. Said he was only sixteen when his sister disappeared and now he's older he wants to find her before his father dies – to set his mind at rest. Or if not to find her, to learn what happened to her.' Ida glanced up at her sister. 'He hardly mentioned his mother, which was odd.'

Georgina steadied her voice before speaking. 'I understand she took to drink – with the grief. That was the last I heard. It was all so dreadful.'

'And you didn't keep in contact with the Prestons? I never understood that. I thought surely you would want to know if Leonora had returned home safely.'

Georgina did not like the way the conversation was going. She felt an implied criticism in her sister's questions. She said sharply, 'You have no idea, Ida, what that family put me through.'

'Meaning Leonora.'

'Meaning the family. Her parents wrote a very unpleasant letter after she . . . after Leonora walked out. They seemed to suggest that I was somehow to blame! Their daughter ruined my son's life and also mine. She . . . she abandoned her children. *My grandchildren*. Did the parents offer any condolences for her behaviour? Not a word!'

'But in your shoes I . . .'

'You were never in my shoes,' Georgina snapped, 'so you cannot understand. No, I did not want to keep in touch with the family. Leonora was jealous because Neil and I . . .' She tried to swallow but her throat was dry. 'She wanted to be the only woman in his life. Some women are like that. Selfish. It was because of her that I lost Neil. If he hadn't insisted on trying to find her when she didn't want to be found he might still be alive. The car crash . . .'

'You poor thing. I know how you must have felt.'

Georgina's eyes glittered. 'Don't talk nonsense, Ida! I've just explained at length that you could not possibly know how I felt. You've never had a child!' She felt herself starting to tremble and made an effort to calm down.

Ida was now whisking cream to add to the jelly, which she felt looked too plain for a special birthday party. She said, 'Richard Preston wanted to know what I thought had happened to send Leonora off like that. He said she was so in love with Neil – he couldn't believe she would have left him so suddenly. Or ever! She said it was a match made in heaven and the family adored Neil. Richard said he knows his sister would never have left her husband and children.'

'Well, she did! That's all I can say.' Georgina noticed the catch in her voice and counted to ten. She marvelled that Ida could not hear the thumping of her sister's heart.

'He asked me if Leonora and Neil had quarrelled.'

'I don't think so but Leonora *had* tried to stir up trouble between me and my son.' Georgina watched impatiently as her sister spread the cream and decorated the cream with glacé cherries. 'What no one understands is that that woman was a born trouble maker – a beautiful but dangerous trouble maker.'

'If you say so, Georgie. I hardly knew her.'

'You were fortunate! What else did he ask?'

Ida shrugged. 'I can't remember everything he said . . .' She carried the finished jelly back to the larder and closed the door. 'If they see the jelly, they won't want to eat the sandwiches,' she explained. 'Now, where did I put the chocolate biscuits?' She stared round the kitchen. 'Oh, by the way, I thought you'd like to stay overnight so I've made up the bed in the—'

'Oh no!' cried Georgina. 'I mean, it's very kind of you but ...' Her voice quivered and she was afraid she might cry.

'In the spare bedroom.' Ida smiled at her. 'You can sleep in the big bed and one of the twins can have the small one. The other one can sleep on the sofa bed in my room.' She held up her hands. 'I won't hear any arguments, Georgina. You seem quite exhausted and I'm not surprised. Such a responsibility at your age, even with the governess. I can see you're not really fit to travel and those trams are so noisy and rattle about so! We can have a nice quiet break-fast tomorrow and then you and the twins will be on your way.' She smiled fondly at her sister. 'Now, let's rejoin the children and see who's won the jigsaw competition. Ivan's mother will be back from the dentist shortly and then we can sit down to tea.'

Back at The Poplars, Marianne hung up the telephone, a little startled to realize that she would be spending the night alone in the house. Mrs Matlowe had been persuaded to stay with her sister overnight, although her tone of voice had suggested that she had agreed somewhat unwillingly. Neither the cook nor the maid lived in at The Poplars and had already left.

Standing at the base of the stairs in the gathering gloom, she shivered but her mind was already considering possi-bilities. 'Six thirty-five,' she muttered. What could she do? An evening stroll in the park, maybe, or along the river bank? That would pass an hour. She could catch up on some mending – the hem of one of her skirts was down ... She could play the piano or explore the house ... or the garden. Her eyes narrowed. 'Or explore the boat house while there is still some natural light!'

She grinned suddenly, aware that her employer had given her the perfect opportunity to see for herself exactly what was in the boat house. 'If I can find the key.'

The keys to various parts of the house were kept on the back of the pantry door, on a board full of small hooks.

At first glance these appeared to be a baffling selection.
Marianne began to decipher them. B1, B2, B3 . . . up to B5.
Then there were CB and MB. 'Can't imagine.' But the
numbered Bs were presumably all bedrooms. Much easier
than she had expected. 'DR must be dining room and K is
definitely the kitchen. FD . . .?' It took less than a moment.
'Front door! So there'll be a BD for the back door . . . Yes.
And this . . . LC? It's probably the linen cupboard!' She felt
pleased with herself until she saw that the hook labelled
BH lacked a key.

Staring at the vacant space she wondered why the only
missing key was the one belonging to the boat house.
Obviously to discourage anyone from entering it. 'But why?'
she asked aloud. Maybe over the intervening years the place
had been unused and had become unsafe. For a moment
she hesitated but curiosity overcame her fears.

'The key is somewhere!' she decided and before she
could change her mind, she went upstairs to the study and
began to search the drawers of Mrs Matlowe's desk. She
found the key almost immediately and minutes later was
hurrying across the lawn in the direction of the boat house.

Last time she had taken a look inside, it had been a sunny
day and the children were with her looking for their leaves.
Today the sky was overcast and the boat house looked
almost grim, like a fat toad crouching at the far end of the
garden. It had rained in the night and the wooden frame
had a sodden, almost sullen look, Marianne thought nervously, but she went up the three steps carefully and thrust
the key into the lock. It turned, but only so far. 'Try the
other way,' she told herself and tried to reverse it. It moved
both ways but only part way and had presumably rusted
within the movement of the lock.

'Bother!' she said loudly and then, in a lower voice,
'Damn!' Shielding her eyes from the reflection in the glass,
Marianne peered in at what she could see of the interior.
It seemed to her that the water level was slightly down but
there were locks on the river in both directions so the water
could not rise and fall with the tide. It was gloomy inside
the boat house and it took some time for her eyes to adjust

but then she could make out the wooden walkway around the edge and in the middle, on the water . . .

'That's odd!' Where was the boat she had seen previously? The narrow, flat-bottomed boat that she had assumed was a punt. There was no sign of it. Just the water, which barely rippled, reflecting the small amount of light allowed in by the windows.

On the riverside she could make out the outlines of the gates, which opened out on to the river, but now she fancied they resembled heavy doors rather than gates, and Marianne could just make out a chain and padlock that secured them. So how could a boat have made its escape? Unless, she thought, the boat house was being used by someone from outside – from beyond the house – with or without Mrs Matlowe's permission. Or was it possible that she rented it out to someone?

Now she could also make out a few sacks to one side on the right-hand walkway and a few utensils hanging on the wall – one which she guessed might be a boat hook. On the left-hand walkway she could see a couple of baskets – possibly abandoned picnic baskets – but they seemed to be decaying fast and leaned almost drunkenly towards each other.

'I think I've seen enough,' she told herself. 'Too depressing!'

But how wonderful it must have been, she mused, when the young people were there. Marianne sighed with envy. She could imagine them punting up the river – the women elegantly dressed with shady hats or parasols, the men wearing straw boaters – with the picnic basket stowed between them. Maybe a salmon mousse in a circular mould, or chopped vegetables in aspic. Maybe a game pie and potato salad, or better yet a still warm chicken wrapped in a cloth, and a . . .

'Yoo hoo, Marianne! It's me, Mrs Brannigan!'

Reluctantly Marianne surrendered her vision of gracious living and returned the neighbour's wave. She walked over to the hedge where Mrs Brannigan held out a paper cone filled with something that promised to be sweet.

'My husband just spotted you from the landing window,'
she told Marianne. 'And I've just finished making these
coconut creams. I hope you like coconut.'

'I do. Thank you.' She took them gratefully.

'The rest are for the Methodists' Church Bazaar. I always
make something for them – it's such a good cause.' She
watched Marianne taste one and waited for her reaction.

'Mmm! Quite delicious!'

Satisfied, Mrs Brannigan said, 'All on your own then?'

Marianne nodded. 'The twins have been invited to a
birthday party and Mrs Matlowe has taken them. Her sister's
persuaded her to stay the night so I'm footloose and fancy
free.' She seized the moment. 'Does anyone else have
permission to use the boat house? I ask because last time
I looked I thought I saw a punt in there and now it's gone.'

Mrs Brannigan frowned. 'A punt? Oh no. You must have
been mistaken. No one is allowed to . . .'

'I'm wondering if someone is using it without permission. First we see a man in the garden – or the twins do –
and then I thought I saw a punt, which has now vanished.
Unless I'm seeing things – or going quietly mad!'

Mrs Brannigan's expression changed. 'You're not
psychic, are you? Some people are, you know, but often
they don't know it. My aunt lived next door to a psychic.
She was quite famous and people paid her to contact their
dear departed.' She shuddered. 'Can you imagine? A seance.
That's what it was called. I think she called herself a psychic
medium.'

'But surely a punt couldn't be a ghost. A ghost is the
spirit of a person, isn't it? The punt I saw – or thought I
saw – was empty.'

Mrs Brannigan folded her arms across her chest.
'Whatever it is I want nothing to do with it. It gives me
the shivers. More likely a trick of the light. Mind you,
people pay to visit haunted houses and nothing bad happens
to them, so I daresay they're not dangerous or anything.'

'Just the spirits of people who cannot find rest, even after
they die. That's how they've been described. It's rather sad,
I suppose.'

At that moment Mr Brannigan called from the kitchen door to say he'd lost a sock and his wife said, 'Oh! Hark at me, chattering away. I quite forgot. We're going out tonight to hear a talk about Africa, given by a friend of ours. Poor Lydia – she sings in our choir and her husband's a missionary or some such.' She paused for breath.

Marianne said, 'How very admirable.'

'Oh it is, isn't it? But poor Lydia – she cannot bear the climate for more than a week or two so she cannot stay with her husband. Their grown-up daughter takes her place at the mission. They're a very devout family. Well, enjoy your coconut creams, Marianne. We'll chat some other time.'

Slowly Marianne made her way back into the house. She returned the boat house key to the drawer in the desk and wondered how to spend her evening. She boiled an egg and cut three slices of bread, and buttered them. It was strange eating alone at the kitchen table. Her thoughts reverted to her conversation about ghosts and spirits and she wondered if the man the children had seen really *had* been a ghost. Could it have been their father's ghost, she wondered. Maybe his spirit had returned to the last place where he had seen his children playing . . . Or, as Mrs Brannigan suggested, nothing more than shadows and her fertile imagination.

'No.' Neil could never have seen his children playing because they were only babies when he and Leonora left and they would not have been old enough to play in the garden – although they were probably outside in their prams whenever the weather permitted.

She washed up after her frugal meal and then spent twenty minutes playing the piano – a very small medley of tunes she had learned as a child – and searched the bookcase for something to read. Finding Mrs Matlowe's choice of reading not to her taste, she trimmed a few dead leaves from the roses that Mrs Matlowe had placed in a bowl in the hall.

Finally, in desperation she went up to her room and wrote a letter to her closest friend who had been at school with her.

Imagine me, she wrote, *in my somewhat spartan room –
a frayed carpet, one upholstered chair, a bed which creaks,
a very small fireplace with a coal scuttle to match and a
view over a haunted boat house! I'm beginning to feel like
someone created by Jane Austen!*

She rolled her eyes. Perhaps she was being over-dramatic.
Alice would laugh, remembering how prone Marianne had
been to exaggerate.

*My employer is rather odd and very strait-laced, but her
beloved son is dead and she has sole care of his twin girls
whom I am attempting to educate. They, the twins, are very
sweet and the neighbours seem pleasant enough and to top
it all this is Henley-on-Thames and in a few weeks it will
be time for the regatta – sorry, the Henley Royal Regatta,
to give it its new title – and the entire area will be filled
with spectators for the various races. All those charming
young men in boaters and striped blazers! Surely they cannot
all be accompanied by equally charming young women.
Maybe I will meet Mr Right!*

The daylight was going and Marianne stopped writing,
rubbed her tired eyes and glanced out over the lawn. Clouds
were rolling up beyond the boat house and for a moment
she thought she saw a flickering light within its dilapidated
frame.

'Stop it, Marianne!' she told herself. 'It's probably the
light from a boat moving up river, or from a fisherman on
the opposite bank.' Just in case there was no rational explanation, she decided to draw the curtains. If there *was* an
unhappy spirit trying to attract her attention, she wanted
none of it. *I have quite enough to deal with in the present*,
she thought, *without getting involved with the past.*

FOUR

The next day, when the twins had arrived home full of excitement following Ivan's birthday party, they sat with Marianne on a seat set alongside the river while the latter attempted to explain about different languages. Emmie appeared vaguely interested but Edie seemed to find the lesson boring.

Marianne pointed to a lady and gentlemen who were walking past with a small white dog on a lead. 'We call that a dog,' she said. 'In France they would call it a *chien*.'

Emmie said dutifully, 'A dog is a *chien*.' She turned to her sister. 'Say it, Edie.'

Edie swung her legs. 'Why don't they just say dog?'

'Because we're learning what French people say,' Emmie told her loftily. 'Grandmother wants us to learn some French words and . . .'

'Here comes a boat!' Edie jumped from the seat and rushed towards the water's edge to get a better view and Emmie followed. Marianne moved closer to them as they all watched a young man who propelled the slim wooden boat by pushing a long pole against the river bottom. He waved to the twins and, by doing so, made the punt swerve a little so that the woman who accompanied him gave a little shriek and said, 'Tommy, darling, do watch what you're doing!'

The twins waved back.

Edie said hopefully, 'Are they going to fall in?'

Marianne laughed. 'I hope not.'

'What do they call a boat in France, Marianne?'

'*Bateau.*'

'So dog is *chien* and boat is *bateau*.' Emmie gave her sister a smug look.

Edie tossed her head. 'It's silly!'

'No, it isn't.'

'It is . . . Oh look! The swans are coming over. They want some bread!'

They both looked at Marianne who shook her head.

'The bread's all gone,' she told them. 'You gave it all to the ducks.' Seizing the moment she said, 'Bread is called *pain* in France.' She pronounced it correctly, as *pan*.

Emmie frowned. 'Like saucepan?'

While Marianne tried to explain, a man approached them and Edie cried out with delight. 'It's the lollipop man!'

Marianne turned to find a pleasant-looking man holding out a small white card, which she accepted cautiously.

'Donald Watson – Private Investigator,' she read aloud.

'It's the lollipop man! We met him when we were out with Hattie.' Edie beamed at him hopefully.

Emmie, reading her sister's expression, said, 'We aren't in the park now. There aren't any lollipops here.'

Marianne looked up from the card and said evenly, 'I assume this meeting is not a coincidence, Mr Watson.'

'No. I'd very much like to talk to you some time, some-where convenient. If you would contact me. I've written my office number on the back. We would need to be discreet.'

'Discreet? Oh dear . . .' The suddenness of his appearance had made her wary. 'I'll have to . . . to consider it.'

Edie said, 'Is your wife coming today? We've seen a boat and the man steered the boat with his pole and made the boat go a bit wobbly and the lady said, "Do watch what you're doing, darling!" and his name was Tommy but we don't know her name.'

Emmie, not to be outdone, said, 'We're learning French words to please Grandmother. Boat is *bateau*.'

He smiled at Marianne. 'Your girls are amazing.'

Emmie said, 'Marianne is not our mother. We told you. She's our governess . . .'

'. . . because our mother has run away and our father has died and we don't even remember them . . .'

'. . . but we had a nanny once who was ever so old and Grandmother had to get rid of her. We don't remember her.'

A silence fell between them.

Marianne, disconcerted, said, 'A potted biography!'

Emmie looked at Donald. 'We need some bread for the swans.'

'I'm afraid I don't have any.' To Marianne he said, 'A nanny?'

'Apparently.'

'Do you know her name?'

'If I ever did know it, I've forgotten it. It might come back to me.'

He lowered his voice. 'It really is rather important that we talk, Miss Lefevre. If you would be kind enough to get in touch.' He said, 'Goodbye,' to the twins and walked quickly away.

Emmie, disappointed, said, 'He's not as nice as I thought he was.'

The swans had grown tired of waiting and now swam away and Marianne decided they must bring the French lesson to an end and walk home.

Donald Watson – Private Investigator.

What on earth could he want with her? she wondered.

As soon as they arrived back at the house, Georgina sent the children into the schoolroom with instructions for Marianne that they should sit down quietly and learn a piece of poetry.

'They are hopelessly overexcited,' she told the governess. 'My foolish sister has that effect on them, I'm afraid. She has the same effect on me! I want the twins to calm down completely before they start to eat their lunch.'

'Certainly. I'll find a suitable poem – unless you have something particular in mind.'

Georgina frowned. 'I'll leave that to you. That's your job, not mine.'

'Then perhaps "*One, two, buckle my shoe. Three, four, knock at the . . .*"'

'Yes, I know it. That will do very well. I shall be . . . *busy* for the next hour or so and am not to be disturbed.'

Hurrying along to her special room, Georgina let herself in and locked the door behind her. Leaning back against

the door she closed her eyes and let out a long sigh of
relief. She was safe for the moment. She stayed with her
back to the door as her eyes became accustomed to the
gloom.

'That wretched woman!' she murmured. How was it, she
wondered, that Ida always managed to catch her wrong-
footed in some way, so that a few hours in her company
left her nerves jangling. Here, alone in the darkness, she
could find some peace of mind. Here, she could talk to her
son without fear of interruption.

'Neil,' she whispered. 'It's Mother. I'm back.' Her son
had died in a foreign country but Georgina had no doubt
that his spirit had returned to Henley-on-Thames where he
belonged; where he was welcomed with open arms; where
he was still needed.

Opening her eyes, she looked slowly round the room
with a sigh of pleasurable relief. Crossing to the altar, she
felt in the hidden drawer for the matches and lit the two
black candles with a hand that trembled. Watching the small
wicks flicker into light, she was comforted, and already she
felt some of her anxiety slip away. A faint smile touched
her face as she knelt carefully, resting her knees on the
hassock that had once belonged to her mother. She knew
every detail of the faded embroidery – every stitch that
Ellen Matlowe had applied all those years ago.

'I'm back, Mother,' she whispered through her clasped
hands. 'I've been with Ida and she's given me a terrible
headache, as usual.'

She always waited for a whispered reply, faint as a breeze
but audible. It never came but Georgina understood that it
was just a matter of time. Ida had never been close to her
mother, and Georgina had always known she was the
favourite.

She said, 'I'm home, Herbert,' and smiled for her dead
husband. He had always told her how pretty she looked
when she smiled. 'It's like the sun bursting through the
clouds!' he had said one day – the day he had proposed
marriage and she had accepted.

Now, she bowed her head. If Herbert came to her now

he would find her very changed, she thought. She was no longer young and beautiful, happy and serene. Now she was growing old, her life had become fearful and full of agonizing regrets – the days too long, the nights filled with terrible dreams.

'Dear Lord, hear my prayers.'

Dutifully she began the short series of prayers to which she felt He was entitled. The Lord came first and she spoke to him with cautious reverence. Afterwards she would relax her vigilance and talk to Neil.

Further down river, below Henley Bridge, Donald Watson found what he was looking for – the boatyard. It was an unpretentious enclosure containing about thirteen boats of various shapes and sizes but this would soon change, he knew. From past experience he understood that as the time for the regatta drew near, more boats, mainly punts, would be taken in for a final check before the big day. The event lasted from the first Wednesday in July until the Saturday.

He parked his motor car and took his time, strolling towards the low buildings that were either repair shops, stores or offices. He whistled cheerfully as he made his way across the rough ground – patches of thin grass surrounded by stony ground and stretches of mud baked hard by the sun – not wishing to give the impression that he was 'nosing around' or that he had no right to be there. Trespassers were never welcome.

All around him men were working on boats – painting, sawing, polishing, caulking and otherwise intent on their labours. No one gave him more than a curious glance but Donald felt reasonably at ease among them because his earliest memories were of hours spent as a boy in his uncle's workshop where he worked in his spare time on an almost derelict dinghy. Strangely the work never ended and the boat was never declared seaworthy. His aunt insisted that her husband simply wanted somewhere to hide away when she started to nag him.

'Can I help you?'

Donald turned, smiling. It was more a challenge than an

offer of assistance but he knew better than to alienate anyone. 'Good morning! Is the boss around?'

'Might be, might not.' The man, thought Donald, might fairly be described as 'grizzled'.

From somewhere the sound of wood being planed carried on the breeze and with it the unmistakable tang of wood shavings and sawdust.

Donald said, 'Is it still Leo Croom? It's a long time since I was last here.'

'It's Mr Croom, yes. He's in the office.' He pointed a calloused finger. 'A bit older and a bit crustier, if you get my meaning! Doesn't like being bothered.'

With that he turned sharply on his heel and walked away.

Donald muttered, 'Thanks for the warning,' and made his way to the squat building that served as the boatyard's office.

Before he could knock on the door it opened and a man in his fifties stepped out, a disgruntled look on his face.

'Mr Croom! I don't know if you remember me but . . .'

Leo Croom eyed Donald sourly. 'I do and I'm busy so make an appointment with my secretary.'

'I won't take up much of your time but . . .'

'I know you won't because I'm due somewhere in ten minutes and it'll take me twenty to get there! Excuse me.'

Donald was not at all rebuffed by this rejection but gave a polite nod of understanding. In his opinion secretaries were often a very fruitful source of information so he opened the door of the office and made his presence known.

Miss Batt, turning from the filing cabinet, stared at him as if she had seen a ghost. 'Donald Watson!' she said at last. 'Gracious me!'

'I can't deny it,' he laughed. 'And you look as young as ever!'

'Now then, Mr Watson.' She wagged a finger at him but blushed as she did so. 'And it's Mrs Warner now.'

'Well, congratulations! I envy Mr Warner.'

Pleased by the compliments, which nonetheless flustered her, she drew herself up, pushed her spectacles up and sat

X Secretaries were nearly always male until WW1, when so many were killed.

down at her desk. 'How can I help you, Mr Watson?' she asked with an attempt at formality, indicating a chair.

Donald sat down and quickly explained that he needed to make an appointment with the boss. 'They are reopening the file on Mrs Leonora Matlowe. Do you remember? She went missing about seven years ago.'

'The young American woman?'

'That's her.'

'So she didn't turn up?'

He shook his head. 'No sign of her but now I need to refer to the old files in case we missed anything. Leonora's younger brother is coming to England, determined to find out what happened to his sister. He's employing me to help him simply because I'm familiar with the original investigation.'

'And because you're good at what you do.'

He tried a modest smile but was secretly flattered. 'We'll see if there's anything new to discover,' he said.

Minutes later an appointment had been arranged for him to talk with Leo Croom and Donald rose as though to take his leave. However, he hesitated. 'I don't suppose you'd know what happened to the punt the Matlowes once owned. I'd like to know if they purchased it from here. It seems to have disappeared over the intervening years since the young woman went missing. There may or may not be a connection.'

She raised her eyebrows. 'You think maybe she took the punt out and was drowned? Something like that?'

'Who knows? Something certainly happened to her.'

'And you want "private" information?' She looked at him sternly but there was a twinkle in her eye. 'You'll get me into trouble, Mr Watson!'

He nodded. 'You're quite right – and that would never do!'

She regarded him earnestly. 'I recall all the excitement although I was only seventeen, but everyone was talking about it. A real mystery, wasn't it?' She glanced towards the door to make sure they were alone. 'Do you have *any* idea what happened to her? I mean, maybe the police *do* know something but can't prove it so you all have to say

nothing . . . because the police seemed to think it might
be the husband who . . .' She frowned then lowered her
voice. 'He might have killed her and just pretended she'd
run off.'

Ah! Light dawned for Donald. Mrs Warner wanted something in exchange for the information about the Matlowes'
boat, which was fair enough. 'Mrs Matlowe said something
to the police about a quarrel the husband and wife had had
the night before she disappeared and I daresay that made
them suspect him. There was never any other evidence that
he might have harmed his wife but . . . mud sticks.'

She was rising to her feet now and his hopes rose. He
said, 'This young man – the brother – has come over from
America and wants to know the facts. I think he wants to
prove to his parents that his sister didn't just abandon the
children willingly.'

'I suppose that if they find out she is definitely dead they
can start to grieve. It must be dreadful to go on hoping year
after year!' She was now opening the top drawer of one of
the filing cabinets and riffling through the various files.

At last she drew one out and opened it. 'The Matlowes
purchased one of our punts in 1898 – that's fourteen years
ago. Paid for by cheque in the name of Herbert Matlowe.'

Donald made a quick note as she turned over another
sheet.

'They have never sold it back to us . . . nor have they
advertised it for sale on our notice board.' She closed the
file and returned it. 'Not much help, is it?'

'You never know what might come in useful.' He smiled.
'You've been a real brick! Thank you.'

He said his goodbyes and had reached the door when she
said, 'They say that Mrs Matlowe hated the punt. She was
terrified of the river. One of her uncles drowned in a boating
accident when she was a child and she never forgot it.'

He stared at her. 'That's news to me.'

'And you're the investigator!' She grinned.

'If I ever need another colleague . . .' He left the sentence
unfinished.

She shrugged. 'Working here you pick up all sorts of things.

People gossip. Especially river people. They love tittle-tattle.'
Changing the subject she asked, 'Will you be watching the
regatta this year or are you too busy?'

'We might snatch a few hours' free time. It would be
something to see the King and Queen go down the river.'

She wished him well with his investigation and he strolled
back to his motor car in high spirits. Thank the Lord, he
thought, as he swung the starting handle, for the Miss Batts
of this world. Sorry! Make that the Mrs Warners.

The Sutton Ladies Charity Group were rightly proud of
their home for the dispossessed, which catered solely for
impoverished gentlewomen. Six women, to be exact. The
Sutton Group consisted of thirty-seven dedicated 'women
of means' who had come together to provide a final resting
place for gentlewomen in Sutton who had fallen upon hard
times and had nowhere else to go. The house, known only
as Number 24, stood in a quiet side street by the name of
Dickens Drive, well removed from the noise and bustle
of the nearby shops.

It was staffed by carefully selected young women like
Agatha who took pride in her work and was a credit to
the entire project. Agatha cooked the meals. Nora did the
cleaning. Nesta and Mary cared for the inmates' physical
needs – helping them at mealtimes, washing them, changing
their clothes, emptying their commodes.

Ivy Busby was one of the current six who enjoyed this
attention and she was properly grateful. Not that she needed
much help – she could feed herself without assistance, and
dress herself each morning in whichever assortment of
clothes had been allotted to her from the recent collection.
Her shoes were a size too large but she had stuffed paper
into the toes. The shapeless dress had once been let out
with two side gussets. She felt that she was wearing a sack
but then told herself that no one in the entire world cared
how she looked so why should she.

It was not an ideal existence but thankfully she suffered
from no disease and still had her wits about her. She was,
however, distinctly frail and was the oldest resident.

At ten past eleven in the morning she sat fully dressed
in a comfortable chair, speaking to one of the home's spon-
sors – a Mrs Margaret Beck-Holmes whose husband was
'something in the government' and might one day be granted
a knighthood. She most definitely belonged under the
heading 'woman of means'.

'You look well, Miss Busby.' Margaret Beck-Holmes
smiled. 'A little more colour in your face, I think. Now when
was it I saw you last?'

'Last Tuesday.'

'Ah yes, that was it, and you had a few sniffles, I recall.'
She patted Ivy's speckled hand and in doing so admired
her own hand, which was adorned by three rings of various
shapes and sizes – all of them valuable. She smiled gently.
'But you've recovered. And you are quite happy here?'

Her husband, Ivy knew, was a boring man with no imagination, but he was rich. He came to Number 24 occasionally
and Ivy had taken an immediate dislike to him. A typically
British pompous ass. That was her impression.

She nodded dutifully but added, 'Happy enough. It's all
relative, isn't it?'

Mrs Beck-Holmes hesitated, unsure how to take the
comment and decided to ignore it. 'Quite settled in this old
country of ours?' she asked Ivy. 'A far cry from America.'

Mr Beck-Holmes must be about fifteen years older than
her, Ivy reflected, and might well die before his wife. If he
did his money would be hers and she might well put
some more of it into Number 24. If he didn't drink it all.
She thought his reddened nose was rather suspicious.

Ivy nodded again. 'Settled, yes, thank you.'

On the opposite side of the room Miss Allen glanced up
from her crochet – a mass of tangled loops and missed
stitches which would never be finished because her faltering
concentration made it impossible. 'Miss Busby comes from
America,' she announced in a quavering voice.

'I know she does.'

'She used to be a nanny. I was a ladies' maid. I never
married.' For a moment Miss Allen considered her crochet
work. 'I had suitors but I chose not to marry,' she continued.

'My ladies needed me. I made them crocheted collars, which they valued. I was highly regarded.'

'I'm sure you were.' Margaret Beck-Holmes smiled apologetically at Ivy and turned to share a few words with Miss Allen. The door opened and another resident was led in, leaning heavily on Nesta's arm.

Ivy muttered, 'Here comes sleeping beauty!'

Miss Spinks was given a strong sleeping draught last thing at night to prevent her from wandering in the early hours, which meant that she was always very sluggish in the mornings.

America. The word tugged at Ivy's heart strings. Was she happy here? No, but she was comfortable. Was she settled? Certainly not, but she was resigned. Did she ever long for home? Every minute of every day. As a girl of eighteen, she had been nanny to Leonora's mother and had stayed with her when she married. She had been nanny to Leonora and to Richard and stayed on as a valued family friend, until Leonora's twin girls were born.

Nesta was settling Miss Spinks in a chair beside the window. Ivy watched the familiar scene without much interest. The poor woman would remain there until lunch was served, staring blankly out of the front window at a red pillarbox and a misshapen plane tree, seeing and understanding nothing.

Do I feel cheated? Ivy nodded in answer to her unspoken question. Am I bored? Yes I am. It was all so predictable. Today Agatha would produce fatty mutton stew, tomorrow steamed fish but not much of it, the next day a vegetable pasty with potato, carrots and onions and tough pie crust. It was meagre fare but the Sutton Ladies did their best with whatever money they could raise and they were justly proud of their small enterprise and were widely applauded in the community for their efforts.

And who was she to complain, Ivy asked herself bitterly. She paid nothing for her bed and board because, like the other five unfortunates, she had nothing. Not a penny in her purse. In fact Ivy no longer owned a purse. She was a charity case. They all were. Thank the Lord the Prestons

back home had no idea of her situation. At least she hoped
not.

'I have my pride!' she whispered.

Nesta said, 'What's that, dear?'

'Nothing.'

Nesta, young and pretty with soft dark hair, was engaged
to be married and would shortly be leaving.

She greeted Mrs Beck-Holmes and turned to go but then
turned back. 'I nearly forgot. There's a letter for you, Miss
Busby.' She drew it from her uniform pocket.

'A *letter*?' Ivy stared in disbelief. 'For me?'

'It was delivered ten minutes ago.'

She handed it to Ivy and bustled out of the room.

Mrs Beck-Holmes smiled broadly. 'Well! A letter! You
are lucky. Would you like me to read it to you?'

'No thank you. I can read.'

The words sounded sharper than she intended and Mrs
Beck-Holmes' smile faltered as she hastily turned her attention to Miss Spinks.

With some difficulty Ivy pushed herself up from the chair
and began to move slowly towards the door. She would
read the precious letter in the dormitory where she hoped
she would be alone.

FIVE

Donald threw open the door of the office and almost bounced in. Today was the day Richard Preston was coming by to discuss the progress of the investigation, if any, and Donald could hardly wait.

Judith looked up from her typewriter. 'Pigs will fly!' she said. 'Only *five* minutes late!'

'Has anyone ever told you that you have a sparkling wit?' he demanded, hanging his jacket on the coat stand and rolling up his shirt sleeves.

'Not lately, no.'

'I wonder why that is.'

She grinned. 'Has anyone ever told you that sarcasm is the lowest form of wit?'

'Preston will be here in precisely ten minutes,' he informed her. 'Are we ready for him?'

'Except for the red carpet. I dusted off the spare chair and have a tray set for three cups of tea.'

'No biscuits?'

'I bought some custard creams, Donald, but you ate them all yesterday. I did warn you.'

'Where's the copy of his letter to us?' he asked.

She placed it on his desk. 'And here's a copy of the letter you wrote to Ivy Busby. She would have received it yesterday.'

'I want him to see it . . . And the notes about my meeting with Miss Lefevre?'

He looked harassed, she thought. Panicking as always. He had no idea how good he was at his job. 'In your folder, Donald. Where else would they be?' She handed the folder to him.

'How do I look? Honestly,' he demanded.

'A little mad and your hair is somewhat dishevelled.'

'So, in a word – utterly professional?' He tried to flatten his hair.

She grinned. 'I'd be impressed – but then, I'm your cousin and a great fan.'

'Thanks. Now, wait while I read this aloud and then pop out for some custard creams.'

'Must I? The chances are he won't like custard creams anyway – and being an American he'll want coffee instead of tea.'

'Get whatever we need,' he instructed. 'No expense spared. Honestly, Judith. I want to impress him . . . And I'm your boss, remember. You're the secretary. Don't make jokes at my expense.'

'As if I would!'

Pacing what was available of the cluttered floor, he began to read.

'*Dear Mrs Busby, as you can see from the enclosed business card, I am a private investigator and have recently been hired by Mr Richard Preston to look again into the disappearance of Leonora Matlowe, née Preston. Richard Preston is coming to England in a bid to discover the truth about Leonora's disappearance.*'

Judith sighed loudly. She had heard the letter several times already.

Ignoring the hint, Donald continued. '*As you were once a nanny to Leonora and Richard Preston and were also, for a time, the nanny to Emmeline and Edith Matlowe, I understand that Richard Preston will wish to meet and speak with you, partly to renew your acquaintance after all these years but also in the hope that you may be able to shed some light on the unfortunate affair especially as you were still caring for the twins at the time of her disappearance.*'

Judith studied her nails. She thought the letter very well done, clear and concise, but she had given him her opinion previously and had no intention of repeating herself.

He glanced up. 'If she is no longer able to read, no doubt someone will read it to her.'

'Almost certainly.'

'*Will you be willing to see Leonora's brother? I am told you are being cared for by the very splendid Sutton Ladies*

Charity Group but I hope this will not deter you from considering a meeting, especially as it might provide new leads into the case and help our investigations.

'*However, I realize that you may well consider this an intrusion and, although Richard Preston will be disappointed, I feel sure he will understand.*

'*I look forward to hearing from you as soon as possible and will show a copy of this letter to Richard Preston when I see him.*

'*Your obedient servant, Donald Watson.*'

He glanced across at his cousin. 'How does it sound?'

'The same as it did when you read it last time. You know my feelings. I think it's sneaky not to tell her that Leonora's brother is going to try and get custody of the twins.'

He rolled his eyes, exasperated at her lack of enthusiasm. 'I explained that. I think she's an old lady and probably can't take in too much at once. The shock might finish the poor old thing off!'

'How do you know she's a poor old thing? Just because she's a woman it—'

He held up his hand. 'Stop! There's no time for the lecture. Just pop out for the coffee and biscuits, please, Judith. He'll be here soon.'

There were footsteps on the stairs and they watched the door, hoping that it was a client for the solicitor on the floor above. The door opened.

'Mrs Montini!' they cried, dismayed.

Judith snatched up her purse and, with a wicked wink for Donald, slipped past her and out of the door.

Mrs Montini was small and shapeless, her dark brown eyes hidden behind spectacles. She carried a large and apparently ancient handbag. Puffing from the exertion on the stairs she sank uninvited on to a chair and waved the letter she had received.

'What is this?' she demanded. 'A letter to settle the account?' Her voice still held a trace of her Italian ancestry. 'Why do you stop looking? You have no . . .'

Donald drew in a long breath and sat down beside her. 'Dear Mrs Montini, I have to remind you of a very sad fact.

Your husband wandered away one night because he was very muddled in his mind, and he . . .'

'Muddled in his mind?' Her tone was indignant.

'And it was dark and he stumbled into the road and . . .'

Hugging her large handbag she leaned forward. 'Muddled in his mind! My husband . . .'

'And he was knocked down by a car and killed. I'm sorry to have to remind you but now that we know he is no longer considered missing *but dead*, we cannot go on looking for him. The bill for our services is very small. If you wish to settle it now . . .' Leaving the sentence unfinished, he glanced desperately at the clock. Please, he thought, let her be gone by the time Richard Preston arrives.

Slowly Mrs Montini drew the letter and the bill from the envelope. 'Yes, it is a small amount.' She seemed to sink lower in the chair. 'You are saying my husband is dead?'

'You went to his funeral. My cousin, Judith, came with you.'

'But I have been to the churchyard and there is no head-stone. How can he be buried?'

'He was buried, Mrs Montini, but you have to pay for the headstone to be installed – with his name on it.'

'Ah! A headstone! Maybe . . .'

'Mrs Montini, I have another client due at any moment. Suppose you . . .' He froze. More than one set of footsteps were approaching.

The door opened and Judith came in with a young, good-looking man who stepped quickly forward and held out his hand.

Donald shook it. 'Mr Preston . . .' He glanced helplessly at Judith.

'Good morning, Mrs Montini!' she cried cheerfully. 'How nice to see you.'

Mrs Montini rose to her feet, eyeing the newcomer dubi-ously. 'My husband wandered away . . .' she began.

Richard Preston turned to Donald for enlightenment.

Donald said, 'Judith, Mrs Montini now realizes that her husband's grave needs a headstone and . . .'

'A headstone? But of course.' She smiled. 'Mrs Montini,

suppose I help you with that? We could meet here at the office one day next week and I will take you to a man who makes headstones. We can decide what you want to put on it.'

Donald crossed his fingers behind his back.

'A man who makes headstones? Oh yes, I think I should like that. But I have this small account to . . .'

Donald said, 'We'll leave that until you come next week.' He lowered his voice. 'I'll make a cup of tea – or coffee – for Mr Preston while you see her out.'

Richard Preston said, 'Coffee, please, black.' He strolled tactfully to the window and watched the traffic go past while various things were set in motion and Mrs Montini finally made her way out, smiling bravely as she went.

Richard Preston turned from the window. 'She sounded the way I felt when I first heard that Leonora was missing. All shook up. That's how we'd put it back home. What happened to her husband?'

Judith took over from Donald, leaving him free to explain and to settle their client into a chair. Judith opened the bag of biscuits and arranged some on a plate. Five minutes later the meeting proper began.

At nine o'clock the following day, as the twins scurried down the stairs, the telephone rang.

'That made me jump!' cried Emmie.

'Me too! I jumped.'

They continued their flight through the kitchen and out into the garden where their assignment was to look for butterflies or bees and to see which flowers they preferred.

At a leisurely pace, Marianne prepared to follow them down the stairs. The sun was shining and it was very warm so she had decided that they would also sit in the garden to do their verbal spelling. For this reason she paused at the landing cupboard and found a picnic rug, determined not to give her employer any excuse, such as damp grass, to send them indoors again.

Lorna answered the telephone and fetched Mrs Matlowe. Poised on the landing, Marianne remained where she was, rather than interrupting her employer by making her way downstairs.

'Who is this? Richard who?'

Already Mrs Matlowe sounded irritable, thought Marianne.

'Oh!' It was more of a gasp. 'My sister told me to expect ... What's that? Come here? Certainly not. That is, I see no need, Mr Preston ... I see no need for a meeting of any kind. To be plain, Mr Preston, I very much object to your visit to my sister. I consider it snooping. An unpleasant habit, I'm sure ...'

Embarrassed, Marianne withdrew quietly until she was out of sight but she stayed within hearing distance, intrigued by the one-sided conversation. Was Mrs Matlowe going to refuse to see Leonora's brother?

'Don't take that tone of voice with me, Mr Preston. I am not accustomed to being bullied and I ...' Mrs Matlowe let out an exaggerated sigh. 'Naturally I understand that you want to learn what happened to your sister but I have no such need. To be frank, I did not like her and the feeling was mutual. She ran off after a stupid row and abandoned the children. As far as I am concerned she ...'

Intrigued, Marianne moved forward a little so that she could see her employer. Mrs Matlowe was sitting on the chair beside the telephone, one hand clasped to her chest.

'Police investigation?' Her voice rose. 'I see no need for ... Mr Preston, I would call that a threat! In fact I would call it blackmail!' Her voice was rising. 'No, you are not trying to be nice, Mr Preston. You are being most unpleasant, trying to thrust your way into our lives ... Don't you think the twins have suffered enough already?'

Marianne could imagine Cook and Lorna, hidden behind the kitchen door, also anxious not to miss a word.

'An offer? How dare you suggest ...' Mrs Matlowe raised her eyes heavenward, as she listened intently to the voice on the other end of the line. 'Just once? You are sure of that? Well, maybe just once – if that means we shall be shot of you. It's all most inconvenient and I shall ... Certainly not. I insist that I shall be present at each interview. In fact

we shall all come together. There will be nothing under-
hand . . . Very well, one visit, tomorrow at eleven o'clock.
And if you do harass me further, I shall speak to my lawyer.
Is that understood? Goodbye to you, Mr Preston.'

She hung up the receiver and sat staring into space, her
chest heaving with emotion. Then, as the anger drained
away, she lowered her head and covered her face with her
hands.

Marianne counted to ten and then made her way downstairs. Mrs Matlowe sprang to her feet. 'Fetch Cook and
Lorna, Marianne, and come into the lounge.'

Two minutes later she turned from the window to face
them. She had calmed herself, Marianne saw with reluctant admiration, and even managed a smile. 'The children's
uncle, Richard Preston, is coming tomorrow for a short
visit – to see them. He is in England hoping to find his
sister – a stupid wild goose chase, but we must humour
him. I've agreed that he speaks to all of us for a few
moments to satisfy himself that none of us knows
anything that will help him solve the mystery of Leonora's
disappearance.'

Lorna said, 'We wasn't even here, Mrs Matlowe, so we
don't know anything – except what we've heard.'

Mrs Matlowe turned gimlet eyes on her maid. 'What
you've heard? I hope you haven't been listening to gossip,
Lorna. You won't last much longer in my employ if you
have!'

'She hasn't, ma'am,' Cook said quickly. 'But you know
how it is. People will talk and it was in all the papers and
such. People have long memories.'

Mrs Matlowe straightened her back. 'Her disappearance
was unfortunate. The police – rightly in my opinion –
quickly lost interest. Wives leave their husbands. Husbands
leave their wives. No one expects the police to waste time
on them . . . My son, sadly, felt he should go after her and
bring her back. If he hadn't been driving in search of her,
he would be alive today. Indirectly Leonora killed the children's father and I, for one, will never forgive her.'

Cook took a chance. 'So do you think she's dead, ma'am?

Or do you think her brother will find her? I mean, it would
be wonderful if he did . . . wouldn't it?'

They had to wait for Mrs Matlowe's reply. 'After all this
time . . . I think it would be a miracle if she were to be
found . . . because . . .' She swallowed hard. 'If she is still
alive and hasn't come back to the twins then it would mean
she has abandoned her own children. Doesn't love them
enough to come back for them. You see what I'm saying?
Emmie and Edie are old enough to understand these things.
They would be distraught.'

Lorna said, 'Poor little mites.'

'Exactly! Better that she's dead – and stays that way.'

The ticking of the clock seemed to grow louder as they
waited to be dismissed.

On impulse, Marianne said, 'If she's dead then . . . do
you think she was murdered?'

'Murdered? Of course not. Don't be so melodramatic,
Marianne. If she's dead then she must have been in an
accident or . . . or contracted an illness.'

Lorna said, 'People do die young of illnesses because
my cousin's friend got whooping cough and then it went
on to her chest and got much worse and . . .'

'Thank you, Lorna. You can spare us the details. Get
back to your work, please, and remember – eleven o'clock
tomorrow morning sharp. We'll give the wretched man his
answers and then send him packing.'

Richard Preston, thought Marianne next morning, was
disconcertingly attractive for someone so young. Too
young for his personality to show through the bright green
eyes, classically shaped features and humorous but vulnerable mouth. His brown hair shone with cleanliness and
had been well cut. Easy to see that a few years ago he
might have been head boy in a good school, or played
for the college baseball team. She wondered how her
employer could possibly manage to dislike him, but she
surely would.

Looking quite relaxed, Richard Preston stood in front
of the household, who had been told to stand in line before

him – rather like naughty schoolchildren, Marianne thought, amused. Mrs Matlowe sat in an upright chair, her hands folded in her lap. Upstairs the twins had been given some sums to do and had been threatened by their grandmother to early bedtimes for a week, if they dared to come down from the schoolroom before they were sent for.

'I'm Leonora's little brother,' Preston announced himself with a smile, 'and I guess you all think I'm wasting my time here in England but I'm making one last attempt to trace my sister – and, of course, I want to meet my young nieces, Emmeline and Edie.'

From the corner of her eye Marianne saw that Mrs Matlowe was keeping a sharp eye out for any sign of rebellion from her staff. She had given them another warning about gossiping and a hardly veiled hint as to the penalties for disobeying. But she had reckoned without Richard Preston. Cook was eyeing him with obvious favour while Lorna was positively ogling him, her eyes wide, her mouth slightly open in what promised to be a smile were she given the slightest encouragement.

He went on, 'I won't pretend Leonora and I were close because I was too young and didn't move in her circles, but I loved her in my way. She was the bright star in our family, funny, light-hearted, wanting to please. I'm sorry that most of you weren't able to meet her.'

Mrs Matlowe coughed and glanced pointedly at the clock.

'Leonora was just twenty when she met and fell in love with Mrs Matlowe's son, Neil. It was obvious that they were made for one another and when they ran off and were secretly married—'

'They had no right to marry in haste that way.' Mrs Matlowe glared at him. 'I should have met her first. That is a normal courtesy in this country.'

Ignoring the interruption, Preston said, 'My parents were upset. My mother had hoped for a very lavish wedding but they were so happy together that—'

'Could we move on, Mr Preston? Get back to the point of this meeting.'

Her jarring tone finally unsettled him. His expression changed to one of hurt. 'I'm sorry you feel . . .'

Cook, greatly daring, said, 'She sounds a very nice woman, Mr Preston. I do hope you find her.'

Mrs Matlowe gave her a withering look. 'Could we get on, *please*?' she repeated coldly. 'Does anyone have anything to tell our visitor that might help him in his search?'

Lorna raised a hand. 'I heard from Mrs Brannigan next door that the people on the other side of us took some nice photographs of your sister with the children. He might let you see them.'

Marianne's pulse speeded up at the look on Mrs Matlowe's face.

'Did he, Lorna?' Richard Preston was positively beaming at her. 'Thank you. Any photographs of my sister with the twins would be . . .'

Mrs Matlowe said, 'I think it most unlikely, Mr Preston. I certainly never gave him permission to take photographs of my family.'

Lorna rushed on while she had their visitor's full attention. 'Oh, he didn't need permission. He took them from one of his windows. His name's Edward Barnes and he's quite famous for his photographs. I mean, that's what he does for a living. The Derby, the regatta, he photographs them all.'

Preston nodded his thanks. 'I'll go round later and speak to him about them. They probably won't help with my search but it will be great to see them.'

Through clenched teeth, Mrs Matlowe sent Lorna back to the kitchen. 'You've had your say,' she told her. 'Go back to the kitchen and get on with your work.'

Marianne asked, 'Did you ever hear from Mrs Matlowe's son while he was searching in America? Did he have any idea why Leonora left the way she did?'

Mrs Matlowe stepped forward. 'Mr Preston is here to ask his own questions, Marianne, not answer yours. If you have nothing useful to contribute . . .'

'No, please let her finish, Mrs Matlowe,' he said. 'This is the sort of dialogue I was hoping for – random talk that might somehow trigger a memory or a clue.' He smiled at her to soften the words.

Marianne persevered. 'I have heard rumours that the boat house is haunted. Did your sister ever comment on that?'

'Strange that you should ask that,' he replied. 'I have several letters with me that—'

'Letters?' cried Mrs Matlowe. 'From your sister?' The idea clearly dismayed her.

'Yes. She was a great letter writer!' He smiled. 'The letters always rambled, nothing formal with Leonora, but they came straight from the heart. I've brought them with me and I want the private investigator to read them. They might help in some way.'

Marianne asked, 'Were any of them written after she left here – because the postmarks on the envelopes might . . .'

'Sadly not. They would have been useful, but no . . . But to return to your question, Leonora did mention the boat house once or twice. It seemed to fascinate her although she didn't think it was haunted. She talked about the Henley regatta and was eager to go out on the river in a punt but she seemed to have the impression that the boat house was unsafe in some way. She was hoping . . .'

He broke off as Mrs Matlowe suddenly groaned. Her head was bent so that her face was hidden but it was immediately obvious to Marianne that she was in some distress.

Marianne said, 'Mrs Matlowe, are you all right?'

Mrs Matlowe raised her head. 'Stop fussing!' she muttered, her voice a mere croak. Clutching her left arm, she groaned again, her face screwed up with pain. With an obvious struggle she somehow forced herself on to her feet but there was a sheen of perspiration on her skin.

'I'm absolutely fi—' she began but then the colour drained from her face and she suddenly swayed. Her eyes closed. 'Neil!' she gasped and would have fallen if Richard Preston had not caught her in his arms and lifted her on to the sofa.

A shocked Cook cried, 'I'll fetch a glass of water,' and hurried out of the room.

Marianne knelt beside her employer, took hold of her hand and felt for a pulse in the wrist. Before she could

determine either way, Mrs Matlowe snatched back her hand.
'Get away from me!' she mumbled, blinking, one hand to
her head. 'I'm . . . I'm perfectly well. Just a moment's
dizziness and no wonder. All this fuss so long after her
disappearance! I have better things to do with my time.'
She threw an accusing look in Preston's direction and struggled back to a sitting position. 'Just get on with your
questions, Mr Preston, and hurry it up.'

Cook returned with the water but Mrs Matlowe waved
it away.

There was a moment's silence while they watched her
nervously. She was breathing deeply, trying to regain her
composure. And trying, thought Marianne, with a twinge
of compassion, to restore her position of dominancy, which
had slipped during her fainting spell. She remained sitting,
however, so was obviously not confident enough to stand
up again.

Richard Preston cleared his throat. 'I guess I can't answer
that question, Miss Lefevre – about the boat house being
haunted. Why do you ask?'

'Because I glanced in one day out of curiosity and saw
a punt floating on the water. At least I thought I did . . .'

Lorna slipped back into the room unnoticed.

'. . . but it's very gloomy in there,' Marianne went on.
'Last time I looked in the punt was gone.' She turned to
Mrs Matlowe. 'Could anyone be using the boat house
without your knowledge?'

'Quite impossible, Marianne. The outer gates – those that
open on to the river – are firmly locked. A bolt on the
inside. You have an overactive imagination . . .' She took a
deep breath. 'Perhaps I should explain that I have a great
fear of water and particularly of the boat house. I was only
ten when my favourite uncle was drowned during the regatta.
His punt overturned at one of the locks and the other boats
closed over him. My mother said it was so crowded with
boats it was a log jam. His body was washed ashore further
down the river the following day.'

'My dear Mrs Matlowe!' cried Preston, with genuine
concern. 'What a terrible thing to happen!'

Cook said, 'Lord help us!'

'I've never forgotten the grief . . . and that's why I didn't want a punt in the boat house. I have never set foot in a boat since then and I didn't want anyone else to do so, but as soon as I married, my husband insisted on replacing it. Leonora wanted to go out in the punt with Neil and I couldn't allow it.'

Marianne frowned. 'So what happened to the punt?'

'It was sunk. It became rotten and dangerous and . . . I sank it.'

After a pregnant silence Mrs Matlowe suddenly forced herself to her feet. 'I think that's quite enough in the way of revelations, Mr Preston. If Cook and Lorna return to their work, I shall busy myself upstairs and Marianne will bring the twins down to spend half an hour with you as arranged. Marianne can then see you out. Good day to you.'

Somehow she made a dignified exit.

Cook said, 'Come along, Lorna, we've work to do.' She hesitated, unsure of the protocol, and finally said, 'It's been nice meeting you, Mr Preston.'

Lorna said, 'Yes – and I hope you find your sister.'

They left the room with a reluctant Lorna waggling her fingers by way of 'goodbye'.

Left alone with the visitor Marianne said, 'I'm afraid she's rather prickly, Mrs Matlowe. It's just her way, I suppose.' Then she wondered why she was apologizing on behalf of her employer. 'I'll bring the children down.'

Five minutes later Emmie and Edie came shyly into the room where Preston, with outstretched arms, was waiting to greet them.

Marianne gave them a little push. 'This is Uncle Richard, children. Give him a nice hug and say hello.'

Edie moved forward and was hugged but Emmie hung back.

Their uncle pretended not to mind. He straightened up then sat on the sofa so that he no longer towered over them.

Emmie said, 'Did you know our mother?'

'Of course I did. She was my big sister. I was her little brother. She wrote to me and told me all about her lovely new babies – that was you and Edie.'

Edie retreated a little, frowning.

Emmie said, 'Grandmother says that our mother wasn't a very nice lady and she ran away and left us behind.'

Taken aback by her directness, his smile faltered. 'Well now, your grandmother only knew her for a short time but I knew her for sixteen years and that's a very long time. So I got to know Leonora and she was very nice. She loved you both very much. She wrote nice things about you in her letters.'

Edie took a step nearer to her uncle. 'Our father went to look for her when she ran away but he couldn't find her and then he died.'

'In a car accident,' Emmie added.

It seemed to Marianne that they both sounded wary and somehow resentful and her heart went out to them as well as to their uncle. She said, 'I'm afraid they are a little prejudiced but it's understandable, in the circumstances.'

He nodded. 'It's only natural. Orphaned at such a young age – I think they are coping very well, don't you?'

'I do. They are very resilient.'

Emmie said, 'But we aren't orphans now, are we, because we have an uncle.'

'Uncle Richard,' said Edie.

He smiled at them. 'How would you like to go on a big ship and sail to America with me and see your other grandmother? Would that be fun?'

The twins conferred in whispers for a few moments.

Emmie said, 'Would Marianne come with us?'

'Because we like Marianne.'

'Ah! Well, that depends.' He glanced at her for help.

Thinking quickly, Marianne said, 'We'll have to ask Grandmother, won't we?'

'Then maybe we'll do that. But not yet. We'll get to know each other first.'

'You could stay here,' Emmie suggested. 'You could stay in the spare bedroom next to Neil's room.'

'Neil's room?' Startled, he glanced again at Marianne.

'It used to be his bedroom,' she explained, 'and now it's unused.'

Emmie said, 'Oh, but Grandmother uses it when she wants to talk to our father. He doesn't answer but she does talk to him. I've heard her.'

They stared at Emmie but Edie said, 'Emmie listens at the door. It doesn't matter and it isn't really sneaky, is it, Marianne?'

The two adults exchanged smiles. Marianne said, 'It is a bit sneaky but I don't think your father would mind.' *But Mrs Matlowe would*, she thought, wondering nervously what else the children had discovered.

Richard Preston decided to change the subject. 'I thought we might go to the zoo tomorrow, twins. Would you like that?'

Emmie shook her head. 'Grandmother doesn't like us to be out of her sight because we're such a responsibility and she's past her prime. She wouldn't let us go to the circus with Aunt Ida.'

'But if she says yes – would you like that?'

They both nodded and Marianne said, 'Just the three of you. I'll stay home and write some letters.' Smiling, she told their uncle, 'You'll get to know each other quickly without me.'

'If she will allow it.'

It was arranged that he would telephone later to ask permission from Mrs Matlowe. They spent ten minutes in the garden and then he decided to leave because the children were getting overexcited and Marianne warned him that if their grandmother noticed, she would have the perfect excuse to refuse his request for the outing.

When he finally said goodbye, Marianne watched him go with mixed feelings, wondering what the next day would bring.

SIX

When Georgina left the children with their uncle she made her way slowly and carefully up the stairs, along the landing to Neil's room where, as always, she locked the door behind her. Trembling and struggling to breathe she crossed the darkened room, bent down to unlace and remove her shoes, then climbed on to his bed and lay down.

The pain in her arm had frightened her but she hoped she had hidden that from the others. There was no way she must show weakness, she reminded herself. They would all take advantage of her in their various ways, given the opportunity. Especially *him*. Oh yes! She had seen through Mr Richard Preston the first moment she set eyes on him. He wanted to take Neil's children from her. It was glaringly obvious to anyone who had their wits about them.

'Oh, Neil!' she whispered. 'They will drive me to distraction. Did you hear them – questions and lies and half-truths. They confused me so that I . . . If only you could have been beside me . . . I know we could have . . .' She put a hand to her head. 'Did you see what happened, dear? I had this terrible pain. I think I may have fainted because I found myself on the sofa with all of them glaring at me! I know they hate me. Yes they do, Neil. They were gloating. On and on about the wretched boat house until I was forced to tell them all about my poor Uncle Walter.'

For a while she was silent, trying, as she often did, to picture her uncle but she could only recall his hearty voice, his smile and the tickle of his moustache when he kissed her. Uncle Walter used to tease her in the nicest way, making her laugh even while she protested. He called her Georgy Porgy. Smiling faintly, she recited the verse. *'Georgy Porgy, pudding and pie, kissed the girls and made them cry. When the boys came out to play Georgy Porgy ran away!'* She used to pretend to be cross with him and he would run away, pretending to be frightened of her . . . So different from her dour father.

Suddenly shivering and close to tears, she remembered the dressing gown and slid from the bed to stagger across the room to the wardrobe. She cast a guilty look at the altar. She would speak to Him when she felt better. Tugging open the wardrobe door Georgina pulled her son's warm plaid dressing gown from its hanger. Returning to the bed, she lay down and covered herself with its rough wool, taking comfort from its familiarity. 'The pain was in my arm, Neil. I don't think it was anything to do with my heart, do you? I think it was just the strain, you know . . . all this worry. Not about you, dear, because I know you have forgiven me for not loving her the way you did, but . . . Well, we just didn't like each other and . . .' Her eyes closed. She smiled into the darkness of the room and waited hopefully for sleep to claim her.

Sleep, however, refused to come to her aid and her mind continued to buzz with unanswered questions and dire visions of the immediate future with Leonora's brother hovering over them like an ominous shadow.

Abruptly she sat up on the bed. 'Ida! I'll speak to Ida. I'll telephone her later when the staff have gone home and Marianne is in her room.'

With the prospect of support from her sister, Georgina felt marginally stronger and she waited impatiently for the hours to pass before she could make a telephone call that was not overheard.

At five to nine she could wait no longer and, seating herself on the telephone chair, she dialled her sister's number.

'Hello?'

'Ida, it's me. I have a favour to ask you. I was wondering if you'd like to come over . . .'

'What, now? It's nearly bedtime.'

'Not now. Tomorrow. And stay for a few days.'

'Are you all right, Georgie? You sound a bit . . .'

'Of course I'm all right. I'm perfectly all right. Now do you want to come or not?'

'What a charming invitation!'

Georgina raised her eyes heavenward. Please God don't
let her be in one of her awkward moods, she begged. 'Sorry,
Ida. I'm not altogether all right. That is, I had a funny turn
earlier – a pain in my arm. I don't think it was my heart.
I think . . .'

'In your heart! Oh no! What did the doctor say?'

'He didn't come. I didn't want to make any fuss because
he was here. The younger brother. I think I fainted but it's
all a bit of . . .'

'Of course I'll come over, dear. In the morning unless
you feel I should come tonight. I'll just pop a few things
in a suitcase and . . .'

'No, wait, Ida. The morning will do but as early as you
can. The thing is this – he probably wants to take the girls
out and naturally I . . .'

'Oh, how lovely! They'll love that. I thought you'd like
him. Rather a dish, isn't he!'

A dish! How like Ida! 'Hardly! I'm afraid we didn't
exactly hit it off and I don't intend to allow him to take
the girls out of my sight. Lord only knows what could
happen.'

'What *could* happen?' Ida said incredulously. 'What could
happen is they could have a lovely time with their newly
discovered uncle. What are you afraid of, Georgie? I think
it's charming that he wants to get to know his sister's children – and perfectly natural. Legally he is related to them.
I don't see how you can refuse him time with his nieces.'

Shocked, Georgina hesitated, thinking furiously. 'But he
might intend to take them back to America with him. I can't
let that happen, can I? Allow my son's children to be dragged
halfway round the world on a whim? Think what you're
saying, Ida!'

'You're their grandmother but his mother and father are
also grandparents. Whatever you think of the family the grandparents are entitled to see their grandchildren. Look, dear,
I'll come over first thing in the morning and we can talk
again but I don't think you should refuse his request. If you
alienate them they could refer it to the courts. The twins

aren't wards of court or anything, I know, but you surely don't want any kind of trouble with the courts. Much better to sort things out amicably.'

Georgina was finding it hard to breathe. Why on earth had she imagined her sister would be an ally, she thought bitterly. Trouble in the courts? Trust Ida to make things worse. 'Look, maybe it's not such a good idea,' she began, 'you coming . . .'

Ida said briskly, 'We'll deal with it, dear. Don't worry. I'll be there about eight thirty. Goodbye for now.'

Georgina sat there for a long time, newly alarmed, expecting the pain in her arm to return but it didn't, so she went to bed. She would get up early and see to the spare bedroom. Lorna could run a duster round when she arrived and a few flowers from the garden would brighten the window sill. Was she pleased that her sister was coming to stay for a few days? She really couldn't decide.

While Georgina had been surviving the afternoon and evening, Richard had been with Donald Watson and his cousin. Matters were going well, he felt. He had read the letter that Watson had sent to the old nanny and now Judith was handing him her reply. In a spidery hand, Ivy Busby had said, '*Dear Mr Watson, Richard is welcome at any time but please make an appointment first. Tell him not to worry – I am not yet in my dotage. Ivy Busby.*'

'Sounds promising, doesn't it?' Donald asked, sure of the answer. 'The point is, as far as I can gather, the nanny was part of the household when the drama took place and was not sent packing until some time later.'

'I wonder if she was in touch with my sister *after* she left.'

Judith glanced up from the file through which she was patiently sifting. 'If Ivy Busby was Leonora's nanny as well as being nanny to the twins, they were probably close and may have kept in touch by letter after Leonora left. Leonora might have confided in her.'

Richard frowned. 'But surely if Nan had anything to tell she would have contacted the police.'

Donald said, 'Not if she had been asked specifically to keep Leonora's whereabouts a secret. Even if Ivy Busby had no concrete evidence but just suspicions, she may have decided it was prudent to keep them to herself. And she was also probably mortified that she had been abruptly thrown out into the wide world after a long sheltered existence within a supportive family.' He looked at Richard. 'She may have thought, "To hell with the lot of them!" or words to that effect.'

After a moment's silence it was Judith's turn. 'Do you know if your family heard from the nanny after she was banished from the Matlowe household?'

'Not to my knowledge. But hey! I was only a youngster, remember, so my parents didn't tell me everything. But Leonora wrote to me until she disappeared. We weren't close while we were at home together but she seemed to need the contact after she'd left for England. Nothing, however, after she disappeared. I have a few of her letters that give a pretty clear idea of relations between Leonora and Neil's mother.' He produced a letter from his own file. 'Shall I read it out?'

'Please,' said Donald. 'Then Judith can hear it. She's not just my secretary. She's my partner most of the time. Right now she's putting the Montini file to bed but she'll be listening.'

'Try and stop me!' she laughed.

'Here goes then. *Dear Richie, Here I am again! Thought you'd like a few words from far away. I'm well and so are the babies. I am longing to bring them home. You will adore them. I know it's a cliché but I truly believe that our two girls are the sweetest, the prettiest and the cleverest in the whole world. Neil is quite infatuated by them and whenever they fall asleep he waits impatiently for them to wake up again so he can amuse them with rattles and whatnot. He calls them 'double trouble' but in a nice way . . .'*

He glanced up. 'I can imagine that. He was so excited by the idea of becoming a father.'

Judith shook her head. 'And then it all turned sour. Poor soul . . . But do go on.'

'*But you asked me about my new mother-in-law. I'm sad to say that Mrs M took one look at me and hated me! I know you won't believe me but she did. I have taken her baby boy from her and she is never going to forgive me. Even Neil agrees that she is behaving like a jealous shrew and nothing I can do will please her. He is totally at a loss.*

'*Neil has sprung to my defence on more than one occasion but that makes the old bat worse than ever. I never imagined that being a daughter-in-law would be so difficult.*

'*Don't say anything to Mother or Father, they will only fret about me and there's nothing they can do to help.*'

He glanced up. 'I think she was pretty unhappy around that time. It infuriated me that I was too young to help her in any way.'

Judith said, 'I suppose she needed to let off steam to someone and you were the one.'

Donald said thoughtfully, 'What are you actually expecting to discover, Mr— sorry, Richard. Her where-abouts? What happened to her? Are you hoping to *find* her after all this time?'

Richard shrugged, hesitated and said, 'A very good question! I don't think I have an answer. *All I could do to please her would be to quarrel with my beloved Neil and walk out of his life forever. Then she would have Neil and the two babies all to herself. But guess what, Richie? Your big sister is made of sterner stuff. I'm not leaving! Do write again. I long for letters from home. Your loving sister, Leonora.*'

Judith sighed. '*I'm not leaving!*' she quoted. 'And then we are expected to believe that she did just that.'

Richard folded the letter then looked up. 'I want to satisfy myself that nothing bad happened to her. I want to be sure that nobody . . . killed her. I've never felt easy in my mind that she just walked out on her husband and the twins. I tried to believe – we all did – that she had been on her way back to us when she met someone else and started a new life. That's my parents' version and it gives them some relief to believe that.'

'But not you.'

'Not me. I think she met someone on her way back to us – someone evil. I think she was murdered.'

'But the police found nothing to indicate foul play.'

'That doesn't mean there was nothing to find.'

Judith had closed the Montini folder and now slid it into a drawer in her desk. 'Mr Montini will soon have his headstone.' Smiling, she leaned forward, resting her arms on the desk and clasping her hands. 'So where do we go from here?'

Richard smiled faintly. 'You're going to ask me if I suspect anyone. The answer's no, but I *am* beginning to wonder about Mrs Matlowe's part in all this. She seems so repressed. So hostile towards me. I wonder if she knows more than she's willing to say. In other words, is she protecting someone? Her son, for instance. You say, Donald, that the police suspected him at one stage in the proceedings but they found absolutely no evidence.'

Donald looked thoughtful. 'From what I deduced from the police file it almost seemed at one stage in the investigation that Mrs Matlowe had suspected her son, although it seems very unlikely. Apparently it was Mrs Matlowe who first hinted that maybe something bad had happened to Leonora that prevented her from coming home when she'd cooled off. But that may be why Neil went off, allegedly in search of his wife but actually to avoid arrest.'

Richard considered this for a moment. 'You mean she alerted the police to the fact that it might have been her own son. A bit far-fetched, isn't it?'

Judith leaned forward. 'She probably didn't intend to – it might have slipped out. Maybe she heard them having a row . . . maybe Neil had a violent temper and she feared it might get out of hand. Then when she ran off Neil went after her and . . . maybe he found her and they had another row over his mother and he lost his temper, killed her accidentally and hid her body somewhere.'

Her cousin frowned. 'And then someone went after him and . . . What do we know about that car accident?'

Richard shrugged. 'You know, I went to that site where he was killed in the car crash. I spoke to the police and they were puzzled. The patrolmen insisted there was no other vehicle involved. Neil drove off a mountain road on a bend. One of them reckoned he had killed himself deliberately. Another reckoned he was just driving too fast for the corner. But he could have swerved to avoid a coyote or something. Or to avoid another vehicle that didn't stop because the driver didn't know he'd gone over the edge. Or claimed he didn't know. There was a whole heap of possibilities.'

'Do you think,' Donald asked, 'that Neil's death and Leonora's disappearance were somehow linked?'

'I can't figure that out. I can't find a link yet but there may be one. I promised my folks if there was anything to be found I'd do my darnedest to find it. I'm taking the twins to the zoo tomorrow but the following day I'll go see Nan. I hope she recognizes me. Nobody is sure of her age, it was always a well guarded secret, but she may be becoming forgetful, to say the least.' Richard shrugged. 'If she *does* know anything that will help me find Leonora – or even just find out what happened to her – it will be a bonus.'

Judith smiled. 'It will be a thrill for her to see you again.'

'She last knew me as a troublesome sixteen-year-old, because we haven't seen each other since she left for England with Leonora and the babies.' His grin broadened. 'I wanted to stop calling her Nanny because it sounded so babyish and offered to call her Nan instead but she fought me tooth and nail. She said she was a nanny, not a nan.'

'Who won the argument?' Donald asked.

'Neither of us. I guess you could say it was a truce. I didn't call her anything, and she pretended not to notice. But this time I'll call her Nanny – for old times' sake!'

Judith smiled. 'An amazing reunion, then.'

'You can say that again!'

SEVEN

Ten minutes before they closed for the day Judith broke the news to her cousin that she was expecting a child.

'A child?' He stared at her. 'You mean you'll be leaving me? How on earth will I manage without you?'

She gave him a frosty look. 'Is that the best you can do, Donald? I tell you the most exciting thing of my life and all you can say . . .'

'Judith! Oh my God!' He rolled his eyes. 'What a selfish brute I am. Please forgive me.'

'Well, I won't! Selfish, inconsiderate, insensitive . . .' She sighed theatrically. 'I tell you you're going to be an uncle and all you can think of is . . .'

'An *uncle*!'

Suspiciously she narrowed her eyes. 'So, Donald, you have one last chance to put things right.'

He adopted an expression of exaggerated delight. 'Dear Judith, what extraordinary news. You are expecting a child! Wonderful!'

'Not convincing, Donald!' she told him crossly. 'This is me, about to become a mother. Your cousin and business partner.'

'Secretary!' His mouth twitched.

'Business partner! Donald, you have to be impressed.' She looked at him imploringly.

At last he grinned and moved close to give her a congratulatory kiss. 'Congratulations, my dearest cousin, friend, confidante – and business partner. You are incredible, Judith. Not only do you do my typing, answer my telephone, file my letters, make the coffee and help me with the investigating – you also, in your spare time, manage to produce a child!'

'Oh stop it!' Exasperated, she laughed.

'No seriously, I'm bowled over. When will you be leaving? No! I'll put it another way. When is the happy event? Have you told your parents? Do you want a boy or a girl? Tell me everything.'

'It's due in January, yes, and we'd like a boy.' She pulled the cover over her typewriter.

'Am I old enough to be an uncle?'

'You're almost too old! You should be a father by now, Donald. Why don't you find yourself a nice girl and settle down?'

'A nice girl who can type . . . yes.' He kept his face straight.

'Donald! You have a one-track mind! There's more to life than "Donald Watson, Private Investigator" – or there ought to be.'

'Is Tom pleased?'

'Thrilled to bits. We both are.'

'It's great news, Judith, and it calls for a celebration. Open the door of the cupboard.'

'The cupboard? Why?'

'You'll see.'

He watched her face as she threw open the door and saw a bottle of champagne nestling in a basket of straw and two champagne flutes. 'Oh, Donald!' She turned to him, accusingly. 'You knew all along! You rotter! Leading me on like that. Who told you? Not Tom?'

'No. You told your mother in confidence and your mother told my mother in confidence . . .' He collected the bottle, opened it and carefully filled the glasses. 'I wanted you to tell me in your own time and in your own way.' He handed her a glass and raised his own. 'Here's to you and Tom and your first baby!' They clinked glasses and sipped, both beaming with pleasure.

Judith said, 'But seriously, Donald, you know I wouldn't leave you for any other reason. I expect to leave in October, so you must try and find a replacement so that we can overlap for a week or two. I want to make sure she is going to be suitable for you.'

'She? I might choose a male secretary.'

'Oh no, Donald! That wouldn't be at all suitable. You need a woman's intuition – a woman's way of looking at things – to complement your own. I've thought about it, and when you interview the applicants, you must choose someone with tact and discretion and warmth. Why are you looking at me like that?'

'Are these the traits I lack?'

'Now would I say such a thing? No, but women can sympathize with, say, a woman whose husband is seeing someone else.' She regarded him earnestly. 'She could cry all over me but not you. And she needs to have good grammar for the letters and a pleasant telephone manner . . . and lots of patience and be willing to do overtime. Also have an interest in investigative work.'

Donald drained his glass and waited for hers to be emptied. As he refilled them he said, 'Why don't you do the interviews for me, Judith?'

Her serious expression was instantly replaced by one of intense satisfaction. 'Oh, Donald, of *course* I will. I thought you'd never ask!'

Ida arrived promptly at eight thirty while Georgina was still eating breakfast, and decided that she could eat 'just a little more'.

Georgina, fully dressed and looking nervous, said, 'There are stewed apples, also toast and marmalade. Help yourself while Lorna refreshes the teapot.'

She was still unsure whether or not it had been a mistake to invite her sister to stay but the thought of the coming confrontation with Richard Preston was making her stomach churn and Ida's large, noisy presence made Georgina feel slightly less anxious.

'So they're going to the zoo.' As usual Ida was straight to the point. 'I've thought about it on the way over, to take my mind off the crowded tram. Lord, what a rabble! Old, young, dogs on leads, cats in baskets, babies in arms, toddlers bawling, couples arguing – and all before eight thirty! I pitied the conductor. I'd have stopped the tram and sent them all packing but that's public transport for you!

Mm! Very good marmalade. Did your cook make it?'

'I bought it at a bring and buy sale, if you must know, but seriously, I do wonder, Ida, if I should let the girls go with him. Suppose he doesn't bring them back or one of them has an accident? I'd never forgive myself. I feel I owe it to Neil to . . .'

'Now don't start all that nonsense about Neil. It's morbid, Georgina. I don't mean this unkindly but neither he nor Leonora stayed around to care for the girls so you don't have to apologize to either of them for anything.' She sipped her tea and pulled a disapproving face. 'I do wish you'd buy some Earl Grey, Georgina. This is much too strong. All that tannin!' She added more milk. 'But as for today, why would Richard want to keep them? How can he look after them at his age? And anyway, I thought he was here to try and find his sister – or find out what happened to her.'

'That's what he says but . . . would you trust him? If he's anything like Leonora . . . I wouldn't trust him further than I could throw him!'

'You're prejudiced, dear, that's all. You must give him a chance. He could take your Marianne to the zoo with him, couldn't he?'

'Marianne said he suggested that but she wants to write some letters so doesn't wish to go with them. I can hardly insist. She's a governess, not a nanny.'

'If I were you, dear, I'd let them go. I really don't believe they'll come to any harm . . . and you and I can have a little expedition of our own. I'll take you out to tea in that little tea shop you like and we'll have cucumber sandwiches and chocolate eclairs!'

In spite of herself, Georgina smiled. As children, a visit to a tea shop was a rare treat. It was kind of her sister to think of it.

Ida said, 'Don't you think, Georgie, it would be better to give in gracefully than to argue the point and lose? And isn't it good for the girls to have some more family? You look after them very well but their world is very narrow.'

'But suppose he wants to take them back to America!'

'It would be an adventure for them.'

'An adventure? Are you mad? You know how I feel about a sea crossing, Ida. Their safety cannot be guaranteed, no matter how the ship is built. Just imagine if he had come earlier and taken them back on the *Titanic*'s maiden voyage! They would all have died.'

'Not everyone died, Georgie. The women and children went into the lifeboats first . . .'

'Not all of them were saved.'

Ida pursed her lips, exasperated. 'You are just being stubborn, making that an excuse. A trip to America when they are a little older would be wonderful for them and they might make some friends and then they can come home and write to each other. Pen friends. That's what they call it. It broadens the mind.'

'You're on his side, aren't you?' Georgina said bitterly. 'I might have guessed.'

Ida wagged a finger at her. 'I'm not taking sides, dear, but I'm worried about the strain you're under. This fainting fit you had yesterday. If you're not worried I certainly am.'

'That was nothing, Ida!'

Ida ignored the interruption. 'And the time will come when the children grow up when they will be less tractable and you'll be older. They'll be very demanding and you'll be exhausted by them. You'll be glad to hand them over to their other family for a few weeks.'

'It was nothing,' Georgina repeated. 'It was just so sudden. I was frightened. Looking back it was just a dizzy spell.'

'It sounds like a heart problem to me and I'm taking you to the doctor. *My* doctor.' She held up her hand. 'It's no use arguing with me; I've already made an appointment for next week and I shall come with you. Do you want to die, Georgina?'

'Die? Certainly not, but . . .'

'Then listen to reason. You cannot let the twins down by neglecting your health.' She wiped her mouth with her serviette and smiled. 'Now then, what time is he coming?'

'He's going to telephone first and . . .'

'How thoughtful of him. Then let's set to and tell the twins. I'm looking forward to those cucumber sandwiches – and I shall eat two eclairs!'

'Ida!'

'I don't care, dear. I shall eat whatever I like. I realize life is slipping away. I don't want to end my life with any regrets. Once or twice recently I've treated myself to a glass of sherry before I go to bed.'

'Tut! You're incorrigible!' In the face of Ida's determined enthusiasm, and still exhausted from the previous day's events, Georgina decided not to argue further about the zoo but, crossing her fingers, she uttered a silent prayer for an uneventful day and a safe return of the twins.

Mcanwhile, in the charity home, Ivy Busby was arguing with Nesta who was unpleasantly surprised by the change in her manner. Gone was the quiet, almost morose woman who kept her thoughts to herself, rarely engaged with the other women and almost never grumbled. Now, since receiving her letter, she had become argumentative, almost demanding.

'How can I wear these clothes?' she cried indignantly. 'Tomorrow I have a young man coming to visit me and I will look pathetic! Whatever will he think? Richard grew up to think of me with respect. He will be shocked, Nesta, and I cannot bear to imagine his expression.'

'You don't look at all pathetic, Miss Busby. Truly you don't.'

'And I tell you I do!' She glanced around for confirmation and her gaze rested on Magda Llewellyn. 'Magda, please tell Nesta that I look pathetic.'

'You do. Yes! So very pathetic!' Magda, a Polish immigrant, had married a retired English colonel a year before he died and left her penniless. She was knitting a small square, using recycled wool – a square which was destined eventually to join other squares to form a blanket. 'Most certainly you are looking pathetic. We all are the same. Tragic figures. What are we but the world's rejections?'

Nesta, feeling understandably betrayed by this ungrateful utterance, turned on her. 'Please, Magda. This is a private conversation. Get on with your knitting.'

'Pah! Who wants blanket made of squares?'

'The homeless. It's in a very good cause.'

'Blankets for people worse off than us?' Magda tossed her head. 'I do not care even to be thinking about it. And as for your *private* conversation, is not so very private after all!' Magda sniffed. 'I hear every word.' She tapped her chest then indicated another inmate, who was bending forward short-sightedly, attempting to do a jigsaw puzzle. 'And look at Miss Spinks. She listening also to this so very private conversation. She not missing a word.'

Miss Spinks looked up vaguely. 'Oh, I am, dear, I am.' A lifetime of needlework as a dressmaker had ruined her eyesight and robbed her of her way to earn a living. She now spent hours peering at the jigsaw pieces and trying to force them into the wrong gaps.

Magda pointed a trembling finger. 'See! Even the cat is listening!'

As though it understood and was insulted by this slur, the large tortoiseshell cat leaped to its feet and dashed from the room.

Nesta said, 'Oh, the poor thing!'

Annoyed by the distraction, Ivy nevertheless made use of the interruption.

'There you are! Magda agrees that I do look pathetic. I'm not losing my reason. I look in the mirror and what I see depresses me. The figure I see cannot be me!'

Nesta was at a loss. 'You mustn't upset yourself,' she begged.

Ivy went on, her voice rising. 'I am not at all ungrateful for all the Sutton Group has done for me over the past years, but look at this cardigan . . .'

'Green suits you, Miss Busby.'

'I don't deny that, Nesta, but see the elbow – it is so frayed it is almost a hole . . .' She poked at it savagely and a small hole appeared. 'There! What did I say? And this skirt hangs on me like a sack and makes me look as if I'm wasting away! Please, Nesta, ask Mrs Beck-Holmes to arrange for me to have some better clothes just for tomorrow. My first visitor. I must look my best.'

Nesta sighed with exasperation. 'But he won't notice your skirt because you'll be sitting down and you can keep the frayed sleeve out of sight.'

'Sitting down, you say? Ah, but I might not! I might walk in the garden. Get away from the smell of boiled cabbage and liniment!'

Magda, thoroughly enjoying her grumbles, sniffed again. 'Is it a garden we have here or a very large window box? So small it is!'

Ignoring her, Ivy persevered with her sentence. 'Walk in the garden with him in hopes of a little privacy. We have things to talk about, you see. Important things. Important questions to answer.' She glanced triumphantly at her companions. 'And my young visitor comes from a wealthy American family and . . .' Her eyes narrowed suddenly. 'He might well make a small, or a not so small, donation to the Sutton Group. I shall encourage him to do so if he appears at all impressed by what he sees.' She resisted the chance to glance at Nesta to see whether or not she had noticed the mention of a donation.

Nesta said, 'I'm sure he will be impressed.'

Ivy sighed loudly. 'A pathetic old woman – that is what Richard will see.'

Nesta rolled her eyes but gave in gracefully. 'Well, I shall do as you ask, Miss Busby, and pass on your request.'

Ivy looked up at her in feigned surprise. 'You will? Oh what a dear you are. I'm sure they will understand. I am *so* looking forward to seeing him again.'

The visit to the zoo went ahead as Richard had hoped it would but only after an ill-tempered argument with the twins' grandmother, which only ended when she became breathless and Ida warned her about her heart.

After an initial shyness, Emmie and Edie had relaxed and the animals had proved wonderfully exciting so that by the time they had seen the bears, the tigers, the chimps, the giraffes and elephants, the girls were giddy with excitement and Richard was worn out by their constant questions.

At ten to five he suggested it was tea time and they gladly agreed. While they waited for the waitress to bring sandwiches and cakes, the bombardment of questions continued.

'Do the giraffes like having those long necks, Uncle Richard? 'Emmie asked.

Uncle Richard! He smiled, still trying to get used to the idea that he was an uncle in England, taking his two nieces on a trip to the London Zoo.

'I guess they get used to it,' he suggested. 'I guess they are wondering if we like having very short necks.'

Edie said, 'We've got used to our short necks, haven't we?'

'I've got used to having very small ears,' Emmie said thoughtfully. 'I suppose the elephants like their big flappy ears because they can hear lots of things.'

The waitress arrived with a tray and set out the food. She smiled at Richard. 'I've put three of each cake on the plate so there'll be no squabbling.' To the girls she said, 'You be good for your daddy!' and gave Richard a wink.

Emmie said, 'He's not our daddy. Our father is dead. He was in a car and it fell over a cliff. Uncle Richard is our new uncle from America.'

Edie nodded. 'We like him. He's fun. He makes us laugh.'

'Does he? Well, that's nice.'

'His big sister was our mother but she's disappeared. We don't remember her.'

'Oh dear!' The waitress appeared rather disconcerted by this gloomy news.

Edie reached for a sandwich but her sister hissed, 'Wait to be asked!' and she withdrew her hand and glanced guiltily at Richard to see if he had noticed her transgression.

To the waitress Emmie said, 'Grandmother didn't like our mother but Uncle Richard . . .'

'Hey, girls! That's enough!' Richard said hastily.

The waitress started to say something, thought better of it and turned away.

The twins exchanged anxious looks but Richard said blithely, 'What a great waitress – and hey! Look at the cakes she's brought us!'

'Jam tarts,' said Edie, 'cream puffs, date slices, butterfly cakes . . .'

Emmie looked at her uncle, frowning slightly. 'Are we really going to go to America to see our other grandmother?'

'I guess so, if your grandmother agrees, but she might say no because it's a long way to my home and she might worry about you.'

'She does love us,' Emmie explained earnestly. 'She prays for us every night so that God will make us good. She might miss us if we went away. She might be lonely.'

Edie finished a mouthful of sandwich and added, 'She might cry if we went away.'

Richard said, 'Let's not worry about that right now. Let's eat our tea before the sandwiches get cold.'

Two pairs of eyes regarded him with suspicion.

Edie said, 'Get cold?'

'He's joking!' Emmie explained.

Five minutes later the sandwiches had been devoured and they were making rapid inroads into the fancy cakes. Richard watched them with a heartfelt longing that it would be possible for them to visit his parents. They looked so much like Leonora. He also had instructions from his mother that if Nanny was fit enough, he should take her home as well. Years ago the Prestons had assured the nanny that she would have a home with the family until she died. Then Neil Matlowe had disrupted their plans by marrying Leonora and whisking her, the two babies and their nanny to England and within less than a year all their good intentions had been blown away by events. Georgina Matlowe had summarily dismissed the nanny for reasons best known to herself. By the time the Prestons had discovered what had happened no one knew where Ivy Busby was.

Richard was determined to right the wrong if it were not too late. He intended to take Ivy Busby back where she belonged.

The next day, Richard went to see his nanny, and Ida took the children to London to see Buckingham Palace and go up the Thames in a river bus. Georgina had been persuaded to have a day in bed to rest her heart and Marianne took the opportunity to find Donald Watson in his office.

He jumped to his feet, obviously delighted to see her.

'You've managed to slip away at last,' he said. 'Well done!'

'It wasn't difficult.' She explained the situation.

Judith beamed at her. 'The spy in the camp!'

'Oh dear! Is that what I am?'

Donald Watson said quickly, 'Of course not! Not a spy in that way. Let's say you are our eyes and ears. A very necessary part of the equation. Does that sound better?'

'Much better, thank you.'

The woman was giving her a rather strange look, Marianne thought, as though she were weighing her up, but then she smiled.

'Miss Lefevre,' she said, 'I am in the middle of a letter to a client – a will has gone missing and the entire family is in an uproar . . .'

'And you have to find it?'

'We *have* found it but I have to explain to them that we shall need a special warrant to get at it. Anyway, as soon as I finish this letter I'll make us a pot of tea.'

Donald said, 'My cousin Judith is my partner as well as my secretary. I don't know what I'll do without her when she leaves.'

Judith smiled. 'I'm expecting a baby early next year and we'll be interviewing candidates for my job. If you ever decide to give up being a governess . . .' She raised her eyebrows. 'Can you type?'

'I can but my speed could be better. I learned for the pleasure of a new skill and I started to teach myself shorthand but gave up on it when this job with Mrs Matlowe came along.'

Laughing, Donald intervened. 'Judith has volunteered to find me the perfect replacement. You must forgive her enthusiasm, Miss Lefevre. I'm expecting her to advertise the post in *The Times*, at least, and she'll probably have posters stuck on every lamp-post!'

'If I do a job, I do it properly,' she told him loftily and returned to her letter.

Donald settled himself to hear whatever Marianne had to tell him. 'You may know very little about past events but you can give me background information about present events which might make my job easier.'

'There really isn't much,' she admitted. 'Of course, Richard Preston has brought photographs of the Preston family to show to the twins . . . and some letters from Leonora, which he is also taking today to show to Ivy Busby – but you probably know all this already. He's hoping the nanny might recall something – anything at all – that might be a clue, but to tell you the truth, I don't feel very hopeful. He will obviously learn more from the old lady if her mind is still sharp.'

'According to Leonora's letters home,' Donald told her, 'Mrs Matlowe hated the new wife for "seducing her innocent son"! That's how she described the romance! That's how the disastrous chain of events was set in motion.'

'Did you know that Mrs Matlowe is unwell and her sister has made an appointment for her to see a doctor?'

'I didn't know. That's rather unsettling.'

'It seems to be her heart and I overheard her sister reminding her that their aunt died of a heart attack when she was only forty-one.'

'Oh dear! More worry for poor Mrs Matlowe.'

Marianne liked the way he spoke of her – avoiding the temptation to demonize her. 'I do feel sorry for her,' she agreed, 'even though she can be very overbearing and bordering on paranoid. But she has the twins' best interests at heart. They are all she has to remind her of Neil.'

'And the sister, Ida – what is she like?'

Not wishing to be disloyal, Marianne hesitated, then chose her words carefully. 'Very different. Chalk from cheese, in fact. Very down to earth, kind hearted, loves the twins – and tries her best to help Mrs Matlowe, who is often rather ungrateful.'

Judith looked up. 'Right, that's done. I'll put the kettle on to save time. I'll pop this in the pillar box as I go past.'

'Go past?' he echoed.

She put on her hat. 'We're out of sugar.'

He looked as though he was about to argue but
she gave him a look that silenced him and made her way
out.

Embarrassed, he smiled. 'I think my cousin is giving
us time for you to decide I would make the perfect
employer! You'll have to forgive her. Once she gets a bee
in her bonnet . . .'

Marianne laughed. 'If I didn't already have a job that I
love, I might be tempted. It all sounds very intriguing and
worthwhile. Helping people with their problems. Very satis-
fying, I imagine.'

'It is, actually – when we solve the problem. Of course,
we fail sometimes . . . and sometimes, even when we
succeed, the end result can mean heartache for someone.
Being the bearer of bad news is never easy, whatever the
circumstances. Being given proof that a man you love has
deceived you, or discovering that a trusted business partner
has cheated you or stolen money . . . People very often
blame the messenger.'

'But better to know than to remain in ignorance.'

He shrugged. 'Easy to say, Miss Lefevre, but it can often
be a painful business. We have to take the rough with the
smooth in this line of work.'

'I can imagine.'

Aware that he was watching her, Marianne glanced down
at her hands.

He said, 'If the children go to America you would be out
of a job.'

'I might be asked to go with them.'

'Go with them? Oh, I hope you don't!'

Marianne raised her eyebrows in mock protest. 'Would
you begrudge me a great adventure, Mr Watson?'

'I might miss you!'

She stared at him. 'Miss me? You don't even know me!'

'You're right,' he said, in some confusion. 'Forget I said
that, please.'

'It's a nice thought, nevertheless – that someone might
miss me.' She was touched by the implied compliment and

smiled. 'We might know each other better by the time the investigation ends.'

Encouraged by her words, Donald Watson brightened. 'I'll make it last as long as possible!'

They both laughed, relaxing a little. It was now Marianne's turn to be confused. *Marianne*, she thought, *you are flirting with Mr Watson! Whatever has come over you?* Without being aware of it, she sat up a little straighter and studied him. Not handsome in the way Richard Preston was handsome, she decided, but pleasant-looking in a comfortable way. She had just admitted to herself that getting to know him better might be pleasant, when Judith returned.

Donald Watson said, 'Where's the sugar?'

'Sugar? Oh that . . . I decided we didn't really need any because . . . because we have some sugar lumps somewhere.' She smiled ingenuously and made her way into what Marianne supposed was the kitchen area. When she reappeared a few moments later with a tray set with tea and biscuits, she settled it on the table and turned to Marianne. 'Did you say you could do shorthand?'

'I said I started to teach myself but . . .'

'Oh yes. I remember. Why don't you carry on with it just in case? Milk and sugar?'

'Yes. Two sugars, please. I suppose I could but . . .'

'You never know – you might fall out with your present employer.'

That wouldn't be too difficult, thought Marianne. 'Or I could simply leave . . . but that wouldn't be fair to the girls. No, I couldn't just leave.' She shook her head, surprised by the regret she felt.

Judith handed her cousin a cup of tea. 'There's no hurry, Miss Lefevre,' she said airily.' I shall be here for some months yet.'

Donald stared. 'But I thought you wanted time to train your successor and . . .' His voice trailed off as Judith shot him a warning look.

She smiled at Marianne. 'Honestly, Miss Lefevre, he doesn't listen to a word I say. Men don't, do they, because they think of us as the weaker sex.'

Marianne laughed, Judith bit into her custard cream and Donald Watson said, 'I know when I'm outnumbered! Maybe we should return to work!'

Magda's unkind reference to the size of the garden was a little exaggerated but not much. It was in fact a sizeable paved yard where the inmates could sit outside if the weather was reasonable and if they didn't mind sharing the area with the washing from time to time. Potted plants of various sizes stood around the outer edge and a white painted trellis supported a wilting honeysuckle plant, which was obviously unsuited to the permanent shade in which it found itself.

Ivy, however, was unaware of her surroundings, as she sat down on a long seat that boasted a made-to-fit cushion. Richard would have to make do with a canvas-seated deck chair, placed opposite her. She was wearing a green blouse with a darker green skirt, and a paisley shawl was draped elegantly around her shoulders. Nesta had taken care with her hair and she was wearing buttoned shoes that shone with recent polish. In fact, she thought she looked as well as it was possible to look at her age and she waited impatiently for Richard to arrive.

When Nesta ushered him into the garden it was obvious that the young woman was overcome by his good looks and lazy American charm.

He stared at Ivy for a moment then a wide smile lit up his face. 'Nanny!' He came forward to plant a kiss on her cheek.

'So,' she said, 'here we are!' She was trying to sound casual and composed although her throat was tight with emotion and tears threatened. 'I thought the day would never come. I didn't expect to see you again and that's the truth. Sit down, do, but carefully. I never trust deck chairs. I knew a man once who trapped his thumb in a deck chair.'

'I'm sorry I couldn't get here earlier but . . .'

Blinking furiously she said, 'So how's your poor mother? It must have hurt her – losing Leonora.'

'She was broken-hearted, Nanny.' He sat down gingerly, looking very insecure.

'You can call me Nan now,' she conceded. Breathing
deeply, she felt her composure returning. 'So disillusioned
when I last saw her and never a word since. It must have
broken your mother's heart. It did mine!' She swallowed
hard and pulled herself together. 'And look at you – grown
so tall!'

'And an uncle!' He grinned. 'Can you imagine me
yesterday with the twins at the zoo?'

'Yes I can. An uncle they had never met! They must be
thrilled.'

'But look at you, Nan! You're looking very chipper.'

'Chipper? *Chipper!* What sort of word is that, for Lord's
sake?' She laughed shakily. 'You're a handsome devil,
Richard, like your father. How is he now?'

'He's not well. His kidneys. Just soldiering on – but he
sent his love to you. He's not much help to Mother but
she's made a terrific effort in the last six months. I told
her I couldn't leave her to come over here until she had
. . . well, conquered the drink. I promised to take the twins
back with me for a holiday so she's determined to be at
her best.'

'Take them on a liner? Good Lord! Mrs Matlowe will
never allow it. She has a perfect phobia about water. And
now we have lost the *Titanic*! One iceberg – that's all it
took! She'll be terrified at the idea of her grandchildren
crossing the Atlantic. You'll see!'

'I'll have to try. I promised Mother and Father.'

Ivy reached out a scrawny hand and clutched his wrist.
'If you *do* manage it, Richard, don't bring them back! Keep
them out there. They will have a better life with your family.
Georgina Matlowe! What a dreadful woman she is. If she
hadn't made Leonora's life such a misery, none of this would
have happened.'

Richard tried to intervene but she went straight on.

'I mean it, Richard. If you care at all for those twins,
take them back with you. Your mother should bring them
up. I'm sure she would rise to the challenge.'

He didn't at once agree but nor did he reject the idea,
she noted, and she drew back satisfied.

Changing the subject, he said, 'I've brought some of the girls' pictures for you . . .' He drew them from the slim case he carried and handed them to her.

Hiding her envy, she asked about the children's current nanny.

'There isn't a nanny. Mrs Matlowe decided they were too old and instead should have a governess. Marianne Lefevre is very nice and they are genuinely fond of her.'

'*Fond*? Of a *governess*?' Ivy looked sceptical. 'I doubt it. In my experience such people are very overrated. Emmie and Edie should be at school by now.'

He nodded hastily and went on. 'You need not worry on that account. Marianne is very professional. The girls have also each written a letter to you . . .'

She was suddenly anxious. 'But do they remember me, Richard? Do they even understand what I was to them? They were babies when I was sent packing by that miserable old woman. Her excuse was that I was constantly interfering between her and Leonora when they quarrelled. Naturally I spoke up for your sister. I had to protect her. Poor Neil was too soft with his mother. Terrified of upsetting her.' Her face darkened. 'Poor dear Leonora. She turned up at The Poplars a happy, sunny bride, so much in love with Neil, so full of life and bubbling with excitement.' She shook her head. 'But within days Mrs Matlowe had cast a gloom over the entire household by her behaviour. Sick with jealousy! By the end of the first week Leonora was in tears and Neil was in despair.'

Richard's face twisted with pain at the thought of his sister's unhappiness. 'She adored Neil! Poor Leonora. What a mother-in-law!'

'And poor Neil, torn between them,' Ivy said quietly. 'He quarrelled with his mother, you know, although he loved her. He was anguished. I'll give him his due. Must have been hard for him but he had to defend his wife from her attacks. Not physical, you see, but verbal abuse. Ruining the marriage. That's what she was trying to do. She wanted Leonora out of her son's life. That's what she hoped for, I'm sure of it.'

While he fumbled in his case for the letters from Emmeline and Edith, Ivy was studying the pictures they had drawn for her. Frowning, she asked, 'What are all these spiky things just outside the boat house?'

He laughed. 'I think they're the roses – the prickles are a little oversized!'

'Roses?'

'Yes. There's a small rose bed just in front of the boat house.'

Ivy was shaking her head. 'There were no roses,' she said firmly. 'Mrs Matlowe said she thought they were over-rated. Roses, I mean. Too prone to disease, she insisted, when Leonora wanted to plant some. Your sister thought it would be fun for the children to plant them in memory of their visit to England but Mrs Matlowe refused the idea.'

He frowned. 'So when were the roses planted?'

'It must have been after I left. That was a rockery. I remember distinctly because there was one of those horrid little statues – a mermaid combing her hair. Such appalling taste, I thought, for a woman in her position.'

Richard said, 'There's no rockery now. Just a neat bed with four rose bushes in a straight line.'

Ivy frowned. 'Maybe she dismantled the rockery. Obviously somebody did. She might have had Mr Blunt move it. I wasn't in perfect health during that period – too much friction for me. I had a great many headaches and didn't spend much time in the garden.' She tried to cast her mind back. 'Maybe after she had driven Leonora away she felt guilty and went ahead with her wish for the roses. Four rose bushes in a straight line.'

'Yes. A bit like the rest of the garden – unimaginative.'

'It must look a bit thin.' She glanced up as Agatha appeared to ask if they would like tea and sandwiches.

Ivy said firmly, 'Not if it's fish paste.'

Agatha forced a smile. 'It's cucumber or egg and cress.'

'We'll have some of each then. Thank you, Agatha.' She smiled at Richard and added pointedly, 'Isn't that wonderful? They're making us some sandwiches! They look after us very well here, you see. Tea in the garden. Just like old times!'

When they were alone again, Richard said, 'Mother wants you to come home with me, Nan. Are you up to such a long sea journey?'

Ivy closed her eyes and whispered a prayer. When she opened them Richard could see tears glistening and offered her his large, clean, well-ironed handkerchief. She whispered, 'I would travel in a hot-air balloon if I had to!'

He said guiltily, 'We didn't intend to leave you here, you know, Nan, but the news was so bad and everyone was distracted by Leonora's disappearance and then, when we did try to contact you, no one knew where you were. Later, when we heard that Neil had been killed, we worried afresh and . . .'

Ivy was shaking her head. 'They wouldn't have known where I was. When I left The Poplars I went to stay with an old friend but almost immediately she fell ill and I nursed her for months but she died. I was put out on the street by the bailiffs because I had no money! Can you imagine that?' She sighed heavily. 'The Sutton Ladies Group were notified by the police who found me wandering in a state of shock – and they rescued me.' She smiled at the memory. 'When they said I was reasonably fit, they brought me here.' Her glance rested briefly on Nesta who was bringing the sandwiches. Raising her voice a little she said, 'I know I'm crotchety but I'm not ungrateful. These people saved my life and my sanity, Richard. I can never thank them enough. They exist on donations, you know. Entirely on donations!'

Richard immediately grasped her meaning and said, 'Is that so? Then my family will want to contribute. I shall write to them at once.'

Nesta gave him a brilliant smile as she set out the refreshments on a small table and retired to give them back their privacy.

He said, 'They will be delighted to support the group. Thank you for suggesting it. But back to what we were talking about. Forgive this question, but can you walk unaided?'

'Walk? Sure I can walk . . . but slowly.' She smiled. 'I rarely run, mind you! I can talk and eat and remember things from years ago. My hearing's good but my sight's failing a little. Otherwise I'm a fully functioning woman of seventy-one . . .' She lowered her voice. 'And when I die, if I die here, it will be of boredom!'

Richard had the grace to look suitably crushed. 'I'm only asking because the journey may not be easy. The Atlantic is prone to storms and . . .'

'I'd like to go home, Richard,' she pleaded softly. 'I want to end my days in America.' Her shoulders went back as she straightened up. 'If I have to, I'll *swim* the damned Atlantic!'

Richard held out his hand. 'Then hey! Let's shake on it, Nan!' he said huskily. 'You've got yourself a deal!'

EIGHT

The following day Richard returned to Donald Watson's office and told them about his visit to Ivy Busby. They listened attentively to all he had to tell them and afterwards an intense silence descended as they each considered what had been learned, if anything, from the visit.

Donald glanced at his cousin and she said, 'I know what you're thinking. The same thing occurred to me.'

They both looked at Richard.

'What do you mean?' he asked. 'Ivy Busby seemed willing enough to travel back with us. She still has her wits about her and can walk, although . . .'

'Not the nanny,' said Donald. 'The rose bed.'

Richard stared from one to the other then frowned. 'What about it?'

'We could be wrong,' Judith said hastily.

'Certainly we could . . . but suppose we're right?' Donald turned to Richard who still had no inkling of what they were suggesting. 'It's a fairly common thing that . . .' He took a deep breath. 'To be blunt, when someone is murdered the body is often buried close to . . .'

'Oh my God!' Richard leaped to his feet, knocking his chair backwards in his panic. 'You surely don't think . . . I mean, you surely don't imagine that my sister's body is . . .'

Judith said, 'Please sit down, Richard. We are only speculating. That's what we do here. We have to look at every possibility. We have to look at the black side as well as the bright side.'

'Sorry. Yes, of course but . . .' Slowly, looking somewhat dazed, Richard sat down, his pale face reflecting his shock. 'You're thinking *someone in the family* murdered her? My God!'

Donald said, 'As Judith said, we have to consider every possibility. We may be completely wrong but we may have just stumbled on the truth.'

'But who would do such a thing?'

Judith frowned. 'It could have been an accident, I suppose.'

'Then why hide the fact?' Richard demanded. 'Why make things so much worse? I can assure you that Neil would never agree to such a plan. Bury his beloved Leonora in the family garden after an accident! Never!'

Donald said thoughtfully, 'There's another possible scenario. Could your sister have taken her own life? In which case the family would have panicked . . .'

'Don't! *Don't!*' he begged. Horrified, Richard covered his face with his hands.

Donald and Judith exchanged worried looks. Richard was young and still vulnerable. For a while no one spoke.

When at last Richard looked up he said hoarsely, 'Not the Leonora I knew. She would never deliberately leave the twins . . . and she loved life. But if that woman drove her to it . . .' He gulped in another breath. 'I'll see that Georgina Matlowe spends the rest of her life behind bars!'

Judith said stoutly, 'From what we hear, if I had been your sister, I'd have been tempted to murder Mrs Matlowe!'

'Judith!' Donald glared at her. 'Don't talk like that, please. We are supposed to remain impartial. *Impartial.* Gather the facts of the matter and hand them over to whoever needs them.'

There was another uncomfortable silence.

At last Richard said, 'So we are thinking that just maybe Leonora might have been driven to suicide and to hide the scandal she was buried under what was the rockery? That's terrible!'

Judith said, 'You will surely admit it has to be considered.'

Richard whispered, 'Suicide! I can't believe it . . . but if she was driven to it . . .' He shook his head. 'That would mean that Neil and his mother-in-law colluded to hide the death. I cannot believe that.'

'Maybe to shield the twins?' Judith sighed and glanced

at Richard. 'I'm beginning to wish that you hadn't reopened
the case.'

'Damned right!' he muttered unhappily.

Donald said, 'I'm sorry, Richard, but I'm duty bound to
pass this on to DS Ackrow – just in case there is anything
in it. If someone dug up the rockery, it has to be a possible
lead. I agreed to liaise with the police at the beginning of
the enquiry and I'd be failing in my duty if . . .'

Richard said, 'And he might want to . . . to exhume the
. . . Damnation!'

They each avoided the other's eyes.

Judith said, 'If they follow this up I don't see how it
could be done without alerting Mrs Matlowe to our suspicions.' She looked at her cousin. 'Could it be done without
her knowledge? The digging, I mean.'

'I don't see how.'

Richard said, 'Unless we could get her out of the house
on some pretext?' Richard continued eagerly, 'Then if
we're wrong she need not have to be antagonized. If I'm
to get permission to take the twins back with me to
America, I'd rather not make an enemy of her if it isn't
necessary. She's difficult enough already and she *could*
fight me in the law courts for the children. I wouldn't put
it past her.' He shook his head in disbelief. 'This can't be
happening!'

Judith said, 'We could be wrong, Richard, but if you
want to know the truth . . .' But she sounded less than
convincing.

'What I want is to find her alive and well!' he protested.
'When I decided to come over here I was clinging to that
thought. I didn't even allow myself to consider the alter-
natives.' He looked from one to the other. 'Should we give
up before it's too late?'

Donald said, 'That's up to you entirely. We'll follow your
lead.'

'Haven't the twins had enough bad news in their short
lives?' Richard looked desperately from Donald to Judith.
'To grow up knowing what we *do* know is bad enough, but
if their mother killed herself or was murdered . . .'

Baffled, Donald held up his hands in a gesture of surrender. 'Please. Let's call a halt for the moment. I suggest we sleep on it and make contact first thing tomorrow. We might see it differently. But if it still seems suspicious – that is, the rockery being dug up – and if a crime *may have* been committed, I shall have to notify DS Ackrow or I could be charged with withholding evidence or misleading or impeding the police.'

'This is all my fault.' Richard sighed deeply then nodded. 'I'll accept that because I have no alternative. Sure – we'll sleep on it.'

And there, reluctantly, they left it.

Meanwhile the young smiling receptionist came into the doctor's waiting room and said, 'Mrs Georgina Matlowe?'

Georgina rose slowly to her feet but Ida sprang up beside her.

Georgina glared at her. 'I've told you – I don't need a chaperone, Ida!'

'Yes you do, dear. We've already discussed this. I'm coming in with you so don't start to argue again.'

The receptionist smiled tolerantly, obviously used to this kind of exchange. 'Your friend is welcome, Mrs Matlowe. Dr Hammond-Green has no objection.'

Georgina counted to ten, heaved a deep sigh and gave in. It was too humiliating to stand arguing with Ida while other waiting patients listened with interest. She hadn't wanted to see this doctor, nor any other doctor, but Ida had made the appointment and she could not afford to upset her sister. Not at a time like this when Richard Preston was trying to stir up troubles best forgotten. She needed Ida for support even though her sister's imperious manner frequently grated on her. What about her own?

Dr Hammond-Green – plump and bewhiskered – was brisk and to the point and wasted no time with idle chat about the weather but asked her at once to describe the incident that had first alarmed her.

Georgina had planned the answer to this question.

'I suspect it was an unfortunate culmination of events,'

she told him, silently praying that her sister would not contradict her version. 'I have a very busy life with my two grandchildren and now their uncle is over from America and our quiet routine has been overturned by his enthusiasm. I feel quite exhausted each morning when I wake and am finding it difficult to cope. I felt a little dizzy and someone helped me to . . .'

'You fainted!' Ida corrected her sharply.

'I thought I might faint but . . .'

'You fainted!'

'I was helped to a seat and . . .'

'You fainted, and Richard caught you just before you fell. You might have injured yourself otherwise.' She turned to the doctor. 'Georgina clutched her arm as she fell and afterwards complained of a pain . . .'

The specialist worked steadily throughout the next quarter of an hour. He checked her heart and lungs, discussed her medical history and silently studied his findings while Georgina glared at her sister with resentful eyes and a tightly pursed mouth. If the wretched man concluded that she had a heart problem she would blame it on Ida who had dragged her here against her will. It was perfectly predictable that, with the odious Richard Preston around the house, charming all and sundry, she would feel worried and upset. It was bound to affect her. When he left, which she hoped would be soon, she knew she would recover. There was no need for this ridiculous fuss.

He glanced up eventually. 'I am rather concerned,' he told her with a smile that she presumed was intended to soften the news. 'There is some irregularity and I don't think you should ignore it. Nothing to worry about unless you neglect it.'

As if on cue, Georgina felt her heart rate increase but she tried to ignore it, telling herself that the doctor was deliberately trying to frighten her. Ida was giving her a triumphant look, delighted to be proved right.

Ida said, 'So, Doctor, was it a minor heart attack?'

Georgina felt like strangling her.

He put his head on one side, choosing his words carefully.

'Maybe a very minor one but no cause for immediate panic, Mrs Matlowe. I'd like to discuss this with Mr Prendergast at Barts Hospital. We may well be able to put your mind at ease but, if not, he can organize the required treatment.' Ignoring her stammered protest, he continued. 'I'll book you in for a full morning of tests and he will contact you by letter with the date and time of the appointment.' He smiled. 'You were wise to come and see me, Mrs Matlowe. Any problem of this kind is best discovered at an early stage.'

Ida beamed. 'I'll come with you, dear, and afterwards I shall take you out to lunch at the Dorchester and then we'll do some shopping in Bond Street or Regent Street – wherever you fancy. We'll make a whole day of it.' She rose to her feet, a hand outstretched towards the doctor who shook it warmly.

Furious that she had lost control of events, Georgina could barely mutter a 'thank you' to the specialist and she left the room with a face like thunder. She bitterly regretted allowing her sister to become involved but it was too late now. She was eager to get back to The Poplars and see what Marianne and the children were doing in her absence. Hopefully the governess was not allowing them to skip their lessons. It had not escaped her notice that Richard Preston seemed a mite too friendly with Marianne and *that* friendship, she knew, must be nipped in the bud before it became a problem.

Dear Alice, wrote Marianne, that same evening. *I am sorry to hear that your mother's rheumatism is no better. I suppose it is one of the perils of growing old . . . It must make her very miserable but maybe the new doctor will be able to help her.*

Pleased also to hear from you. It was like an echo of the normal world whereas my life here is becoming increasingly disturbing. The twins' uncle (young and charming) has arrived from America and plans to take the twins back to see their American grandparents if Mrs Matlowe will allow it . . .

She glanced out of the window at the garden while she

waited for inspiration. At the far end the boat house lurked darkly and beyond it, on the river, a boat horn sounded eerily on the night air. She tried to imagine the regatta in bright sunshine and failed miserably.

It is too much to expect, I think, that I shall see anything of the regatta. The Matlowe family will not be taking part as she fears the water and considers the event 'dangerous'. Maybe she's right. I cannot imagine Emmie or Edie sitting still for long in a small boat even if we hired one – they are definitely fidgety and would soon get bored . . .

She wondered if Richard Preston would take the opportunity to enjoy one of England's popular society events. If so he would hardly go alone. It was, after all, a social occasion and there was nothing sociable about being alone. Was there the slightest chance that he would ask her to accompany him, she wondered?

Mrs Matlowe's sister, Ida, is still here and took her to see a doctor about a recent incident when she collapsed with a pain in her heart. We have heard nothing about the doctor's diagnosis. When she returned, she went straight up to her son's room and stayed there for the best part of an hour.

While she was at the doctor's I spent some time with Donald Watson and his cousin Judith who works with him as a partner-cum-secretary. I think she approves of me because she deliberately left me alone with her cousin while she went out to post a letter. Donald Watson said he would miss me if I went to America with the twins – not that Richard has asked me to, and anyway he might be taking their family nanny home with him so she would probably look after them. She might even resent my presence.

I confess I was very flattered that anyone might miss me but Donald Watson may be married so I must not read too much into his comment.

Judith also suggested I might take her place when she leaves the agency (to have her first baby), which is food for thought – except that my secretarial skills are sadly lacking, but just in case I now spend an hour each evening working on typing and shorthand . . .

She brought the letter to a close with the thought that no

matter how strange her world was becoming, at least she was never likely to be bored!

The next morning found Georgina on her knees before the altar in Neil's room.

'It's Ida,' she told him, rolling her eyes in exasperation. 'I won't allow her in here, naturally, but she is very curious. Nosy is probably the word I'm looking for. Even as a child she could never bear for me to have a secret . . . But enough about Ida. We went to see a specialist and he has made an appointment for me to see a man in Barts Hospital – but you mustn't worry, dear. I'm sure it's nothing . . .'

She wondered whether to confide in him about Richard Preston's visit to the old nanny. Delaying the decision momentarily, she said, 'Poor Ivan has died as predicted and I am taking the girls to his funeral. It's about time they learned about death and seeing him serene in his coffin will reassure them that there is nothing to fear.' She thought about it. Her own feelings – her earlier fear of dying – had changed with her son's death. Wherever he was, she would be with him and that was reassurance enough.

Gathering her courage she said, 'The brother has discovered the nanny's whereabouts. I was hoping she had died by now but it seems not to be the case.' She sighed. 'Lord knows what she told him. She was a meddlesome woman, as you know, dear, and even now I'm sure she has told Preston a pack of lies. Oh, I know Leonora thought the world of her but, to my mind, she had too much influence in that family . . .'

Closing her eyes she breathed deeply in an attempt to calm her thoughts, which as ever swirled chaotically within her mind, trying to separate the confusion of ideas and suspicions. Clutching at one of them, she said, 'Ivy Busby!' That was her name. Yes, Ivy Busby had tried to cause trouble between her and her son.

'My dearest boy!' she cried. 'You can have no idea how tormented I am by these wretched people! The good Lord knows I am guilty of mistakes – for which I am deeply sorry and would make reparation if I could – but . . .'

The Lord understands, she assured herself. *You must trust Him, Georgina. And stay calm. That's very important for your heart. Trust Him and stay calm.*

Detective Sergeant Ackrow could hardly contain his excitement. His colour rose as he stared at his two visitors. 'They dug up the rockery? God Almighty! Why didn't we find this out years ago?'

Donald Watson shrugged. 'Probably because no one thought to interview the nanny.'

Richard said, 'Or couldn't find her. Poor Nan had been kicked out, remember. Literally thrown out on to the street. Really, it beggars belief!'

It was hot in the police station and Donald was beginning to sweat around his shirt collar but the window remained shut and no one else seemed troubled by the heat so he suffered in silence. Richard Preston had agreed, after some persuasion, that they take the news to the police and it was immediately obvious that DS Ackrow placed a lot of importance on the information. Donald had to admit to a certain excitement himself. But how was it to be done, he wondered anxiously, without Georgina Matlowe becoming aware of their suspicions? If the police decided to dig up the rockery in the hope of finding a body, Georgina would probably throw a fit and send at once for her solicitor.

'We'll need a warrant,' the detective was saying, scribbling frantically in his notebook. 'However, that means we alert her to what we are doing.' He glanced up. 'The thing is that if we find a body it's possibly a murder investigation so we have to step carefully. If we don't follow the regulations, meaning the correct procedures, we could end up with egg on our faces.'

Donald and Richard exchanged glances.

The latter said, 'We might be wrong. Would Mrs Matlowe be able to sue us if we did it without her permission and she later found out what we'd done?'

After a long silence Donald said slowly, 'How long would

it take to dig up the rose bed and, if there's no body, put it
back again as it was?'

DS Ackrow brightened. 'I'm with you! You mean, if we
got Mrs Matlowe out of the way and did it . . . would she
notice? Does she ever go into the garden?' He looked at
Preston.

He was taking the suggestion seriously, Donald thought,
and was immediately nervous.

Richard said, 'Probably she would notice.'

DS Ackrow squinted thoughtfully at his notes then turned
to Preston. 'Could you get her out for a day?'

He shook his head. 'She'd never go anywhere with me.
I'm the devil incarnate in her eyes. And anyway, what
about Marianne and the twins – and the staff? Cook and
maid. There's also a gardener by the name of Blunt,
although he only comes about once a week if I remember
correctly . . . Ah! I have an idea.' His eyes narrowed
thoughtfully. 'I believe she has to go to the hospital in
London one day – or it maybe a specialist of some kind
– and her sister is going with her. I could take Marianne
and the twins somewhere but that would leave the kitchen
staff. We'd have to get rid of them . . . And what about
the neighbours?'

The detective frowned. 'They would certainly notice
police gathering round the rose bed, but if there was only
one man digging . . .' He sighed. 'Hmm! It's difficult.'

Donald said, 'I suppose working at night is out of the
question.'

'Risky. We might be spotted. Come on, Watson. You're an
investigator. Think of something!' He was only half in jest.

Donald nodded. 'All I can think of is to take the neighbours into our confidence as to the real reason for the
excavation . . . maybe get the cook and the maid over to
the police station on the pretext of answering more questions – or give them the day off – all to go ahead on the day
. . .' He faltered to a stop.

'When Mrs Matlowe is at the hospital in London!' DS
Ackrow finished the sentence for him and had the good
grace to add, 'Well done!'

Richard said, 'I think it's too complicated, isn't it? I mean, too many things could go wrong.'

The detective shrugged. 'It's all we've got, though. It just might be workable. It's risky but . . . If the gardener notices anything afterwards he'll think it was the others who dug over the plot and the others will think it was Mr Blunt!'

Richard said, 'I'm sure Marianne will help us with dates and so on. She'll be in the know.'

Donald looked at him. 'I don't think you should be there when it happens – for your own sake. If there is a body, and if it's Leonora . . .'

Richard agreed quickly. 'I shall be taking the children somewhere nice and Marianne will come with us. That way I shan't be there if . . .' He shook his head, unable to put his feelings into words.

DS Ackrow said, 'Well, I think that's all for you, Mr Preston. Watson and I will carry on, settling the details.'

Preston was about to protest but then he realized that the detective was trying to spare him any more unpleasantness. He stood up, thanked them and made his exit.

The two remaining men got down to business, planning the excavation.

There was a routine plan for such operations, Donald learned. Tarpaulins would be laid around the bed; the rose bushes would be lifted and set aside in a box while two men took turns to dig out the soil.

'And if we find her?' Donald asked.

'We'll have a blacked-out vehicle parked nearby and the body will be carefully wrapped, carried out and driven to the mortuary. Immediately the soil will be replaced, the roses replanted and the surface flattened. Say two to three hours at the most.'

Donald didn't know whether to be pleased or not. It was his plan but, like most plans, it could go wrong.

As if reading his mind, the detective said, 'Don't worry. It'll be my neck on the line but I'll clear it first with those higher up. It'll be quite a coup if it *is* her!'

'Tough on the brother, though.'

Ackrow shrugged. 'The family want to know the truth.

They've initiated it. They need to know what happened to her. That's why he's over here.' He stood up.

Time to go, thought Donald. He made his excuses and left. No time for doubts now, he told himself. The sooner it was over, the better.

NINE

Georgina had bought the twins identical black outfits despite Marianne's protest. Black skirts, black jackets with black stockings and shoes.

'You don't seem to understand, Marianne, the importance of death in the minds of young children. This is life, Marianne, not a fairyland where everything ends happily. I want them to realize that life is fleeting and they must be good children if they want to go to heaven. That's where Ivan has gone. They will accept that.' She gave her a sharp glance. 'I expect you to wear black also.'

Marianne nodded. She was on shaky ground, she reminded herself. She was only the governess and had no right to interfere.

When the day came the children dressed in their new outfits with excited giggles, admiring themselves in the long swing mirror in Marianne's room.

Emmie said, 'I look like a witch!' and rolled her eyes. She held out her arms, wiggled her fingers and said, 'I shall turn you into a frog!'

'You can't because I'm a good witch.'

'You can't be a good witch because good witches are white and we're both dressed in black.'

Marianne was adjusting her own black straw hat and deciding that it suited her. 'Don't let your grandmother hear you being silly, girls. Wearing black to a funeral is a mark of respect. It shows you . . .' She picked up a hand mirror to see the effect of the hat from the back. 'It means that you liked Ivan and you're sorry he died.' She gave herself a final glance in the mirror and, satisfied, said, 'Now come along. Your grandmother has ordered a hansom cab to take us to the church. Isn't that exciting?'

Outside the front steps, the vehicle waited, the horse snuffling impatiently. Georgina was already seated in the back, clutching her large black handbag. She indicated the space beside her, and Marianne sat down while the children scrambled on to the small seats opposite. The interior of the taxi smelled of leather polish and cigar smoke. The driver flipped the reins and they drew out carefully into the traffic.

'That's enough from you two!' Georgina told the twins who were fidgeting excitedly. 'A funeral is a solemn occasion and I want you to behave yourselves. Think only good thoughts and ask God to forgive your sins.'

They nodded dutifully.

Emmie asked, 'Does he forgive *your* sins, Grandmother?'

'My sins?'

She seemed flustered by the question, Marianne thought.

'I don't have any sins, Emmie,' Georgina replied loftily, 'but if I did He would forgive me. He also forgives mistakes.'

'I make mistakes,' Edie offered eagerly. 'I thought five times five was twenty but it's not. It's ... um ...' She looked at her sister for help.

'Not that kind of mistake, Edie. The sort of mistake that one makes – unintentional mistakes.' Marianne saw that her hold on the handbag had tightened. 'Mistakes that turn out badly but ...' She fell silent.

Marianne said, 'Everyone makes mistakes sometimes. God understands that.'

Georgina nodded gratefully. 'Exactly.'

Edie cried, 'Oh look! Those two horses are pulling that bus!'

Georgina gave it a cursory glance. 'I never trust those horse buses,' she said. 'Very unsteady – and they will insist on racing each other. It leads to accidents. I don't care for trams either but they are steadier on the whole.'

Emmie said, 'But if they have an accident then that's a mistake and God would forgive them.'

Georgina rolled her eyes despairingly. 'No more talking, girls,' she instructed. 'We are going to a funeral and you must think proper thoughts.'

Marianne considered herself rebuked also. Her thoughts

lately, with regard to her employer, were certainly not very proper.

After the service Marianne, Ida, Georgina and the twins returned to the home of the bereaved parents with another eight mourners, for a simple meal of ham and salad followed by fruit jelly and cream. There was also a cake with Ivan's name on it, made by Ida.

While Georgina was in conversation with Ivan's aunt, Ida took Marianne's arm and led her into the passage where they could talk without being overheard.

'I'm relying on you, Marianne,' she told her. 'I shall stay here for a few days to be of help and support to Ivan's parents and during that time you must keep a watchful eye on my sister. I'm worried about her health and not only her physical problems. One of our aunts died of melancholia – it was terrible. She took her own life – there's no other way to say it.'

'Good heavens! How sad!' Marianne was genuinely shocked.

'It was. She threw herself off a bridge. Very nasty – a truly terrible way to go – and she was only twenty-one. Georgina and I were quite young at the time but we heard about it as we grew up.' Ida glanced back towards the dining room but seeing no one within hearing distance she went on. 'I have to ask you something. Have you ever seen the inside of Neil's room? The door seems to be permanently locked and I fear the worst. She idolized that boy. Absolutely idolized him. I imagine she has preserved the room exactly as it was when he was . . . unattached.'

Marianne's mind seemed to move at a snail's pace as she considered how best to answer Ida's question. It would be foolish to reveal that Lorna had shown her the room because that would not reflect well on herself or on Lorna, but if she pretended to know nothing about it . . . She frowned. Perhaps it was important for Ida to know the truth.

She would have to lie, she decided. Or rather, deliver a series of half-truths.

'I did see inside the room once,' she said. 'The door was

open and it was being cleaned. Lorna was brushing the carpet . . .' She threw out her hands in a gesture that meant 'nothing of importance'.

Ida's eyes narrowed. 'And?' she encouraged, waiting for more. 'You haven't answered my question, have you?'

Marianne said, 'No.' She hesitated.

'What aren't you telling me, Marianne? I'm trusting you to be frank with me. We both, I'm sure, have my sister's welfare at heart.'

Marianne drew a deep breath. 'There's a sort of altar in there. I expect that's where Mrs Matlowe . . . The thing is that she never goes to church so she probably prays there . . .'

Ida's mouth fell open with surprise. 'Never goes to church? What are you saying? Of course she goes to church!'

'What I mean is . . .' She was flustered. 'I mean that some people do like to pray in private . . . and maybe the altar makes her feel closer to God.' She realized it sounded lame.

Ida pounced. 'Some people do, do they?' She raised her eyebrows.

'I assume so.'

'You're saying that my sister no longer attends church? Since when?'

'Never since I've been with her.'

Ida, finally and reluctantly convinced, shook her head. 'This is very worrying. I hope she isn't becoming obsessed with death. She's never been the same since Neil's marriage to Leonora. Not that I disliked her, because I couldn't – she was a lovely girl – and because she made Neil so happy . . .' For a moment her eyes filled with tears but she quickly produced a handkerchief and dabbed them away. 'Poor Georgina was convinced that Leonora would take Neil back to America forever. She thought the young woman was trying to drive a wedge between her and Neil. It was sheer panic on her part.'

'And when she disappeared?'

'I think in her heart of hearts Georgina blamed herself and I daresay Neil also blamed her. I saw a change in her – in Georgina, I mean. She became very withdrawn – introverted

possibly. Didn't spend much time with the twins. Then fell
out with the family's nanny and sent her away. Hired a replacement and then later decided it was time for a governess. The
first one didn't suit and then you arrived.' She smiled briefly.
'She trusts you, Marianne, and that's why I'm enlisting your
help. I want you to promise that if you see any further signs
of what I shall call "unresolved grief", or deterioration of
her mental state . . .'

Marianne, now feeling guilty, opened her mouth to
protest but Ida ignored her obvious reluctance and went
on regardless.

'. . . or increased melancholia, you will notify me at
once. A missing daughter-in-law and a dead son are quite
enough to throw most people out of kilter and my poor
sister is no exception.'

'I'll do my best,' Marianne told her, trying to ignore
the feelings of disloyalty. She was well and truly caught
in the centre of the intrigue but could see no way out of it.

'I don't want another tragedy, Marianne. I don't want her
to follow our aunt's example. You are in a good position
to help me avert one. Georgina will miss me. She finds me
overbearing but . . .'

'Oh I'm sure she doesn't!'

'She does but she's always drawn strength from me
without understanding that she does it. She has always been
the same. She was bullied at school on one occasion and
I found her in tears in the cloakroom. I soon sorted things
out for her. She rarely asks me for help but that's because
I act on her behalf before she needs to ask.' She patted
Marianne's arm. 'Do you have any sisters?'

Marianne shook her head. 'I've an older brother in India.'

'India? Not much use to you there, is he!' Frowning, she
forced her thoughts back to the matter of her sister. 'As
long as you understand the situation, Marianne. I'm relying
on you. Please don't let me down.'

Marianne lay in bed that night tossing and turning and
wondering how her life had suddenly become so complicated. Her job as a governess, apparently so straightforward,

had now developed complications. The past was impinging on the present in an uncomfortable way, leaving her loyalties in some disarray. Her first duty must be toward the twins, who were in her care for much of each day and who deserved her full attention.

Donald Watson, however, considered her his eyes and ears within the Matlowe household and she could plainly see that uncovering past events would probably seriously affect the children's lives in the future. The suspicion that someone had killed Leonora, if proved, would certainly have a most damaging effect on those closest to the twins and would indirectly affect their own attitude to life as they grew older. If it turned out that Neil, their father, had killed his wife, Emmie and Edie would surely grow up full of insecurities. Discovering that Leonora had been buried beneath the roses would be a nightmare for them – one from which they might never recover.

Maybe, she thought unhappily, it would have been better if Richard Preston had not come to England in search of the truth. Not knowing what happened to his sister might have been a better option for the Preston family.

And now, on top of everything else, Ida had recruited her to watch for signs that Georgina might be sliding into a state of melancholy – a state of mind that had prompted one of her aunts to throw herself off a bridge!

Marianne liked Ida. She found her refreshingly honest and full of commonsense and was quite willing to help her by watching Georgina. Were the altar and the constant prayers a sign of this inherited weakness or simply a defence against any unhappy or guilty thoughts she might have? There was no way of knowing. Thank heavens that so far the twins showed no sign of a similar tendency – both girls being of a lively, cheerful disposition. But how long would that continue if their grandmother became seriously morose and introspective? Living in The Poplars, the twins' view of the world was a very limited one. They might be better off with the Preston family in America . . .

Sighing, her mind too active, Marianne turned on to her right side, drew up her knees and tried not to think, but it was impossible. Wide awake and full of uneasy thoughts, she slid out of bed and crossed the room, to take a look in on the children sleeping in the next room. Emmie lay straight and calm in her bed, her face pale and untroubled in the moonlight. Edie lay among the twisted bedclothes in an untidy heap, her face scrunched up, her long hair tousled on the pillow.

'Two little sisters,' Marianne whispered. Innocent children whose lives might already be unravelling around them. She whispered a little prayer for their survival as she went slowly back to her own room.

The warrant for the exploratory dig was issued and various preparations were made to ensure that no one was in the house when the police arrived to dig up the rose bed.

To Georgina's disgust, the hospital tests would take up most of the day and they insisted they must keep her in overnight. Ida had then arranged to collect her the next morning and take them out to lunch. Afterwards they would spend time in the shops in Regent Street, possibly followed by a visit to a theatre matinee. Ida was wrongly convinced that, despite her sister's protests, she was actually looking forward to these delights.

The day of the hospital appointment dawned cool but dry and Ida arrived promptly at eight thirty to escort her sister to the hospital. While Georgina was pretending to make last-minute preparations for the short stay in hospital (but was actually locked in Neil's room, praying) Richard waited further along the street as Marianne helped the children into their clothes.

Cook and Lorna carried on as usual, unaware that they were going to be given the rest of the day off as soon as their mistress had departed. Marianne, watching from an upstairs window, saw Richard Preston further up the road, wearing a hat that shaded his eyes. He was talking to a man she recognized as Donald Watson and she hoped that Mrs Matlowe would not glance their way as she passed them – but presumably they would be prepared and would turn away as she passed by.

She guessed that the neighbours would be full of curiosity, as they had been warned of police activity in the back garden although they had been given very few details, but the Brannigans, much to their dismay, had already arranged a week's holiday on the Isle of Wight so would be away from the vicinity and would miss the excitement.

Ida called Georgina down. She arrived with a small holdall, looking flustered and ill at ease.

Ida held up a warning hand. 'A quick goodbye to the twins, dear,' she urged Georgina. 'I don't want to keep the driver waiting. He's an irritable man and won't take kindly to being kept waiting.'

Georgina turned to Marianne. 'Take care of the children, Marianne. I don't care for the seaside visit but you must see that they come to no harm. I shall be back some time during the evening tomorrow as Ida insists on taking us to the theatre.' She tried to smile at the prospect of a hospital visit followed by a day's outing with her sister but failed. 'More for her sake than mine!' she added irritably. 'I have never been a great theatre fan.'

Marianne smiled. 'We'll take good care of the girls,' she assured her.

Georgina leaned towards her and whispered, 'Remember what I told you. Don't let them out of your sight for a moment. I don't trust him.'

'I promise you, hand on heart!' Marianne insisted in a low voice, with an unhappy sense of betrayal. If she was honest with herself, she felt sorry for her employer and understood her anxiety. The worry over her heart problem had obviously raised the suspicion in the older woman's mind that, if she were found to be dangerously at risk from a heart attack, Richard might apply to the courts for permission to take them back to the Preston family, using her medical condition as justification for their removal.

Minutes later she hurried into the kitchen and told the staff they could have the rest of the day off.

'Are you sure it's all right for us to go?' Cook said dubiously. 'I mean, suppose Madam finds out – what then?'

Lorna lingered nearby, equally anxious.

Marianne gave them the answer they had rehearsed. 'It's Mr Preston's idea, not mine. His shoulders are broad! If she does find out, he's going to take all the blame. And anyway it's only for today. You'll be back tomorrow so why should she guess that you had a few hours off today?'

'We-ell, if you're sure it will be all right.' Cook glanced at Lorna. 'Let's go then!'

Lorna gave a little whoop of excitement and five minutes later they, too, had left the house. Marianne leaned from the front room window and waved to the two men who were still waiting further along the road as arranged.

Richard Preston hurried to collect Marianne and the twins. He had hired a motor car for the day and they were off to Margate to sample the delights of the seaside. With squeals of excitement, the twins scrambled into the back seat and Marianne slipped the front door key under the flowerpot where Donald Watson would find it.

The twins chattered non-stop as the car set off on its journey. There was no picnic basket as their uncle had promised to take them to a special place that sold fish and chips and they would have ice creams and buy buckets and spades.

'We're going to paddle in the water!' Emmie chortled, 'and maybe find a crab!'

'Or a starfish! And make sandcastles!'

They were unaware that their grandmother would spend the day in hospital. No one had seen any good reason to give them cause for concern. Richard was determined they would have fun and Marianne had decided not to dwell on what was happening back at The Poplars. She knew how difficult the day would be for Richard Preston but was eager to distract him from the gruesome thoughts of what might be found below the roses.

Under an overcast sky, the small police team went to work with well-oiled efficiency and the Barneses, watching from next door, found it fascinating – a bit of excitement to enliven their somewhat routine daily lives. From time to time they glanced upwards at the cloudy sky, fearing that a sudden shower might muddy the well-orchestrated proceedings and leave tell-tale traces, but it stayed fine.

Donald and DS Ackrow watched anxiously as tarpaulins were carried round the side of the house, across the lawn and laid carefully around the edges of the rose bed. A wooden crate was brought out and the four rose bushes were carefully eased from the soil with a garden fork and then lifted into the wooden crate, each complete with a mass of root soil. Every care was taken with them – it would look very odd if the roses began to wither as soon as they were replaced.

'I don't know what to hope for,' Donald remarked to the DS. 'Finding nothing will only extend the agony of the investigation, but finding a body will cause huge distress for Richard Preston. He gives an impression of confidence but he's quite young for his age.'

'But he set the thing in motion,' the detective replied. 'He'll have to take the consequences.'

'Do you think there's a chance Leonora is still alive?'

'I fear not! I'd like to be proved wrong though.'

The two men employed to dig now began to bring up soil from below ground level and this was carefully tipped on to the tarpaulins.

The detective growled, 'If they so much as drop a spoonful on the grass I'll have their guts for garters! I don't mind telling you this hasn't gone too far up the chain of command. It's a bit hush-hush and I stand to take the blame if anything goes wrong. If we find something I'll get the credit!' He shrugged.

'And if there is a body . . .?'

'We'll wrap it up and call in the unmarked van which we have waiting round the corner. Hopefully we'll get it away within minutes.'

'To the mortuary?'

He nodded. At that moment the church clock struck the hour. 'Nearly an hour so far,' he said and took out his handkerchief to mop his brow. Then he glanced up at the Barnes' window. 'I hope that photographer isn't taking pictures of this.'

'I warned him not to. He's pretty reliable, I think, though, mind you, if she is down there, a few photographs might come in very useful later. Evidence.'

Ackrow said nothing.

The mound of earth grew and another hour passed until one of the diggers straightened his back and turned to beckon them over.

Donald said, 'Oh God! They've found her!'

'Not necessarily. You stay here, if you don't mind. If it is her we can't have too many people cluttering the scene.'

He strode purposefully towards the waiting diggers and Donald watched in frustration as they all stared down into the excavation, heads close together in conversation. Saying what? Donald wondered, with a sick feeling in his stomach.

The detective glanced back at him and waved for him to join them and within seconds he was standing beside the detective, staring down into what was quite obviously a deep but very empty hole.

DS Ackrow shook his head, his expression one of deep disappointment. 'Not a sign of anything untoward,' he reported. 'They would never have gone deeper than this.' He sighed and his shoulders sagged. He instructed the diggers to take a ten-minute break and then to refill the hole as quickly as possible. 'And replant the roses, in a straight row, exactly as we found them. Thanks, lads.'

Donald remained, torn between rushing back to the office to tell Judith the results of the excavation and seeing it through to the finish. When the rose bushes were once more in place and the tarpaulins removed, he was astonished to see that the lawn showed no sign of the recent clandestine activity. It was as though nothing had happened, he marvelled. Very impressive. *The roses would need to be watered in.*

As he parted from Ackrow outside the front steps of The Poplars, he could see that the day's efforts, with nothing to show for them, was a bitter setback for the detective.

The DS rubbed his eyes wearily and sighed. 'Back to square one,' he remarked. 'But that's the job! What's that saying? "Ten per cent inspiration, ninety per cent desperation!" That's about it. Hardly glamorous.'

Donald said, 'But I bet you wouldn't want to do anything else!'

A faint smile lit the detective's face. 'You're right – I wouldn't. That's the dilemma for the likes of us coppers. We're a funny lot!'

Donald grinned. 'It was worth a try, though, wasn't it? There may be other leads. Let's not give up hope just yet.'

'I'll be in touch.'

'Likewise!'

As they went their separate ways Donald felt a secret relief that he had no gruesome news for Richard Preston when he eventually returned from his trip to Margate with Marianne and the twins. He was aware of a pang of envy when he imagined Marianne and Richard sharing the heady delights of the famous seaside town. Would Richard Preston take the twins back to America, he wondered? It would be a great experience for Marianne if she went with them. But would Georgina Matlowe ever agree to such a thing? It seemed unlikely. She was apparently using the sinking of the *Titanic* to prove how dangerous the sea crossing would be. It gave her a wonderful excuse to refuse.

But if Marianne *did* go she might never come back. She might even marry Richard, who was part of a wealthy, prestigious family. It seemed distinctly unlikely that she would ever become his secretary and business partner. Judith would be very disappointed – and so would he. He frowned as he ran up the stairs to his office, sorry that Judith had ever put the idea into his head.

The next morning, Bert Blunt arrived for work at The Poplars and made his way towards the potting shed. He was going to prune back the buddleia, which was threatening to engulf the hibiscus, then he would mow the grass and . . .

Halfway across the lawn he stopped, stared at the little rose bed, hesitated, walked on then turned and went back. He stood staring at it, and scratched his head.

'I'll be damned!' he muttered. 'Damned and double damned! I could 'ave sworn . . .' The two red roses had

been at either end of the bed and the two pink ones had been
between them . . . hadn't they? Or maybe not. He blinked
his eyes and stepped nearer to the rose bed, peering more
closely. No doubt about it. Today the pink ones were on
the ends and the red ones were in the middle . . . but where
were they before?

'They couldn't 'ave moved their selfs.' He shook his
head. 'Course they couldn't!' After a long pause he shrugged
and turned back towards the shed. 'It's you, 'Erbert Blunt!
Silly old fool! You're losing your ruddy marbles!' Rolling
his eyes, he pushed the vexing matter to the back of his
mind, opened the shed, removed his jacket and hung it on
the hook then reached for the secateurs.

TEN

It was eight thirty the same morning. Georgina sat up in bed wearing a hospital gown and a fierce expression. Ida sat on a chair beside her and they both sipped from cups of tea.

Ida said, 'There's no point in upsetting yourself, dear. They are doing the best they can for you. If you do have a heart problem you should let them advise you. If I were in your shoes . . .'

'Well, you're not. Easy for you to talk. If you were sitting here, worn out after all those tests, you'd feel differently. I don't see why we can't just get up and leave.'

'But what's the hurry? You've had a nice sleep and they will soon be bringing round the breakfast. Then you'll see Mr Prendergast again and we'll be off with our lovely day to look forward to.'

'Ida, I've told you . . .'

'Lunch at the Savoy – I've booked a table so you can't refuse – then a matinee. Or a little shopping. You know how you love Harrods and you did say you needed a new handbag . . .'

'I said no such thing!'

'It's looking a little past it, the brown leather . . .'

'No worse than yours – and I have two other handbags so . . .'

Her voice rose and a passing nurse said, 'Anything wrong, ladies?'

'Nothing at all,' Ida assured her, smiling broadly.

As the nurse moved on Georgina muttered, 'They're all so smug!'

'They're professionals, Georgie, and this is their world! You should be grateful that . . .'

'If you call me Georgie again I shall smother you with my pillow!' She set the cup and saucer on the bedside table and glared at the woman in the next bed.

Alice Beddowes, being short-sighted, assumed she might
be smiling and smiled back. Thus encouraged, she leaned
forward confidingly and said, 'It's either porridge or stewed
prunes but the porridge is a bit lumpy. I'd have the prunes,
dear, if I were you.'

Georgina gave her a withering look, which was entirely
wasted, and turned back to Ida.

Ida said, 'You could probably have a little of each if you
wanted . . .'

'God in Heaven!' Georgina closed her eyes but at that
moment the doors swung open at the end of the ward and
a trolley appeared, laden with crockery and food.

Georgina panicked. 'Where are my clothes, Ida? Find
them for me. I shall get dressed and then see Mr Prendergast.'

'But your breakfast, dear. You have to eat.'

'No I do not!' She swung her legs out of the bed and a
nurse veered quickly towards them.

'Now, Mrs Matlowe, you must be sensible . . .'

'I want my clothes, Nurse. If no one will fetch them I
shall walk out of the hospital in bare feet and this ridiculous gown!'

Ida said, 'Georgina! What has got into you this morning?'
She threw the nurse an apologetic glance.

The nurse said, 'You really cannot leave the hospital
without speaking to Mr Prendergast. That would be quite
against the rules – and contrary to good sense. I'm sure
Mr Prendergast will explain everything to you and he
will have planned a course of necessary treatments or
medicines . . .'

They eyed each other for a moment and then, to Ida's
relief, Georgina relented. 'If you allow me to dress I shall
wait to see Mr Prendergast.'

The nurse rolled her eyes. 'I'll speak to Sister and see if
we can arrange something for you.'

When she had left them Ida said, 'Really, Georgie! That
was very high-handed of you. And very unwise. You have
a heart problem and this sort of behaviour will make it
worse!'

'I don't care, Ida. I want to get out of here, spend a little

time with you and then get back to The Poplars. Lord knows
what they will have been up to in my absence.'

'I'm sure everything is going smoothly, dear. Why
shouldn't they be able to manage a few hours without your
supervision? They will be fine.'

'Will they? You think you understand the situation better
than I do?'

'Yes I do. Marianne is very . . .'

'It's not Marianne I worry about. It's that wretched uncle
of theirs! And Margate! The sooner he . . . Ah! Here come
my clothes. Perhaps you'd step outside while I dress, Ida
– and close the curtains as you go.'

The day's outing to Margate had been an outstanding success
full of excitements, even surpassing the visit to the zoo.
The following day, in Georgina's absence, Emmie and Edie
were still full of reminiscences but their usual routine bored
them and they were definitely fractious. Marianne decided
they should spend a quiet day in the schoolroom with a
simple programme of work. She would read to them, teach
them a poem or a song, they would draw and paint. Some
time in the evening their grandmother would return home
and she wanted the twins to be calmer by then.

Mrs Matlowe, however, arrived home earlier than
Marianne expected and almost at once she was called into
the study to discuss the previous day's activities.

'Sit down, Marianne, and tell me everything. I took one
look at the children and I could tell at once that they were
totally exhausted. I knew it! I knew that man would wear
them out. He has no idea about how to bring up children.
In his eyes he has only to give them gifts and work them
up into a frenzy of excitement. Children's minds are deli-
cate and should never be overloaded.'

Marianne jumped at once to Richard's defence. 'On the
contrary, Mrs Matlowe, I must beg to differ. I believe that
from time to time an exciting day is beneficial to young minds.'

'In what way, pray?'

'In a stimulating way. It creates new emotions . . .' She
searched her mind for further benefits. 'And opens them

up to different situations. I do believe it encourages imagination and . . .'

'Hmm. Hardly convincing. Were there any tears or
tantrums? I want an honest answer.'

'None that I recall.' She smiled. 'May I ask if you enjoyed
the theatre?'

'We did a little shopping instead. I don't care for the
theatre and my sister knows it full well.'

'I hope the news from your stay in the hospital . . .'

'For heaven's sake! We are talking about the twins. I
would like a few specifics. I certainly hope you kept them
away from anything hectic. When I tried to talk to Emmie
she was almost incoherent with excitement and could hardly
string a sentence together.'

'Specifics? Let me see . . .' Marianne tried to recall some
quieter moments. 'We played for some time on the beach
with buckets and spades and built a rather splendid sandcastle. The girls tucked up their skirts and paddled . . .'

'Paddled! Tut! Seawater, Marianne, is not as beneficial
as the so-called experts would have us believe! I hope they
wore sun hats. We don't want to ruin their complexions.'

'They were not in the water too long and yes, they wore
sun hats.' She had decided not to tell her that a beach
photographer had 'snapped' the four of them walking on
the promenade. The result had been a charming photograph,
which Marianne would treasure. They had bought four
copies – one each for the girls to discover at a later date,
one for Marianne, and one for Richard to send back to his
family.

She went on, 'They watched a Punch and Judy show . . .'

'Oh dear! I should have warned you. I detest Punch and
Judy. They are nasty, violent stories that frighten most
children.'

'They found it hilarious, Mrs Matlowe, as did the other
children. Please don't worry yourself on that score.'

'I shan't worry myself! It is *you* who are worrying me, with
all these unsuitable details! But I blame myself. I should
never have agreed to the plan. It was simply that I was
distracted by concerns for my health.'

Marianne fumed inwardly at her employer's stream of criticism but the truth was she *had* wondered once or twice if the day was becoming too eventful (she had omitted several events that might be construed as 'hectic'), but Richard's enthusiasm and the girls' joy had persuaded her not to intervene. If their uncle went back to America without them, the twins might never see him again and she wanted the day to be a wonderful memory for them in years to come.

She said, 'We had a quiet lunch in a rather elegant restaurant where the girls behaved impeccably and later Mr Preston rowed us on a small boating lake. Very calming. Very good for their digestion.' She smiled. 'There is no reason to worry about the girls. I'm sure it did them good to see the outside world and have a little fun.'

Upstairs in the schoolroom Emmie was struggling to remember the dodgems they had driven. 'Did the dodgems have wheels?' she asked, frowning.

'I don't think so.' Edie considered the sandcastle she had drawn and gave a satisfied nod. 'I'm going to put the Punch and Judy in my picture *and* the fish and chips and the vinegar bottle!'

Emmie paid her no attention. 'If they didn't have wheels, how did they get around? When Uncle Richard turned the steering wheel they sort of slid around and went *crash*!'

'They went very fast!'

'Very, *very* fast!' Abandoning the half drawn dodgem car Emmie considered a blank area of the page. 'I'm going to draw Marianne eating the jellied eels out of that little dish . . . and Uncle Richard, in his funny Kiss-Me-Quick hat, tasting a jellied eel and pretending to be sick!'

Both girls collapsed into loud giggles.

Edie said, 'You can draw me holding up the dead crab.'

'No, there won't be room. You put it in your picture. I'm going to draw Marianne running after her hat when it blew away!'

Ten minutes later Marianne returned to the schoolroom

to find the paint box open on the table and the two tell-tale pictures bursting into glorious technicolour.

Georgina let herself into Neil's room and carefully locked the door behind her. She was trembling as she made her way to the altar and lit the candles. Lowering herself carefully to her knees in front of the altar she closed her eyes and placed her hands together.

'Dear Lord, hear my prayer . . . I come to you today in great need of help and guidance. The news from Mr Prendergast was not at all good – in truth it was quite the opposite. It seems I have a serious fault in my heart, which I may have had since I contracted measles as a child.' She recalled the illness clearly – the whispered voices, the bedroom darkened by permanently closed red curtains, her mother tiptoeing in and out of the room and the anxious wait for the doctor to arrive.

She paused in mid-prayer and briefly laid a hand on her heart. What was it doing, she wondered uneasily. Was it even now deteriorating? Was the strain of talking about it adding to the problem?

Resuming the prayer, she said earnestly, 'I'm told to take things easily to avoid bringing on a heart attack, but I have the twins to look after. How can I neglect them? At the first sign of weakness that young man will be off to the courts to claim that I am not fit enough *physically* to have the twins in my care.' She pressed a hand to her heart. 'I dare not imagine what would become of them if they were snatched away from this God-fearing, ordered existence to live with a wild American family. If the rest of the Prestons are anything like Leonora and Richard it would be nothing short of tragic for Emmie and Edie.'

She paused again to feel for a pulse in her wrist but found nothing. Was that good or bad? And what about her temperature? Had Mr Prendergast said anything about her temperature? Was that a bad sign also? She really should have paid him more attention.

'So, dear Lord, I need you to watch over me and mine . . . and to be aware of this risk to my health. If you could

just keep me safe and well until the twins are old enough
to be independent. I ask it for their sakes, not mine. If I
feel that you are with me, dear Lord, I can struggle on, but
alone . . .' She gave a long, shuddering sigh. 'I fear I will
not survive long enough without spiritual support.'

Abruptly she added, 'Amen,' and struggled back to her
feet. She had the uneasy feeling that being told that she
had a defective heart had made her more anxious than she
had been when in blissful ignorance of the fact. For that
she blamed Ida for whisking her off to the specialist. But
Richard Preston must share the blame because his presence
had put such a strain on her that she had fainted. They had
all been much better off without him and the sooner he left,
to return to America, the better it would be for everyone.

Collecting Neil's dressing gown she wrapped it round
her and climbed on to his bed. Now at last she could relax
a little, she told herself thankfully.

'It's me, dear,' she began. 'If you wondered where I was
these last few days I was in hospital for tests but it turned
out to be nothing. Nothing to worry about, that is. You
know me. Strong as a horse, to put it in a rather unlady-
like way!' She smiled. 'Your Aunt Ida insisted that I see
someone – you know what a fusspot she is, but it was a
wasted day, really.'

She tried to imagine how it would feel to have a heart
attack. Mr Prendergast had said the first one was usually
quite mild but mustn't go unrecorded. Must on no account
be ignored.

'Your awful brother-in-law took the children to Margate
for the day. A rather vulgar town, in my opinion, full of
rowdy Londoners down for the day, stuffing their faces with
candyfloss and making too much noise. But he was set on
the idea and I don't want to antagonize him too much. It
clashed with my hospital visit so I sent Marianne with them,
to keep an eye on them. I know you and Richard got on
well enough but he was only a boy when you knew him
in America and no doubt on his best behaviour when visitors were present. I don't think you would be so keen on
him now – a sight too confident and pushy. He has insisted

on tracking down that awful nanny. Do you recall Ivy Busby, dear?'

Gingerly she slid her right hand across her chest to feel her left upper arm. Apparently a heart attack often started with a pain in the upper left arm before it moved into the heart proper. So she would have a little advance warning. It felt perfectly normal at the moment so she was in no immediate danger and that was a relief. She now regretted that she hadn't listened more carefully to Mr Prendergast but, if she was honest, she had been in a blind panic, desperate to hear nothing bad and determined to get out of the hospital. In retrospect she could see that Mr Prendergast meant well but at the time she had seen him as the enemy. But she would say nothing more to Neil.

'It's that time of year again, dear,' she told her son with feigned cheerfulness. 'A week or two at the most – I've lost track of the date – and the regatta will be upon us and the town will be seething with hundreds of visitors.' Which was tedious and very inconvenient but her son had always found it exciting. The river, too, would be packed with punts and skiffs, not to mention the inevitable houseboats – a very confused and potentially dangerous situation, as always. 'Cook was saying that there's even a very extravagant gondola for hire! Whatever will they think of next?'

She felt her left arm again. How bad would the pain of a minor heart attack be, she wondered? Would she be able to ignore it? How painful would a major heart attack be? Was it as bad as childbirth? She had borne that stoically when Neil was born. 'You were very brave.' That's what the midwife had told her.

If the pain in her arm was bearable, she decided, she would say nothing to anyone, simply make an excuse and go to her bedroom and lie down. She would alert no one unless it worsened. If it moved to her heart or was intense pain she would have to give in and send for the doctor.

Wrapped in Neil's dressing gown and locked away from the rest of the household Georgina felt comfortable and began to relax. She returned to her conversation with him.

'I know you always thought the regatta fascinating but

I have always realized there is a darker side to it.' She shuddered. 'All that deep water waiting to swallow the unwary – and there'll be plenty of those! People picnicking in the boats and drinking too much champagne! A disaster waiting to happen!'

Now that she was no longer dwelling on her heart problem, some of her anxiety began to slip away and she gave a sigh of satisfaction as she recognized that fact. Perhaps this was the time, therefore, to check that all her affairs were in order – and to finally write that letter.

'I'll start it tomorrow,' she told her son. 'That letter I told you about. I will do it. The truth, the whole truth and nothing but the truth, as they say. No one will understand the way you do, dear, but I must die with a clear conscience. Then, in the hereafter, when you and I are together again, there will be no unfinished business between us. You approve, don't you, dear?' She waited but after a few moments she said drowsily, 'Thank you, Neil. I knew you would.'

Later that evening Cook grinned at Lorna over the rim of the day's last cup of tea – the ten quiet minutes that Cook thought of as 'winding down at the end of the day' before setting off home. 'When the cat's away, the mice will play!' she said.

They grinned like two conspirators.

Lorna said, 'We got away with it yesterday and no questions asked!'

'Not yet anyhow. Just remember to keep quiet. No blabbing to Hattie or Mr Blunt or anybody.'

'Or the butcher's boy.'

'Exactly.' Cook glanced at the clock. 'Mind you, I wouldn't care to try it again. Might not be so lucky another time.'

'So what did you do with your time off?'

'I went round to my aunt's and did her ironing for her. She can hardly stand, she's that bad with her rheumatism, poor soul.' She stirred her tea absent-mindedly. 'But I'm not ironing towels and tea towels. None of that, I told her.

What's the point? They get creased up the minute you use 'em. They're washed and that's enough.'

Lorna looked dubious at this heresy. 'But what about tablecloths?'

'I do iron them – because you see them. Mind you I've only got one decent one and that's a devil to iron because my mother embroidered the corners and they seem to shrink up a bit with the stitching. They're awkward to iron flat . . . What did you do yesterday?'

'I went down to the river with my sister like we do every year, and walked along the towpath to see if they'd started the preparations for the regatta. The King and Queen are going to be there.'

'So I've heard – about a thousand times! Everyone's talking about it. It really will be Royal Henley Regatta!'

Lorna shook her head. 'No, because they're going to call it Henley Royal Regatta – so the blazer badges will be HRR. It said so in the paper.'

Cook shrugged.

'Anyway they haven't quite started but they've got some wood stacked along the path – ready for building the stands.'

'Let's hope no one steals it!'

'Course they won't!' She smiled. 'I love it along the river when it's decorated – flags and bunting everywhere and those coloured Chinese lanterns hanging in the trees and bushes.' She gave a sly grin. 'There was one young chap last year, unloading some crates from a boat – ginger hair and freckles – seemed to take a shine to me. Whistled after us and called out, "How do, ladies?"'

'How do you know he wasn't after your sister?'

'"Cos I'm prettier than her!' She tossed her head. 'Oh! Here comes Mr Blunt. He must smell the tea!'

He tapped on the back door and came in, hat in hand and, without a word, settled himself on a vacant chair.

Cook poured him a cup of tea and Lorna passed the sugar bowl before he spoke.

'Funniest thing!' He spooned sugar into the cup thought-fully. 'Them roses.' He jerked his head in their direction. 'I could swear they've been moved.'

Lorna's eyes widened. 'Moved? Where are they now, then?'

Cook said, 'What d'you mean, moved?'

He took a mouthful of tea, swilled it round his mouth and swallowed noisily. 'Not moved like that. I mean changed.'

'Into what?' Lorna demanded.

'Not into what! Not into something else! Just . . . swapped round.'

Baffled, they regarded him carefully.

Lorna persisted. 'Swapped with what?'

Mr Blunt shook his head. 'You two are as bad as my missus. With each other, of course. They're different colours.' He took another long, noisy mouthful and Cook winced.

Lorna said, 'They used to be pink and red. You saying they're like yellow and white now? Or orange?'

Cook snorted. 'Orange roses?'

'I've seen orange roses, Cook. I *have*!'

They waited for his answer. 'Not exactly,' he said at last. 'That is, they're still the same colours but . . .'

'You said they'd changed! You said they were different colours!' Lorna was growing exasperated by the story. 'He did, didn't he, Cook? He said . . .'

Cook rolled her eyes. It was time they were off home and she stood up pointedly. 'Drink up, Mr Blunt,' she urged. 'Time we were on our way.' To Lorna she said, 'Rinse the cups and dry them. Madam likes us to leave the kitchen shipshape.' She stood up, removed her apron and reached for her jacket.

Mr Blunt took the hint, drained the cup and stood up. He reached for his hat. 'Changed places, I meant,' he said, in a last attempt. 'Don't ask me how.'

Lorna gave him a bright smile. 'We won't!' Behind his back she tapped her forehead and Cook laughed.

'Then I'll be off. See you next week.' As he stepped outside, he put his hat on and then set off round the side of the house.

Cook raised her eyes heavenwards. 'Poor old boy!' she said.

'He gets worse! Let's hope he doesn't try that story on Madam! She'd give him short shrift.' She gave the kitchen a final glance. Satisfied, she asked, 'Orange roses? Have you really seen orange roses?'

'Sort of orangey pink. Like a peach, you could say.'

Lorna threw a shawl round her shoulders and they left the kitchen together by the back door.

Ivy Busby turned drowsily until, realizing she was awake, she smiled triumphantly without opening her eyes. So she had not died in her sleep. That was her biggest worry now – that she would die before Richard took her home to the family. And today was the day that he was coming to take her shopping. He was going to buy her a travelling outfit, which she would wear on the ship. Everyone at Number 24 was green with envy. Her smile broadened as she thought about it. What a change in her fortunes!

They would travel on Cunard's *RMS Mauretania*, which was barely five years old. Under her pillow was a brochure about the ship, which Richard had sent to her, plus the letter he had sent outlining their plans for the journey. Once he had satisfied himself, one way or the other, about poor Leonora's fate, they would book their passage. If they had discovered that she was dead and had found her body, they might arrange to take her body home to America to be buried with the rest of the family. If she had not been found they would give up and return empty handed. Ivy did not know what to hope for.

Selfishly she thought mainly about the change in her own situation and the excitements ahead for her. The ship was luxurious and they would have superior cabins and a steward to see to their needs. Possibly, hopefully, they would also have the twins and she, Ivy, would be caring for them – unless Marianne travelled with them. In her heart Ivy hoped this would happen because she knew the extent of her own frailties and secretly doubted that she had the stamina to look after two lively children. She also doubted that Mrs Matlowe would allow Marianne to leave her service. She might well refuse out of malice. Nothing would surprise Ivy where that woman was concerned.

She shared a breakfast table with Miss Allen and a woman by the name of Frederika who presumably had a surname but never used it.

After a few mouthfuls of stewed prunes Ivy said, 'Four million rivets! Imagine that! The *Mauretania*, I mean. That's how many rivets they needed for the hull.'

Miss Allen said, 'That's wonderful! Four million! It's wonderful, isn't it, Frederika?'

'Is it? I'm not an expert on express liners.'

Ivy scraped up the last spoonful of prunes. 'The interior is frankly luxurious, Richard tells me – plenty of mahogany panelling and tall pillars. And electric elevators – or lifts as you would call them over here.'

Frederika said, 'This Richard is your nephew, I take it.'

Ivy hid her irritation. They all knew that Richard had been one of her young charges when she was a nanny. Frederika was simply being awkward. She forced a light laugh. 'Not a nephew, Frederika. You are becoming a bit forgetful. It happens to us all, dear, in time. No, I was his nanny many years ago. He positively adores me, bless the boy. Not that he's a boy now. Twenty-three, I think, or it might be twenty-four. Time passes so quickly.'

Nesta arrived with a rack of toast and took away the dishes. She smiled warmly at Ivy who had let it be known, albeit discreetly, that the Prestons had made a generous donation to the Sutton Ladies Charity.

'Richard and I will each have a cabin and the twins will share. The cabins are superb. We shall each have a telephone and a private bathroom . . . There is so much to do – a reading room, walking on the promenade deck and even deck tennis!' Ivy laughed delightedly.

Frederika said, 'You won't be playing tennis, surely! Not at your age.'

Ivy concentrated on buttering her toast and bit back the sharp reply that sprang to her lips. Of course she understood that she was now envied by the other residents and that aroused jealousy. She pitied them. Each one of them would give an eyetooth to be in her shoes. She said sweetly, 'I certainly will not – much too strenuous – but I daresay Richard will play. A wealthy, good-looking young man can always find a partner for deck tennis.'

'Anyway, you'll be busy looking after the twins,' Miss Allen reminded her. 'I'm crocheting collars for you to give to the girls. One for each of them.'

Frederika smirked at this unlikely prospect but Ivy said, 'Miss Allen, that is so kind!' and laid a hand on Miss Allen's skinny arm in a gesture of gratitude. 'And the girls will never be bored on-board ship. There is a children's playroom with a huge mural of the five and twenty blackbirds escaping from the pie – and it will be well supervised!'

Frederika said, 'And the *Mauretania* holds the Blue Riband for speed across the Atlantic.'

Ivy stared at her. 'She does, yes. Fancy you knowing that!'

'You told us yesterday.'

Ivy detected a note of bitterness and counted to ten. She smiled at Miss Allen and said, 'Would you pass the marmalade, please? I feel the need for something sweet.'

ELEVEN

D onald looked up as his cousin came into the office looking somewhat harassed. 'Tough assignment?' He grinned.

'Most certainly!' Judith flopped down on top of several files that had been left on a chair. 'Poor Mrs Montini. She was rather tearful and dithered a lot and the man became a bit impatient with her.'

'But that's to be expected, isn't? I mean, being tearful. Choosing a headstone for one's beloved. Rather an emotional time.'

'Of course it is. Not to mention the wording to be engraved on it. The poor soul had nothing prepared and then at first couldn't remember if his name was Carlo Eduardo or Eduardo Carlo and couldn't recall his exact date of birth or . . .'

'So what was the final wording?'

'"Dearly Beloved" followed by "Rest In Peace" followed by the name and date, etc. Nothing dramatic or romantic but . . .' She stopped abruptly. 'You're looking very depressed. Was it very awful this morning?'

'Very. Ackrow was in a foul mood because we found nothing yesterday and wasted money and time and his superiors have been leaning on him. He's been told to drop the case – not that he ever really took it on, but . . . He was so keen to lay it to rest and now we've got nothing we didn't have before and he's in the dog house.' He shrugged. 'In fact we have less than before because we haven't got him or his resources. Reading between the lines I think he blames me.'

Judith sighed. 'It was worth a try.'

'I could kill for a pot of tea.'

'Then why don't you make one?'

'You usually do it!'

'But I'm not your . . .'

'Secretary! I know. You're my business partner.'

He looked so crestfallen that Judith abandoned her protest, put the kettle on and opened the milk. She called from the little kitchen, 'Is there anything more to be learned from the nanny? She was there at the time.' She set out the tray and three minutes later carried it in and set it down on the desk.

He said, 'You be mother!'

'You'll wear that joke out!'

'The nanny? I doubt it. Richard had a long session with her. We got the tip-off about the rockery and the roses, which led nowhere, but nothing else.' He frowned. 'Maybe Richard asked the wrong questions.'

'Maybe Ivy knows nothing. Or it was too painful and she doesn't want to remember what happened and has blocked it out of her mind.'

He looked startled. 'You're not suggesting that we hypnotize her!'

It was Judith's turn to look startled. 'Hypnotize her? Good Lord, no! I think that would be dangerous – especially at her age.' She frowned. 'I keep thinking we could make better use of Marianne but I can't think how. I mean, she is on the spot. And there's the boat house. If only she could get in there and look around.'

'For what?'

'I don't know. A clue. Another lead. Anything!'

He hesitated. 'I'm beginning to worry about Marianne. We've put her in an unpleasant position – acting for Preston against her employer. It can't be very comfortable for her. If that dig had run into difficulties and Mrs Matlowe had found out . . .'

Judith nodded. 'Marianne gave us so much information about the family arrangements. I think you may be right and she did overstep the mark – but only because she wanted to be helpful. If we persuade her to snoop around in the boat house and it gets back to Mrs Matlowe . . .'

'The fat will be in the fire with a vengeance. She might be sacked – and we won't be judged innocent either.'

Judith looked at him. 'We might all be charged with

conspiracy to . . . to dig up the rose bed!' She glanced at him helplessly. 'That sounds ridiculous but I'm sure they could come up with something to charge us with. It was very irregular, to say the least. Could you lose your licence, do you think?'

'I honestly don't know. We could argue that the police encouraged us in the idea but that doesn't mean we're guiltless.'

'If only we'd found her. Then it would have been congratulations all round.'

They fell into a gloomy silence, which was eventually broken by Donald.

'There's the sister, Ida!' he cried. 'We've forgotten her. I wonder how much she knows about what happened – in the past, I mean.'

'The trouble is if we ask her anything she'll tell her sister.' Judith shook her head. 'She's bound to. Blood's thicker than water and all that . . . Who else is there to ask? The cook and the maid weren't there until after Leonora's departure; Marianne's too recent, which only leaves Mr Blunt, the gardener . . .'

'And we don't want to alert him!'

'Are we missing something, Donald?'

He made no answer straight away. After a long pause he said slowly, 'I'm wondering if I should talk to Richard and point out that we are going nowhere and ask if he wants to call it a day. He could take the twins and the nanny and hot foot it back to America.'

'You think Mrs Matlowe will allow the children to go with him? I think she'll fight him all the way.'

'Through the courts, you mean?'

'Any way she can. If he just takes them . . . That would be kidnapping, wouldn't it? She could have him arrested.'

They regarded each other soberly.

Judith said, 'I'm trying to find a happy ending.'

'I'm beginning to think there won't be one!'

Thursday 13th June, 1912. My dear Ida, if you are reading this it is because I am dead and am relying on you to explain everything to everyone. Not a nice task and I hate to ask you but I seem to be surrounded by enemies and do not know where else I can turn . . .

Georgina laid down the pen and reread her words. Hardly elegant but it was not a novel and all she needed to impart were certain truths and her own deep regret at what had happened all those years ago.

You will never know how many times I almost confessed to you but that would have placed you in a terrible position and I could not do that to you. We may not always have seen eye to eye but on the whole I think we love each other and I had no wish to inflict on you the hell I have suffered since that terrible day . . .

Poor Ida. She would have no idea what to expect when she opened the letter. Shock, certainly, followed by revulsion and shame. And then maybe a small amount of compassion for the long, lonely years her sister had endured, unable to share her secret.

It started when I received Neil's letter telling me he had married! Can you imagine how I felt? My own son, married to a woman I had never met. Someone he had scarcely mentioned in his letters home. He described it as a whirlwind romance! To be frank, it felt like a slap in the face! I was totally crushed. Then I began to wonder if he would ever come back to England or would stay in America, as he seemed infatuated with the entire family. It took me days to come to terms with the whole situation but then I told you about the wedding. I needed you to understand what I was going through and sympathize but you were relentlessly cheerful and scornful of my tears. I forgave you but since then I have refrained from confiding in you. You have had no children and I cannot expect you to understand . . .

There were footsteps on the stairs but Georgina knew that she had locked the study door and no one would be able to disturb her. When the letter was finished she would go up to Neil's room and read it through to him. She knew that when it was written she could lock it away until the time came for it to be found. It would be quite safe.

She sat back, frowning. But suppose it was not found for months or years after her death. It should be discovered at once, but how was that to be arranged? Unless she gave it to her solicitor with instructions for it to be sent to Ida immediately. Yes! That was the answer. She smiled, encouraged by the way she was dealing with the matter.

'No hysterics, Georgina,' she said softly. 'You are stronger than you think.' But then she did have to consider her heart and Mr Prendergast had warned her against becoming upset or overemotional.

Dear Ida, please do not think for one moment that I blame you for anything. What I did rests entirely on my own shoulders and I take responsibility for it . . .

'Now where was I?' She reread the last three lines and thought carefully before she continued.

When they came to England I promised myself that I would show Leonora every kindness. I had no intention of allowing either of them to know how I felt about being a thousand miles away when they stood together at the altar, making their vows. But my heart was breaking and it has never mended. Poor Neil. He was infatuated with his bride and spared very little thought for me. Leonora was charming and pretty and very wilful. She liked to get her own way and Neil always sided with her and she knew it and knew that I knew it! It was humiliating, Ida. I wanted to share their happiness but it was impossible . . .

Downstairs the telephone rang followed by footsteps on the stairs and a knock on the door.

'Madam . . .' It was Lorna. 'It's Mr Preston on the telephone and he wants to come round and talk to you – if you could spare a few moments.'

'Tell him I'm busy. He could try tomorrow morning between ten and twelve.' Her heartbeat sounded louder than usual.

'He says it's important.'

'So is what I'm doing!' she snapped. Drat him!

'So what shall I tell him?'

'I've just told you what to say. Tomorrow between ten and twelve. Now please don't interrupt me again.'

After a small pause she heard the girl's footsteps retreating and smiled with satisfaction. 'That put you in your place, Mr Preston!' she muttered.

She tried once more to concentrate on the letter. She wanted to tell Ida that Leonora, in the bloom of youth and bursting with joy, made her feel old, ugly and unwanted. She was sure that Neil had seen her in a different light after he came back because he saw her through Leonora's eyes.

Finally I had an argument with Neil followed by another one with Leonora and the atmosphere became . . .

Lorna was back. 'He says he must talk to you today because tomorrow he is going to take Nanny shopping and . . .'

'Damn him and damn Nanny!' Georgina at once glanced heavenward and said, 'Sorry!' She flung down the pen and saw ink splatter across the page. With a groan of frustration she saw that the letter so far would have to be rewritten. Her heart was racing now and she tried to take deep breaths to calm herself. She thought resentfully of Mr Prendergast and his well-meant advice. How was she supposed to stay calm in her present situation? She felt a wave of faintness and was glad that she was sitting down. Leaning her elbows on the table she pressed her hands against her face and counted slowly to ten. *Don't let them win*, she told herself. *Hold on to your self-control.*

'Madam? Are you all right?' The door handle was rattled. 'Mrs Matlowe?'

'Of course I'm not all right but I shan't let you know that!' she whispered. Without a word she blotted the letter and slid it into the top drawer, locked it and pocketed the key. 'I'm coming!' she called and made her way to the door.

A few moments later Richard replaced the phone and looked at Donald. 'That was fairly painful!' he said. 'I am definitely not in her favour today. Not that I ever was.'

'But is she going to speak with you?'

'She agreed grudgingly to see me at four the day after tomorrow. She sounded wary.'

'As well she might!' said Judith. 'And you said nothing about the reason for the meeting.'

'I didn't want to give her time to start consulting solicitors. I'm resigned to the fact that she will refuse to let them visit my parents and will certainly try to prevent any attempt to keep them in America. She even refuses to allow the twins to visit Nan on the grounds that they don't remember her. I pointed out that *Nan* remembers *them* and she's longing to see them again.' He shook his head. 'She sure is one stubborn old biddy!'

Judith turned to Donald. 'But Richard is their uncle and his parents are the twins' grandparents. Can she stop Richard from taking the children to America for a visit?'

'But their father was English so he would have been the legal guardian, so to speak. Which makes Mrs Matlowe, as next of kin, the new legal guardian. That might give her a prior right to bring them up.'

Donald pursed his lips. 'Perhaps you should find yourself an English solicitor, Richard, who understands our legal system and ask him to talk to your family solicitor in America. Let them fight it out.'

Richard sighed. 'I wish we didn't have to fight over the girls. I admit I don't like Mrs Matlowe – I can't get over the way she behaved to my sister – but I do see her point of view. The twins are all she has. She may also feel she has a duty to her son to bring the girls up.'

Judith said, 'I'm sure Neil would prefer them to be brought up in America. He must realize how narrow-minded his mother is. Their upbringing is very restrictive.'

'But Neil's dead and we shall never know.' Richard rubbed his eyes tiredly. 'If only she would be more accommodating we could arrange part-time custody. Term time in Nebraska and holidays in England, perhaps, but I'm sure she would never agree. She wouldn't trust us.'

'Or the other way round.' Judith was interrupted by the telephone and the two men remained silent as she dealt with a new client. 'Certainly, Mr Warner. Mr Watson is with another client at the moment but is free tomorrow at nine thirty. Would that time suit? . . . Yes, I'll take your telephone number and he will ring you back within the hour for a few initial details . . .' She wrote down a telephone number, nodding as she did so. 'Right then. We'll see you tomorrow – and try not to worry. I'm sure we can be of help. Goodbye.'

Donald looked at her expectantly and she said, 'Trouble over a will.'

'As ever!'

Judith said, 'As I was saying about the joint custody idea – either way the girls would have a wonderful life. Most children would jump at the chance if they understood all that is entailed.'

Richard said, 'So it's shopping with Nan tomorrow and I go into battle at four on the fifteenth. Here's hoping!'

Judith held up both hands. She had crossed fingers on each one.

True to his promise, on the following day, Richard found himself comfortably seated in the ladies' dress department at Harvey Nichols, keeping an anxious eye on Ivy Busby who sat erect on the chair next to him while a solicitous assistant, by the name of Miss Andersby, discussed her needs.

'A trip to America!' she said. 'Oh! How I envy you, Miss Busby. And on the *Mauretania*!'

Ivy nodded. 'The weather may be a trifle cool . . .' she began.

Miss Andersby clapped her hands. 'So you will need something comfortably warm. Something to keep you snug on a chilly day. I believe the ships sail at some speed so there may be a draught. Let me think.' She was a small woman, probably in her late twenties, with softly waved mouse-brown hair and brown eyes, the latter magnified by spectacles. 'What about a lightweight wool? We have a charming skirt and jacket which would suit you perfectly.' She peered at Ivy's eyes. 'Hazel eyes – a very good match would be the soft green, although the lavender would also look well on you.'

Richard looked at Ivy. 'I think you would look well in

the green, Nan, but you could try them both on. I'm sure Miss Andersby would help you with that.'

'Oh, but of course! That's my job. And you'll no doubt need a hat to go with the outfit. I'll take you down myself to the millinery department and introduce you to Miss Larklin. She'll look after you. Now then, I'll fetch the suit in your size and . . .'

'My size?' Ivy laughed nervously. 'I have no idea – unless you have a "skinny" size! There's not much meat on my bones, Miss Andersby. It will have to be trial and error.'

Miss Andersby's smile was full of reassurance. She had quickly realized that her client was very advanced in years and was unused to shopping at such a famous store as Harvey Nichols. She might be finding it a trifle daunting. 'It's no problem, Miss Busby. I'll help you into the fitting room and while you take a moment to rest, I'll pop along and fetch my tape measure. We shall have your measurements in no time. You must not worry at all. Just relax and let me find you what you need.' She smiled at Richard. 'Your mother is in good hands.'

He laughed. 'I'm not the son, Miss Andersby, but you're close! Miss Busby was once my nanny – and a very good one, too!'

Ivy said, 'Richard is taking me back to America to spend my remaining years with the family.'

Miss Andersby clasped her hands. 'Then we must find you the perfect outfit for such a wonderful adventure.' She held out her hands. 'Let me help you rise, Miss Busby, and we'll make our way to the fitting room. I can't wait to see you in the green wool . . . but having said that, we also have a warm tweed with heather tones. I'll show you that one also.'

With some trepidation, Ivy allowed herself to be guided towards a curtained alcove. She moved carefully, determined not to stumble or to exhibit any sign of frailty. Nothing must prevent her from going back to America.

While Richard and Ivy were busy in Harvey Nichols, Georgina was attempting to continue her letter. She had

laboriously rewritten the page that had been spoiled by the
ink splatter and was about to continue when Cook sent
Lorna up to tap on the door.

'Mrs Matlowe, there's a man asking for you. Cook says
will you please come down and speak with . . .'

'A man? What's his name?' Georgina's heart skipped a
beat. Who on earth could this be? 'Is it the police?' She
almost held her breath. How ironic if her secret had been
discovered and she was arrested. The plan was to confess
after her death.

'I don't think so, Madam. He looks just ordinary and he
said Mr Croom sent him.'

'Mr Croom?' Georgina's mind raced. Did she know a
Mr Croom? The name sounded vaguely familiar. Should
she refuse to speak to him? Maybe that would arouse
suspicion. If she asked him to call another day, that would
simply prolong the agony of not knowing what this was
about.

'What's his name?'

Lorna screwed up her face in concentration. 'Cook did
tell me but I forgotten. Sorry, Madam.'

'So you should be, you silly girl! I've told you a dozen
times or more, always ask for the name. The *name*!' Lorna
stared at the floor. 'Because it may be someone I don't
want to speak to. I suppose I'll have to come down but I'm
not pleased, Lorna.'

'I'm sorry, Madam.'

'I'll be down in a moment or two,' Georgina agreed with
reluctance. 'Show him in to the front room, Lorna, and wait
with him.' She hated allowing strangers into the house but
was not going to discuss whatever it was on the doorstep.
Too many nosy neighbours!

Minutes later she found a middle-aged man standing by
the empty hearth. He wore some sort of cape and held a
deerstalker hat and, for some reason, reminded Georgina
of Scotland.

'Your name, sir?' she asked curtly.

'Edgar Lunn.' He paused, smiling, then continued. 'I was
given your name and address by —'

'And your business with me, Mr Lunn? Please be brief. I am very busy.' Turning, she waved Lorna away.

'The thing is, Mrs Matlowe, I've just bought a very expensive boat from Mr Croom's boatyard.' He smiled again. 'Something I've always wanted and an unexpected legacy has suddenly made it possible. They say all things come to those who wait!' He laughed.

Georgina did not return his smile. She disliked his confident attitude. A little too friendly, she thought.

Unaware of her hostility, he continued. 'We live about two miles away – we moved here a few months ago – and the land runs down to the river. All we lack . . .'

She was eyeing him intently. A niggling doubt had entered her mind and was taking hold. Was this man genuine or was he another of those wretched private investigators or, worse, a detective using this rather absurd disguise? If the man was an impostor, she must not be taken in by him. But now she also recalled a Mr Croom whose family owned the boatyard her own family had used on various occasions. 'So you are a friend of Mr Croom.'

'Hardly a friend, Mrs Matlowe. More a business acquaintance, although I do catch sight of him from time to time on the golf course. A pretty neat putter, although I hate to admit it.'

He sounded genuine, she thought cautiously, preparing to relax her vigilance. 'And why are you here?' she demanded.

'It's about the boat house,' he told her.

The boat house! At once alarm bells rang in her brain and she moved quickly to the nearest armchair and sat down in case she was overtaken by the faintness that troubled her recently in times of stress. She indicated that he also might sit and he availed himself of an upright chair.

'The point is,' he went on blithely, 'we are having a boat house built but it takes time and Mr Croom wants us to take delivery of our boat. He wondered, knowing that your boat house is empty, if you might allow me to rent your—'

'Mr Croom said that? He said our boat house is empty?' Her voice was a little shrill. 'How can he say that? He has never seen the inside of our . . .' She stopped abruptly, aware that her visitor might think she was overreacting. But they were trying to find out about the boat house! She should have known it would happen one day but had been lulled into a false sense of security. Her heart thumped against her ribs and she felt a fine perspiration breaking out on her skin. Her breathing was becoming ragged but she fought to remain in control.

Her visitor suddenly realized that she was in some distress. 'Are you feeling unwell, Mrs Matlowe?' He stood up, staring down at her anxiously. 'Can I call someone?'

'Please don't fuss,' she managed shakily and he sat down again.

'He suggested,' he went on, 'that is, Mr Croom suggested that you might be kind enough to rent out your boat house for . . .'

'Rent it out!' The idea immediately terrified her. How could she possibly allow complete strangers the use of the boat house when she could not even risk allowing anyone to enter the place? It was quite out of the question.

'It would only be for perhaps six weeks,' he went on, 'and naturally we would come to some kind of monetary agreement by way of rent. I can assure you I am willing to pay a fair price . . .'

Georgina leaned back against the chair, fighting for breath. Without warning she became aware of a faint pain in her arm. *In her left arm!* She was going to have a heart attack! 'Oh God!' she cried. 'Please go! Please! Whoever you are! I won't rent out the boat house! I don't . . . It's not a good idea. I'm sorry but I want you to go!' She clutched her arm.

'Mrs Matlowe! I didn't intend to . . . Really I just wanted . . .'

She waved her hand weakly, unable to force any words to her lips. Her head swam and she watched through a blur of panic as he finally left the room and let himself out. As the front door closed behind him Cook appeared in the doorway.

'Madam! Are you all right? What's happening? I was making you a tray of tea . . .'

'He was a . . . I don't know who he was. He might have been . . . he said he wanted to put his boat in our boat house. That's what he said but I don't trust him!' She gulped in more air. The pain in her arm had not grown worse and she clung hopefully to that fact.

Cook said, 'Did he threaten you or something? Should I call the police?'

'The police? For heaven's sake, woman! Just bring me a glass of water and hurry! And my pills, please.'

Cook disappeared, obviously flustered. Georgina tried to take stock of her condition. Was the pain in her arm getting worse? No. Maybe it would go away when she took the pills. There was no pain in her chest although her heart was still racing. She found her handkerchief and wiped the perspiration from her face. *Take care what you say to Cook*, she told herself. She must not alarm Cook or anybody else. But who was that man? That was the problem. Had he deliberately mentioned the boat house to study her reaction? Was he a detective? Surely not after all these years . . . but you could never be sure.

'This is not a heart attack!' she whispered. 'It's not! It's . . . it's just fear. Not even that,' she amended hastily. She must not allow herself to become *fearful*. It was anxiety and that was dangerous.

When Cook returned she gave her a faint smile. 'One of my funny turns,' she told her, sipping the cold water gratefully. She took one of her tablets. 'Nothing to worry about.' To Cook she said, 'You may go now. It's nothing for you to concern yourself about.'

No, she reassured herself. It had been a false alarm. The pain in her arm was subsiding. She was sure of it. That wretched man! When she felt better she would telephone Mr Croom and ask him if he really had sent the stranger to her home. A suspicious stranger, at that, who asked suspicious questions. How dare Mr Croom put her through such an ordeal? Rent out the boat house indeed! The boat house had been out of bounds for years and would remain so for the foreseeable future.

She sat for a while, after Cook had gone back to the

kitchen, until she felt fully restored. Gradually her confidence returned. She thought long and hard about Mr Edgar Lunn. He was a fraud, she decided. A cape and a deerstalker hat in June? How unlikely was that? Did he even look like a man who would be familiar with boats? Of course he didn't. He may have fooled Mr Croom but he had not fooled her. The best form of defence was attack. She would waste no more time worrying but take action. She would telephone Mr Croom and warn him not to be so gullible in future – and never to talk about the boat house with anyone else.

Before she could carry out this plan, however, Cook came back, flushed with excitement. 'That man, Madam. Lorna said his name was Edgar Lunn. I said it never is! Edgar Lunn! It can't be!'

Georgina frowned. 'He did say that was his name. Should I have recognized it?'

Cook's smile broadened. 'Only if you read his books, Madam. He's a writer. Writes mysteries. *The Church at Long Eagle* – that's one of his. I've read that twice. And *The Secret of Downey Hall*. And *Once A Villain*. That's wonderful, too. My aunt buys all his books and lends them to me. I haven't read *The Secret of Downey Hall* yet but I know it'll be very good. Edgar Lunn is ever so famous. I knew he'd moved to Henley but I never thought I'd meet him. Well, I didn't actually *meet* him, did I, but I saw him in this very house – although his back was to me so I didn't quite see his face. Fancy him coming here. It just goes to show . . .'

Georgina said faintly, 'Cook, please!'

'Oh yes!' Cook cried. 'I nearly forgot. *Shadow Over Marksby*. That was about a soldier who deserted while on active service and . . . I can't remember how that one ended.' She took a deep breath, beaming with excitement. 'Wait 'til I tell my aunt he was here.'

Georgina sat very still after Cook had returned to the kitchen. An intense relief washed over her and, with clasped hands and a bent head, she gave thanks to God. Despite his eccentric appearance, Edgar Lunn *was* genuine. So why did he have to wear that ridiculous outfit? She thought about the recent scene and wondered what the poor man would make of it. Not that he was poor in any sense of the word if he had just bought a house and an expensive boat.

Oh dear! What a fiasco! Georgina smiled faintly. Maybe he would write her into one of his mysteries as a silly, hysterical old woman! Should she write and apologize, she wondered? No, because how could she explain her apparently irrational fear?

Thoroughly mortified, she did not know whether to laugh or cry. Thank heavens she had not made that irate telephone call to Mr Croom! Cook had saved her from that mistake. Now that she understood she began to regret that she had sent him packing. A famous author coming to her for help. That would have been something to tell the people at her next bridge night – something to impress them . . . Unless Edgar Lunn was at this very moment planning to tell *his* version of the meeting to his cronies at the golf club!

The minutes ticked by and at last Georgina decided there was no way to undo the damage and the entire stupid incident was best forgotten. Water under the bridge. She allowed herself a wry smile. 'Sometimes, Georgina Matlowe, you can be very foolish,' she admitted and her deep sigh was heartfelt.

Ida had bought the twins a dolls' house and had invited them over for the day to play with it. Georgina had insisted that she was too busy with 'various correspondence' but had nominated Marianne to escort them and they arrived around eleven on the Monday following the debacle with Edgar Lunn. While Ida and Marianne chatted, Emmie and Edie explored the dolls' house, discovering that the entire front wall opened and the roof lifted. They gazed into it, enchanted.

'Downstairs it's the kitchen and the front room,' Edie explained, 'and upstairs . . .'

'It's the bedroom and the teeny box room. There's a big bed for the mother and father and a small bed for the little girl.'

'We should give her a name, Emmie.' Edie picked up a

small pegtop child and considered her. 'Does she look like a . . . a Caroline? Or Madeline?'

'Or Jaqueline?'

'Or Angelina? Or Marianne!'

They both giggled.

Edie said, 'Or Maude – like the lady at Sunday School, because they both have dark hair.' Replacing the doll she peered into the kitchen with squeals of delight. 'Look! It's a teeny, tiny frying pan . . . and there's a kettle and a saucepan . . .'

In the kitchen Ida had asked Marianne for a report on Georgina's health and Marianne had described the incident with Edgar Lunn.

Ida shook her head, mystified. 'I've heard of him, of course, but I don't read mysteries. I like romance . . . But what on earth could he have said to upset her? Had he been rude to her?'

'Who knows? I can't imagine why he should be unpleasant in any way. According to Lorna—'

'Who was no doubt eavesdropping!'

'I daresay she was.'

'Servants always do.'

Marianne felt uncomfortable. She was being encouraged to spy on her employer so presumably that made her no better than the servants. 'Lorna thought they were talking about the boat house,' she said, 'and a Mr Croom was mentioned. Mr Lunn was sent packing in no uncertain terms, it seems, and Mrs Matlowe was obviously shaken by the meeting and needed a glass of water and her tablets. Cook said she was terribly pale.'

'Tut! She's not supposed to get upset. It's bad for her heart. Mr Prendergast told her to stay calm.' Ida sighed. 'I do wish she'd confide in me. I'm sure I could help her if she would only trust me . . . Maybe I ought to move back in with you but she seems set against the idea. And what is all this about "various correspondence"? Who is she writing to? I asked her but she snapped that it was private and that she didn't ask me about my correspondence – which is true, but then I don't hide myself away the way she does.'

Edie appeared, holding a bed from the dolls' house. 'There are no sheets and blankets. How can they go to bed?'

Ida laughed. 'I was waiting for you to spot that,' she told her. 'You and Emmie will have to make some sheets and blankets. Now . . . let me see what I can find.'

Emmie arrived with a table that lacked a tablecloth. Within minutes Ida had found a sewing basket and some pieces of material, remnants of earlier sewing activities. Two small pairs of scissors completed the finds. 'Now off you go and measure up the beds and the table, cut out the materials and see how it looks. If you want to you can turn up the edges. You'll find needles and threads in the sewing basket.'

The twins went back to the front room, chattering excitedly over the project.

Marianne said, 'At least she takes the pills regularly.'

'That's something to be thankful for!' After a short silence Ida leaned forward confidingly. 'Not a word about this to anyone, Marianne, but I am thinking about offering to move into The Poplars *permanently* to keep an eye on Georgina. To be close at hand in case . . . Well, in case she has a heart attack.' She sat back. 'You look shocked.'

'Shocked? No, but surprised. Do you think your sister would agree to that? It might be a good idea . . .' She hesitated, certain in her own mind that Mrs Matlowe would fight the idea tooth and nail. But if she did agree to the idea, would it improve matters?

'We don't get on very well, I admit, but now I feel Georgina needs support if she's to survive this wretched heart trouble. I would keep my flat on so that, if things become fraught, I can slip away for a few days and let any friction fade. Even if the idea doesn't work out, I shall have had time to understand more of what is going on with her. I'm convinced that something is troubling her and I'd like to know what it is. She is the only family I have . . .' She sighed heavily. 'Anyway, we shall see. When I think the time is ripe I shall put it to her. I'll think of an excuse that makes me the needy one!' She smiled regretfully. 'I know Georgina better than she thinks I do!'

*   *   *

That afternoon Georgina made another attempt to finish her letter to Ida.

The trouble started with a quarrel between us when Neil was at the dentist and one morning I found Leonora in the boat house, which was against my most strict orders. She had decided to explore, she told me airily. When I challenged her she suddenly announced that, as a surprise birthday present, she was going to buy a new punt for Neil. She said it was such a waste to have the boat house and never use it and that Neil had expressed regret that they never took part in the regatta. Whether that was true or not, I don't know. She told me this, knowing how much I hated the idea of the regatta and anything to do with the river . . .

Georgina shuddered, seeing the scene again with horrible clarity. Time had not dulled the image of herself and Leonora staring at each other with mutual dislike – Leonora smiling in triumph and Georgina apoplectic with fury at being outmanoeuvred. Perhaps that was the moment, she reflected, that her heart had first come under strain.

She insisted that I need not be involved but that she and Neil would watch the races together. I at once imagined them in the punt, opening a bottle of champagne and crowing over her success – and I imagined me at home, fearing at any moment to hear news of a disaster like the one that killed Uncle Walter . . . I then made a fatal mistake by forbidding her to carry out the plan. I swear, Ida, that her eyes lit up and she made up her mind to beat me.

I was so angry that for a moment I was speechless and then I slapped her face. That took the smile off it!

Georgina regretted the last sentence but it was too late. She had written it. It made her sound spiteful and even vicious but it was the truth. Leonora had brought out the worst in her.

Then she made a mistake that was definitely fatal – she laughed and said, 'You really are a bad-tempered old witch! Neil said you could be difficult but boy! He was being generous!' Of course I didn't believe a word of it. I know

*my son better than she did and he would never say that
about me. Never!*

*I lashed out at her again and she took a step back, fell
into the water and hit her head against the old punt as she
went down. I swear I did not mean to kill her. I did not
mean to push her into the water. It was an accident. Somehow
I overcame my fear of the water and looked for her, hoping
to pull her to the side and help her out . . .*

'I didn't mean to kill her.' Georgina spoke in to empty
room. 'I would never deliberately kill the twins' mother or
my son's wife. I'm not a monster.' She closed her eyes and
swallowed, her throat dry as dust. 'Sometimes things just
happen. That was one of those times.'

*But when she failed to come up again and I knew she
must have drowned, I had to decide what to do. How would
it be for Neil to know that I had killed his beloved Leonora?
And for the twins to know that their grandmother killed
their mother? It would be horrific. It would break their
hearts. I knew that if they knew the truth it would ruin all
their lives.*

*I waited and waited alone in the boat house for the body
to come to the surface but it didn't appear. I was dazed by
the tragedy and at a loss what to do next. I dare not ask
for help. Finally I left the boat house, locked its door and
went back to the house. Claiming a bad headache I went
up to my room and lay on the bed, trying to think clearly
but fear and a deep horror had dulled my mind and I lay
there in a confused panic . . .*

Georgina rubbed her neck, which now ached painfully,
and she moved her stiff limbs.

*Even today, eight years later, I can still feel the horror
and dread that seized me, and with it came the weight of
remorse, which almost suffocated me and still does in weak
moments. I started to lie, inventing a quarrel with Leonora
that ended with her storming out of the house in a temper.
Neil was horrified and spent days searching for her until
at last he went to the police and reported her missing.*

*Finally in desperation he decided she had gone back to
her parents in America and set off after her.*

*Then one day I discovered that her body had floated
to the surface and while I tried to decide what to do about
it, the wretched nanny continued to bombard me with
questions – she was definitely suspicious and, when I
could bear it no longer, we quarrelled and I telephoned
for a taxicab and sent her packing. I shall never forget
the look on her face . . .*

The awfulness of Georgina's task suddenly overcame her
and she returned the pen to the ink stand with a trembling
hand.

'Finish it tomorrow, Georgina,' she told herself. 'That's
enough for today.'

Mr Prendergast had told her to 'be kind' to herself and
she thought this was what he meant. There was no point
in making herself ill. No one else cared how she felt or
how much anguish she could bear . . . except Neil. Georgina
took the letter and made her way up to his room.

Two days later, when Ida telephoned to ask if she could
spend a few days at The Poplars, Georgina's first instinct
was to say no, but Ida explained that there was something
wrong with the pipes in her flat and 'the man' would be
coming on the nineteenth to deal with the problem. It
might take several days, she told Georgina, to track down
the fault and she would have no water supply during that
period. Reluctantly Georgina heard herself agreeing.

Ten minutes before Richard Preston was due to arrive at
The Poplars, Georgina began to panic. In some way, the
letter she was writing to Ida had made her doubly fearful
about the meeting. It was as if the presence of her written
confession made her more vulnerable to discovery and therefore Richard Preston could prove dangerous. It was possible,
she thought, that the meeting was some kind of trick to
force herself to reveal things best kept hidden – a trick
conceived by the police. Nothing would surprise her.

Five minutes before Preston was due to arrive, she made
a sudden decision and hurried to the schoolroom.

'Marianne, I want you to sit with me while I talk to

Mr Preston,' she said. 'Please give the girls some work which will keep them usefully occupied for, say, twenty minutes. Then come down to the study. I don't trust the man one inch. Oh, and be prepared. When I decide I have heard enough I shall tell him so and say, "Please see Mr Preston out, Marianne," and you must then immediately stand up and hold the door open for him. I shall know when I have had enough of his nonsense!'

As instructed Marianne made her way to the study where she found a chair had been prepared for the visitor opposite Mrs Matlowe, who would sit in her usual chair behind the desk. The chair for Marianne was to Mrs Matlowe's right but about six feet away, so that it was quite clear she was simply there as a supporting figure and probably not required to say much – which suited Marianne very well. She expected a difficult twenty minutes because she suspected Richard Preston wanted to broach the subject of taking the children to America.

She sat down in her allotted seat and watched as Mrs Matlowe fussed with various papers on her desk.

'Look at that, Marianne! Five minutes late. Not a good start. Now he only has fifteen minutes of my time available to him.'

At that moment the front doorbell was rung and shortly afterwards Lorna brought Richard to the study. They all shook hands and sat down. Marianne expected her employer to explain the presence of a third person at the meeting but she did not do so.

'Well, Mr Preston, perhaps you would state your case,' she said, looking at him severely.

'My case?'

'Why are you here?'

'Ah! I have had a letter from my parents inviting Edie and Emmie to spend a few weeks with them in . . .'

Marianne was impressed. He had plunged straight in!

'Most certainly not, Mr Preston. You need go no further!' Mrs Matlowe's back had stiffened.

'In July,' he went on, as if she had not spoken. 'Most children benefit from a summer break from school and . . .'

Marianne could imagine how hard he had worked on the exact wording of the request.

Mrs Matlowe shook her head. 'Edie and Emmie do not attend school, Mr Preston. They are being educated privately, as you know, by Marianne, and we do not believe they are in need of a holiday. They are not "in need of the benefit of a summer break", as you put it. If and when they do need a holiday, they will be taken by Marianne and myself to Scotland, Devon maybe . . . or possibly somewhere in Wales. They will not be dragged halfway round the world, Mr Preston. Please thank your parents for the invitation but tell them I have considered their offer and refused.'

Marianne found herself holding her breath.

Obviously taken aback by the abrupt rejection, Richard glanced at Marianne.

Mrs Matlowe said sharply, 'Don't look to Marianne for support, Mr Preston. She is in my employ and understands exactly the situation with Edie and Emmie.'

'Isn't she allowed a voice?'

'Not necessarily.'

'Then why is she here?'

Mrs Matlowe was taken aback by this challenge. She muttered something mainly incomprehensible which ended with the word 'impudence' and said, 'Marianne! Mr Preston wants to hear your opinion.'

Marianne cursed inwardly but said, 'I do understand Mrs Matlowe's worries, but in my opinion the twins—'

Mrs Matlowe nodded. 'That's enough, Marianne. Thank you.'

Marianne was wishing that she had had a chance to speak to Richard before the meeting but there had been no time. Had Mrs Matlowe done that deliberately, she wondered?

Richard took a deep breath, trying to hide his irritation. 'Mrs Matlowe, I don't think you are being quite fair. My sister was – is – the girls' mother and my parents are their grandparents. Surely you can understand that they wish to see the twins.'

'I do accept that, Mr Preston. I suggest they come to

England and follow your example. Book into a hotel nearby and make visits to us here. They will not be turned away, I can assure you.'

'But they want the twins to know where Leonora grew up and . . . and to experience the American way of life.'

Mrs Matlowe shuddered. 'The American way of life? Are you under the impression that it is somehow superior to the English way?'

'Not superior but very different. Your son enjoyed it immensely. He spoke of possibly moving to America.'

The silence was tangible. Marianne wondered if it were true and thought it might well be.

Shocked, Mrs Matlowe caught her breath and, quite unconsciously, laid a hand over her heart. 'That is a lie, Mr Preston! We both know it. My son would never have considered such a thing . . . unless your sister had persuaded him. I wouldn't put that past her.' She glanced at Marianne. 'Please try and convince Mr Preston that the twins are in very good hands and enjoying exactly the sort of life their father would have wished for them.'

Marianne drew a deep breath. 'Of course they are well cared for but it may be that, had things been different, your son would have wanted them to visit their grandparents. Possibly he would have wanted you to go with them.' She dared not look at her employer or at Richard, so she stared down at her hands instead. Had she just talked herself out of a job?

Richard said, 'Neil loved America, Mrs Matlowe. If he were still alive—'

'I don't believe you, Mr Preston, and I prefer you should not take my son's name in vain in this way.' Mrs Matlowe was sounding decidedly breathless and her growing agitation was painfully clear. 'You think that by putting words into his mouth, you will persuade me to change my mind but you are wrong. Neil was properly brought up and had no great admiration for the American way of life.'

How, Marianne wondered, could Richard remain so calm? He certainly would not want to antagonize her but he might eventually have no choice.

'Mrs Matlowe, I was hoping you would be reasonable but I see you are determined not even to consider the request. I shall give you a few days in which to think it over but if you continue to deny the girls this opportunity I will be forced—'

Mrs Matlowe's expression changed. 'Are you trying to threaten me, Mr Preston? Marianne, you heard what he said. Does that sound like a threat to you?'

'Oh no!' she cried. 'Not a threat. I believe he is trying to point out that . . . that he may well be forced . . .'

'To do what exactly?' Mrs Matlowe turned to him. Marianne saw with alarm that she was clutching her left arm and all colour had drained from her face.

The silence was broken by the scrape of Richard's chair legs as he rose to his feet. 'I shall be forced to apply to the courts for permission to take the children abroad. For a holiday. The twins are not your property, Mrs Matlowe. My parents are entitled to see them and I'll fight you if I have to!'

'You certainly will have to! Now I am feeling a little unwell. Please leave this house immediately. Marianne!'

Remembering her instructions, Marianne hurried to the door and opened it. Richard swept past her as she called down to the kitchen for Lorna to open the front door for him. Hurrying back to Mrs Matlowe she found her crumpled on the floor, her face ashen, groaning in obvious agony.

'I'll fetch your pills!'

She ran from the room, collected the pills from the cupboard in the bathroom and continued downstairs. She told Cook to telephone for the doctor. 'Tell him Mrs Matlowe is having a heart attack!'

Later, when Mrs Matlowe had to be helped to her bed and they were awaiting the doctor's visit, Marianne telephoned Ida to tell her what had happened.

'Oh! The poor soul!' she cried. 'I'll be with you within the hour.'

'So how is Mrs Matlowe?' Donald asked.

'Not good, I'm afraid.' Marianne shook her head and explained the situation.

It was Thursday afternoon before Marianne found time
to visit Donald. The heart attack had occurred on Tuesday
and Ida had taken charge of the household while Georgina
was recovering with twenty-four-hour bed rest and more
of the same pills. The doctor had been cautious. 'She has
had a mild attack,' he told them. 'It would have felt anything
but mild, but a severe attack might well have killed her.
She must rest and must be screened from any stress. Keep
her calm. The sleeping pills will guarantee her a good
night's sleep every night, which is vital. Calm is of the
essence.'

Marianne told Donald, 'With Mrs Matlowe's sister with
us, the household seems very different. More relaxed and
Ida likes to spend time with the two girls, which leaves me
with a little extra time on my hands. They are out now with
Hattie for their afternoon walk and then, when I get back,
I am taking them to a shop in Henley that sells furniture
and things for dolls' houses. Emmie wants to buy some
crockery and Edie has set her heart on a clock for the wall.'
She glanced up at the clock on the office wall and said,
'Isn't Judith coming in today?'

'She's been in but she began to feel very sick. She said
it's her "condition"! I sent her home but on the way she is
collecting some forms that we need for the will case we're
dealing with.'

'Can I do anything to help? Type a couple of letters,
maybe? I haven't much time but I could do one or two.
I'm slow but careful.'

He jumped at the offer but added, 'Only if you agree to
let me take you out one evening for a meal – by way of
payment!'

'There's no need to repay me, Donald. I'd be pleased to
help.'

'But I've been dying for an excuse to ask you out!' he
grinned. 'Please say you'll agree.'

'It's very kind and I'll accept the offer with pleasure!'
Marianne smiled warmly at him.

'On that happy note I'll show you the drafts of the letters
which I scribbled down after Judith left – to save a little

time when she comes in tomorrow. Assuming she feels well
enough . . . But before we go any further, I have something
I must say to you. Looking back over the past few weeks
I think we've asked too much of you. Or rather, *I* have.
Asking you to deceive your employer over such an important issue. I put you in an awkward spot and I won't do it
any more.'

'I was pleased to help.'

'But the case could have ended in a prison sentence for
someone – or worse, the death penalty. It would have been
on your conscience and I'd be responsible.'

'Then I'll accept your apology, Donald. But don't feel
too badly because I could have refused to help.'

They exchanged a long look and both of them realized
that somehow their relationship was undergoing a change.
Marianne was touched by what he had said and by the concern
he had shown for her. It must have been hard to admit a
mistake and apologize. She had liked him before but now
he had gone up in her estimation. She wanted to say more
but maybe they had said enough for now. One step at a time.

Instead she smiled and said, 'So find the letters for me,
Donald, and I'll make a start.'

When the telephone rang later that evening it was Ida who
answered it. Unused to staff, she found it more natural to
do things for herself.

It was Richard Preston. 'I was hoping to speak to Mrs
Matlowe but I understand she's not well. I'm sorry to
hear that.'

Ida said bluntly, 'It was a heart attack brought on by
your meeting on Tuesday. I'm afraid she became very
anxious and that's a risk with her heart in its present state.
She's dozing and I know she won't speak to you, even if
I wake her – which I won't do. Can I help?' He hesitated
and her heart sank. 'You're taking her to court, Mr Preston
– is that it?'

'No, not at all. At least, not yet. I have found a suitable
solicitor who will be advising me, but this is about Edie

and Emmie. I promised Ivy Busby that I would take the
girls to see her. I was hoping Mrs Matlowe would allow
that to happen.'

'Ah! A tricky problem! Let me think . . .'

'It would only be for an hour, excluding the journey to
and from the home. Not a full day's outing.'

'Hmm. If I don't mention it until they are safely back
here, it might be possible. If my sister doesn't know about
it until it's over . . . You see where I'm going with this?'
She stared at herself in the hall mirror and frowned, seeing
a few more grey hairs. 'On the other hand, is it worth risking
another upset? The twins won't remember the nanny, will
they? As far as I recall they were very young – only infants
when Miss Busby was . . . when Georgina dispensed with
her services.'

'The visit is primarily for Nan's benefit,' he told her.
'She remembers them clearly but hasn't seen them since
she was sacked.'

Ida raised her eyebrows. That was a snub, she thought,
but could not blame him. Georgina could be very auto-
cratic and had often complained that the nanny was
constantly extolling Leonora's virtues. 'I suggest that
tomorrow, about one o'clock, you telephone and ask if you
can take the children to see their one-time nanny. Georgina
will be asleep at that time, which I can use as an excuse
for not asking her permission. But please don't extend the
visit for any reason or my sister will decide you have spir-
ited them away! The two of you may not see eye to eye
but Georgina is my sister and I don't want to risk her health
in any way.'

'I understand perfectly,' he told her, 'and I will bring
them home before four o'clock if you are agreeable with
this timetable.'

'I am.'

'My thanks. I'll see you tomorrow.'

Ida hung up the phone and gave a last regretful glance
at her reflection. 'He'll be a nice catch for some lucky
girl in a year or two. If only I were twenty years younger!'

She went in search of Marianne to tell her what had been arranged.

Marianne looked startled. 'Is that . . . wise?'

'I admit it's devious but . . .'

'The girls are sure to tell her all about it – or draw a picture about it.'

'But I shall tell her afterwards.'

Marianne frowned. 'I hate to interfere,' she said slowly, 'but since the heart attack, Mrs Matlowe has been slightly paranoid about Mr Preston and insistent that he never takes the girls anywhere alone.'

'Then you shall go with them.'

'I suppose I could, but he may not wish to take me.'

'He won't have any option, Marianne. If he doesn't want you to meet the old lady, you can sit in the reception area or stroll in the grounds. I assume there is a garden.'

'Just a small paved area, but you're right. I can amuse myself. If that solves the problem, I'm quite happy about it.'

'I'll tell him when he rings tomorrow. It's my guess he'll enjoy having you along. You're an attractive young woman, Marianne.'

'Oh!' she said, disconcerted by the compliment. 'Thank you.'

Ida laughed. 'Don't be so modest! If I were in your shoes I'd be setting out my stall where that young man is concerned!'

The following evening, after the children were settled for the night, Marianne wrote to Alice.

I must tell someone and I fear it has to be you, Alice, she wrote. *I am still recovering from a ghastly afternoon. It was arranged that I would accompany the twins and their handsome Uncle Richard to the charity home where the children's nanny now spends her days – until, that is, Richard Preston whisks her back to America to be reunited with the family!*

The idea was that we would all spend time with her, but that I would slip away discreetly at some stage and leave them on their own. I imagined I would then wander elegantly through the garden or rest my idle bones on a sofa in Reception. It was not to be . . .

Marianne sighed, recalling the reality of the visit. Ivy Busby had appeared, walking unaided, wearing a wool suit that was quite unsuitable for the very warm weather. Her face was flushed, her gaze very direct and unsmiling. Richard, somewhat taken aback, had then explained to the nanny, as tactfully as possible, that it had been a condition of the visit that he should not have sole control of the children and introduced her as the twins' governess.

Ivy Busby, however, made it quite clear that she was offended by this information and gave me a withering look that would have stopped an elephant at ten paces! She said, 'That dreadful Matlowe woman! How very like her to impose conditions. If she was trying to offend me she has succeeded!'

I felt deeply slighted but for the children's sake I hid my feelings. I immediately apologized and offered to withdraw but Richard said, 'Please, Marianne. This is not your fault.' But Ivy Busby waved a hand in my direction and said, 'I know exactly whose fault it is! Just get rid of her, Richard, and let us enjoy the visit.'

Marianne had hesitated, unsure what to do. The twins had been listening wide-eyed and could obviously see that something was wrong.

Edie began to cry and turned to me for comfort and Emmie took hold of Richard's hand, regarding the nanny with dismay. Desperate to save the afternoon I said brightly, 'Say "Hello" to your nanny, girls. She's been looking forward to seeing you both.' Neither of them spoke and I really could not blame them . . .

Richard was by then crimson with embarrassment and Marianne's heart went out to him but she had no idea what else to do or say to help him.

I lowered my voice and said to him that if I withdrew things might improve and, before he could argue, I slipped out and closed the door behind me. I went back to the front entrance where there was a solitary sofa, rather the worse for wear, and I sat on it feeling slightly hysterical and not knowing whether to laugh or cry! Can you imagine it, Alice?

I had heard such wonderful things about the 'dear old family nanny' from Richard that it was hard to reconcile the myth with the bad-tempered old woman.

A few moments later a woman came out to me and introduced herself as Nesta, one of the staff . . .

According to Nesta, Ivy Busby had slept badly in spite of a sleeping pill and had woken feeling overexcited and very anxious about the coming meeting with the twins. Someone called Frederika had given her a couple of glasses of sherry to 'calm her nerves'.

'Strictly against the rules, of course,' Nesta insisted. 'We don't allow any alcohol at Number 24 because it upsets the various medicines and pills that the residents take. Someone had smuggled in a bottle for Frederika and we made her give it up. But too late, of course. It had the unfortunate effect of making poor Miss Busby feel argumentative. She can sometimes be difficult but I could say that about all of our ladies. They are all in a rather sad position and can be irascible.'

She lowered her voice although there was nobody nearby to hear, and said that Ivy tended to boast about her recently improved situation and the others were a little jealous. She thought Frederika might have given her the sherry deliberately, knowing how it might affect her! Lord save us, Alice, from such a fate!

So the wonderful nanny was tipsy and I was grateful for my early escape. It seemed that there was no garden but only a small area at the rear of the building and that it was currently strung with lines full of washing so I took myself off for a long walk round the block . . . three long tours, in fact!

We were unable to talk on the way home for fear of 'little pitchers' but I shall presumably get to hear about it at some time.

Marianne felt slightly better when the letter was finished. Putting pen to paper about the disastrous afternoon had somehow taken the bitterness from the memories. She had also told Alice about Donald's invitation to dinner and that had restored her natural cheerfulness. Weary from the day's emotions, she signed her name with a flourish, slipped the folded letter into an envelope and sealed it.

As she pulled off her clothes and put on her nightdress, her bed looked very inviting.

THIRTEEN

Donald and Richard sat together in the office regarding each other unhappily. Richard had just described the previous day's visit to Ivy Busby with an attempt to make light of it – an attempt which failed dismally.

He said, 'I feel so bad for Marianne and the twins. It was a wretched experience. When Nan realized that she had cast a blight over the afternoon she was very apologetic but it was too late then. The damage was done.'

'So you weren't able to ask Miss Busby any more about what happened when Leonora disappeared? I was hoping she might volunteer something useful because, to be honest, Richard, I feel we have nowhere else to go.'

'I managed to ask her what she thought had happened to Leonora and she said she believed that she stormed out after the row with Mrs Matlowe and was then killed – either by accident or design. She thinks she's dead. She says that she was tempestuous and quite likely to storm out and frighten everyone but that she almost certainly intended to return. She would never desert the children.' He leaned forward. 'Are you about to tell me you're giving up on the case?'

'Regretfully I am. I can't see any way to move forward and you may be better off going home. You did your best.'

'I saw a solicitor before I came here and he is writing a formal letter to Mrs Matlowe asking her to agree to me taking the twins for a holiday. She should receive it tomorrow morning.'

'She'll refuse, of course.'

'Unless I can persuade her sister to put in a word for me. Ida is quite a forceful personality! I also handed the solicitor a letter from my parents making the same request. It may help our cause.'

Donald frowned. 'I'm rather hoping that you won't need Marianne. My cousin is expecting a child and suffering bouts of sickness. She may give up earlier than intended and I am about to sound Marianne out about taking Judith's place. She's very bright and she's been helpful throughout the last few weeks – and she can type!'

Richard's face fell. 'Actually I was going to ask her to travel with us, spend a week with the family and travel back. Hmm. When and if we are allowed to take them out of the country, that is.'

Donald grinned suddenly. 'We might have to fight a duel for her!'

'I'd win!' he laughed. 'I've had fencing lessons!'

'I'd choose pistols at dawn!'

Richard shrugged. 'It's a damned nuisance that Nan and Marianne are hardly on friendly terms. God! Why is everything so difficult?'

Donald hesitated. 'I'm taking her out to dinner tonight. I shall bring up the question of the job here.'

Richard raised his eyebrows. 'Lucky you! If she accepts, that is. Do you think she'll abandon Edie and Emmie?'

Donald stood up and strolled to the window. 'According to Marianne, Ida is determined that they should go to school and mix more with other people. She feels that their world is too small. Not boarding school, but a good private school somewhere nearby where they could attend daily. Of course, this is not the time to raise the question – it would give Mrs Matlowe another heart attack! But as soon as she improves . . .' He left it unfinished.

'They certainly are very isolated,' Richard agreed reluctantly. 'Our education system is much more relaxed. Not nearly so uptight.'

Donald said, 'Our education system is the best in the world! Ask anyone!'

'Here we go again!' Richard laughed and glanced up at the clock. 'Ten to one already. Let's go and find some lunch.'

It was almost eight o'clock before Donald and Marianne were seated at the small Italian restaurant Donald had

chosen. Marianne felt comfortable from the moment she
stepped inside as they were greeted by a friendly 'Italian'
waiter who showed them to a table in a secluded corner of
the room. Donald whispered to her that his name was Harry
and his accent was false, but she preferred to give him the
benefit of the doubt. An overhead fan controlled the temperature, bright red gingham tablecloths covered the tables and
the walls were painted with scenes from Italian life. Several
lobsters wallowed in a nearby tank and Marianne looked
away.

He said, 'Richard came into the office this morning and
told me about the trip to see Ivy Busby. I'm so sorry you
were upset – and so is he. Have the twins recovered?'

She told him briefly about Frederika's mean trick and
he rolled his eyes. 'So not all sweetness and light at
Number 24!'

'Sadly not. I daresay they get on each other's nerves at
times.'

'So how would you feel if you and the nanny were stuck
on the *Mauretania* for a week?'

'I might go quietly mad!' she admitted. 'In the nanny's
mind I work for the enemy so that puts me on the wrong
side. But will she be going on the ship? She seemed
terribly frail to me and I believe the Atlantic can be very
rough.'

Donald was looking at her intently. 'I'd rather you didn't
go,' he said bluntly. 'I know I have no right to ask but I'm
going to anyway.' He reached across the table and laid a
hand over hers. 'I'm offering you the job with Watson
Investigations – it will be vacant when Judith gives up. I
think that's going to be sooner than we expected because
she is feeling very unwell at the moment.'

She could not resist glancing at his hand as it lay over
hers but he immediately took it away.

'I'm sorry, Marianne. That was too forward of me. I'm
an idiot.'

She smiled. 'I rather liked it,' she confessed. 'But to get
back to Watson Investigations . . . I'd like to accept but it will
depend on what happens to the twins. Ida has suggested . . .'

'That they are ready to go to school. Yes. Richard told me.'

The waiter returned to their table and handed them each a menu and Marianne wondered if Donald knew any Italian but fortunately it was in both languages. After some deliberations she chose braised liver with a salad because she thought it would be easier to manage than the various pasta dishes, which were unfamiliar to her.

'So,' she said, 'the letters I typed for you were satisfactory?'

'Quite excellent!'

'No spelling mistakes?'

'I wouldn't know! It was not my best subject at school.'

'What was your best subject?'

'Horsing around! No, actually it was mathematics.'

'Then why did you become a . . .?'

'It was my father's business. Watson and Sidden Investigations. I went into it when I left school, Sidden died soon after and my father three years ago. I'm the sole survivor but, of course, I've had Judith with me, who is very good.'

A jug of water arrived on the table accompanied by two glasses and a small bowl of olives.

'May I ask about you?' Donald asked tentatively. 'Without sounding too inquisitive?'

'Certainly. I have no dark secrets. My mother married a Frenchman and we lived mostly in France but Papa developed tuberculosis and, as the disease worsened, my mother was terrified of being widowed and alone in a foreign country so we all came back to England.'

'How old were you then?'

'I was fifteen. When the worst happened, the shock of Papa's death made her ill. The doctors called it a nervous breakdown and sadly, after that, she went rapidly downhill. I don't think she wanted to live without him.'

'So she died, leaving you alone – or do you have brothers and sisters?'

Marianne shook her head. 'I have a much older brother but he lives in India and has done for years. I was looking for a job as a companion but saw Mrs Matlowe's advertisement and thought it would be more rewarding to work with children. I had a decent education – and here I am.' She shrugged. 'Although thanks to Ida's intervention on the twins' schooling, the job may not last as long as I had hoped.'

He smiled broadly. 'But I may have a lot to thank Ida for! You might, in desperation, be driven to come and work with me.'

He's very eager, thought Marianne, flattered. She had become very attached to the twins but, if she were going to lose her job, working with Donald would be a very promising second best. She smiled. 'We'll have to wait and see what Fate has in store for us!'

The waiter reappeared and a plate of braised liver was placed before her. It looked and smelled delicious and she suddenly realized that she was hungry. A few moments passed while they explored their food and found it very good.

Then Donald said, 'I have to ask, Marianne, so do forgive me . . . Is there a man in your life? I can't believe there isn't.'

'There is no man, Donald . . . And am I to assume you are unattached?'

He nodded, grinning. 'I have one more question, which may come as a surprise . . . My mother would like you to come to lunch on Sunday.'

Marianne raised her eyebrows. 'You've told her about me?'

'No, but Judith did. She is determined that you are the ideal person to replace her here and to that end she wants us to "get along" – as she puts it. She's always insisted that she knows me better than I know myself and she may be right. She means well, Marianne, so don't think badly of her.' He refilled her water glass. 'She is meddling but with the best intentions. So what do you think, Marianne? My mother is looking forward to meeting you. Can you ask for time off?'

'I think Ida will be reasonable. She's in charge at the moment so I'll ask her. Mrs Matlowe is making very slow progress and gets agitated at times – mainly about a letter she is writing which she wants to finish. She says it's to the solicitor about her will but Ida says there is no hurry and it should wait until she is stronger.'

Abruptly Donald put down his knife and fork. 'I have this nightmare, Marianne,' he said, suddenly earnest, 'that Mrs Matlowe has another heart attack and dies . . . and Richard Preston seizes his chance and whisks the children back to America, taking you with him to look after them!' He swallowed hard, then, aware that he was being too serious, added humorously, 'I wake up screaming! The neighbours are complaining!'

Marianne tried not to laugh. 'I think perhaps a cup of Ovaltine at bedtime,' she suggested. 'Cook swears by it!'

'Marianne!'

'I'm sorry. I promise I won't disappear to the far corners of America without warning you.' She smiled. 'Does that reassure you?'

He nodded. 'It's not ideal but I'll settle for that.'

Cook was making a minced beef pie the following day when Lorna came into the kitchen with a message from Mrs Matlowe.

Holding out a key she said, 'She wants you to fetch a sealed envelope from her top drawer and a pencil and rubber and a book from the shelf which is large enough to lean the paper on . . .' She stopped for breath and, ignoring Cook's startled expression, went on. 'And you are not to open the envelope or tell her sister or Marianne about the letter or anything.'

'What on earth . . .?'

'On pain of dismissal!'

'Dismissal?' Cook regarded her with deep suspicion. 'Is this some kind of leg-pull, Lorna? Because if it is you'll regret it. I'm not in the mood for . . .'

'She said it, I swear. She said she thinks she can trust you.'

'Does she? Hmm. Who's the letter from?'

'It's not *from* anyone. The way she said it and the pencil and everything, I think she's writing it *to* someone.'

'Lordy! Now I've heard everything.' Nonplussed, she abandoned the pie and rinsed her hands under the tap. 'Best do it, I suppose, but I hope I'm not in the firing line if anyone finds out about it.'

She picked up the key and hurried upstairs, grumbling to herself about 'being put upon' and 'being made to feel deceitful'. In the study she found the sealed envelope, picked up a pencil and rubber, and after a quick search, took down an atlas from the bookshelf. 'I don't know what you're up to, Madam,' she muttered, 'but I'm not too happy about it.'

She found Mrs Matlowe in bed waiting for her. 'At last!' she said ungraciously, as Cook handed her the required objects. 'Thank you, Cook. That will be all for now.'

Cook said dubiously, 'Should you be doing this, Madam? That is, you are meant to be takings things easy.'

Ignoring the question Mrs Matlowe said, 'And no one knows about this. You've told no one?'

'No, Madam. Only me and Lorna know.' She frowned. 'Will you be able to write like that? Should I help you sit up a bit?'

'Thank you, Cook. It might be better.'

Cook did her best to raise the patient to a sitting position and was shocked to note how thin her employer had become. Normally, dressed in her usual black bombazine, Mrs Matlowe gave an impression of substance, but here in bed she seemed frail and her arms, protruding from her nightdress, looked thin and somehow helpless. Cook felt a twinge of compassion for her. 'Do you need a bedjacket?' she asked.

'Perhaps I should. There's a blue one somewhere – sent to me by poor little Ivan's mother. She knitted it when Ida told her I was ill. She was so pleased that I took the girls to the funeral.'

Cook found it and helped Mrs Matlowe to put it on. 'Anything else while I'm here?' she asked.

'No thank you.'

As Cook reached the door she turned for a last look and Mrs Matlowe said, 'Remember!' and put a warning finger to her lips.

'I will,' Cook replied and went downstairs feeling deeply troubled.

Georgina breathed a sigh of relief as Cook's footsteps receded. 'Please God,' she whispered, 'let her keep her promise not to tell a soul. If she does keep it I shall give her a small raise for her loyalty.'

She planned to write the last few pages of her confession in pencil and to copy it in ink as soon as she was up and about again.

I was walking in the garden one day, trying to think of a way to make Leonora's body stay down in the water out of sight. One glimpse at her corpse was as much as I could bear. I knew there was no way I could move it from the boat house altogether so I would have to keep it out of sight below the water. I was standing beside the rockery when the idea came to me. I would use some of the rocks to wedge her in the punt then use the rest to sink the punt with her in it. After some thought I decided to come down in the early hours when no one was about and somehow get Leonora's body into the punt. I knew it would be a difficult and utterly revolting task but I felt that it was part of my punishment from God and I deserved it. I promised myself that I would not utter a word of complaint . . .

Georgina sat back against the pillow, breathing deeply as her mind replayed the ghastly scene. She wished she had asked Cook to bring up a pot of tea but it was too late now and she would press on until it was finished.

That night I crept out of the house and down to the boat house. It was a very dark night and I could use no light in case I was seen by someone, so as I let myself in to the boat house I was glad that the worst of the scene would be masked by the gloom. I had no wish to see Leonora's face. First I had to pull her out of the water and on to the wooden walkway, which was a mammoth task. I was revolted by the thought of touching her and when at last my outstretched hand caught hold of her floating body, I touched only her sodden clothing and pulled her towards the walkway . . .

Georgina shuddered at the memory, dropped the pencil

and covered her face with her hands. Her heart was
racing and her insides seemed to churn as she relived the
nightmare moments.

Keep calm, she told herself. *Mr Prendergast told me to
be kind to my heart. I must not get upset.* Was she being
kind to her heart by writing her confession? Definitely not!
But there was no way round it. She reminded herself that
she was obeying her conscience and that was of paramount
importance in the sight of the Lord.

*Somehow I dragged the body on to the walkway and
then I used the boat hook to pull the punt towards me. Even
now I can't imagine how I managed to roll Leonora into
the punt but I did. I was by then very sick and shivering
with revulsion and exhausted by my efforts . . .*

By this time the moon had moved across the sky and had
begun to shine in at one of the far windows, giving the interior of the boat house a ghostly glow, which was too much
for Georgina to bear and she suddenly gave in to her emotions
and fled from the place, stopping only to throw a few old
sacks over Leonora's inert form. She locked the door and
crept back to the house where she poured herself a large glass
of brandy and stumbled up the stairs to her bedroom . . .

A timid knock at the door now startled her, breaking into
her memories. Quickly she pushed paper and pencil under
the pillow and arranged her features into what she hoped
was a neutral expression. 'Come in!'

It was Lorna with a tray. 'Cook thought you might fancy
a pot of tea,' she said.

'Oh! How terribly kind of her! I appreciate the thought.
Please thank her for me, Lorna. Would you pour me a cup
and then I needn't balance the tray on the bedclothes. Two
sugars, Lorna. Ah! Garibaldi biscuits!' She forced a smile.
'My favourites.'

Really, she thought gratefully, she may have underesti-
mated her staff. They were being very kind. She sipped the
tea and declared it suitable. 'You may take the pot and the
tray. I shan't want a second cup. Oh! And Lorna, please ask
Marianne to come at four thirty. I want to speak with her.'

As soon as she had gone, Georgina finished the tea and

set the empty cup on the bedside table. She resumed her
letter.

*The next night I finished what I had started. I carried the
rocks from the rockery into the boat house and piled them
over Leonora's body. It seemed at first that the weight was
never going to sink it but at last, with a horrible gurgle, the
punt slipped sideways, righted itself again and tipped down
at the end near her feet. In an instant she was gone and I
breathed a sigh of relief, knowing – or rather imagining – that
she would never be seen again . . .*

She added a few more lines then signed it, then, on
reflection, added a few more.

*This confession is written to ease my conscience before
God and in the hope that the girls will never have to grow
up believing that their mother abandoned them. My son's
daughters deserve better than that – and so that the police
will never again believe that my son was responsible in any
way for Leonora's death. I alone am guilty . . .*

Marianne went up promptly at half past four and found
Georgina sitting up with an envelope in her hand.

'I want you to replace this in the top right-hand drawer
of my desk,' she told Marianne. 'It is sealed and addressed
to my sister and I trust you not to attempt to open it. It is
to do with my will and is of no interest to anyone else.
When you have relocked the drawer bring me the key. Then
I want you to go round to the doctor and ask him for some
more sleeping pills. Tell him I have been taking a tablet
each day after lunch so that I could sleep throughout the
afternoon.'

'Two a day? Oh, but . . .'

Georgina held up a hand. 'It's none of your business,
Marianne, how I take my medicine. The doctor will understand that the days are long and boring and if I'm awake
all afternoon I simply fret and that is bad for my health.
And bring the tablets straight to me. Ida means well but
she has always been interfering and I don't want her to
know. Is that understood?'

'Yes, Mrs Matlowe.'

'And when you bring me the pills you can bring me up to date on the twins' progress. There has been a lot of disruption in the household, which is not good for them, but hopefully that wretched Preston will soon take himself back to America.' She dabbed at her forehead with a handkerchief. 'We shall be well rid of him.'

Saturday came and with it a visit from Richard Preston which took them all by surprise. He bought carnations for the invalid and a game of bat and ball for the girls and, while Lorna found a suitable vase for the flowers, he, Ida and Marianne were soon sharing a table on the terrace and were in earnest conversation while Emmie and Edie were given time to play in the garden with their new game.

'I'm sorry about the way Nan reacted to you, Marianne,' Richard told her again. 'It was quite wrong of her, but I do want to try again with her and wonder, if the twins came with me to see her without a chaperone . . .' He gave a wry grin and left the sentence unfinished. 'If not, I'm really at a loss to know what to do next. If Mrs Matlowe is refusing to let me take the girls home with me for a few weeks and if Nan is refusing to travel with Marianne – which I'm afraid she is at the moment . . .' He looked at her apologetically. 'I don't know where to turn for advice.'

Ida said, 'Poor you! It's a fair old pickle, one way and another.'

Marianne said, 'I understand she was jealous and I can forgive that, but I can't imagine the two of us getting along – and then there's the twins to think about. They've never once mentioned their nanny since that day and when I tentatively raised the subject they went very quiet and looked at each other.'

Ida laughed. 'I know that look! My advice, Richard, for what it's worth, is to persuade your parents to come over to England to see them here.'

He shook his head. 'My father is too ill and Mother would never leave him.'

Ida shook her head. 'Best laid plans . . .'

He nodded. 'It's so frustrating.'

Marianne said, 'Do you really believe that your nanny will survive the long crossing?'

'I'm not at all sure, but she won't hear of anything else and I can't let her down. She thinks she still has a role to play in their lives.'

Ida surprised them. 'If it were not for my sister I would volunteer to come with the girls – it might be the only way Georgina would agree to let them go – but I can't leave her with this heart problem.'

'She may believe,' Marianne ventured, 'that she might have a heart attack and die while the twins are away. It might make her more determined than ever to keep them here.'

Ida sent Marianne inside to ask for lemonade and biscuits and when she returned with the tray Ida sprang her next surprise. 'Maybe it would make more sense, Richard, in view of all the problems we have at the moment, to let the girls go to America when they are a little older. They might appreciate everything more . . . cope with the changes better. They've led a very sheltered life here.' She glanced at Richard. 'It also might be a good idea to let the dust settle, as they say. Would you consider that?'

He hesitated, thrown by the suggestion.

Ida pressed on. 'The point is that if my sister is not going to recover her full strength – and it does look a little uncertain – I shall make it a condition that I stay with her only if the twins start to attend a normal school.' She looked at Marianne. 'That's not intended as a criticism of your work with them, but they should be widening their experiences, Marianne, and learning to be around other children.'

There was a startled silence. Marianne's first thought was that, if the suggestion were taken up by the girls' grandmother, she herself would be free to accept the job with Donald, but she said nothing.

Ida continued. 'I don't mean sending them to boarding school. I mean a very good private school that takes day girls as well as boarders. Cook says there is such a school by the name of Dewsbury Girls' Preparatory, which is just within walking distance. Of course it depends if they have any vacancies, but we could investigate the idea.'

Before anyone could reply, the telephone in the house . rang and Lorna came hurrying out.

'It's for Mr Preston,' she told them breathlessly. 'From Number 24. They said it's urgent!'

'That's Nan!' Richard jumped to his feet and followed her back into the house leaving Marianne and Ida exchanging looks of alarm.

Then Ida raised her eyebrows and whispered, 'If the old girl has died it might be God's will!'

Marianne considered several comments but uttered none of them.

Richard appeared in some distress. 'It's Nan. She's had a stroke and they've taken her to the cottage hospital. Please excuse me. I'll have to dash!'

Just then Emmie and Edie arrived at the table saying they were thirsty and eyeing the jug of lemonade.

Ida smiled, 'Go and ask Cook for two more mugs and then you can join us. It's a good thing we didn't eat all the biscuits!'

FOURTEEN

That night Georgina waited until the house was quiet and the church clock had struck midnight, then she put her plan into action. She now had nearly a hundred sleeping pills – the small lie had served her well, she thought – and she made her way in her bare feet along the passage to the bathroom at the far end. There she locked the door, poured herself a glass of water and began to swallow the tablets, two at a time.

It was strange to be on her feet again and she did feel a little unsteady, but that was of no concern. The purpose of the exercise, she reminded herself, was to apparently slip away in her sleep so that everyone would believe she had died a natural death. They would read the letter and discover the truth about Leonora and that would be bad enough. She did not want to add the crime of suicide to her legacy because she was trying to save the twins from any more grief. She had caused them enough damage.

When she had taken all the pills she waited for a moment to see if anything immediate happened but, finding that she felt no different, she unlocked the bathroom door and began the slow journey towards the stairs. They would be the worst hurdle, she knew, but she was determined to die in Neil's bed in his room. That way she could talk to him until the end came, knowing that he understood exactly what she was doing and why – and that he forgave her.

Making her way up the stairs was more difficult than she had imagined and took a deal longer but, pausing on every other step to catch her breath, she gradually reached the second landing. Only yards to go, she told herself.

'Come on, Georgina! You can do it. You *have* to do it!'

Gathering her remaining strength, she struggled slowly and silently to the door of Neil's room and then reached into the pocket of her dressing gown for the key.

Minutes later, to her great relief, she had opened the
curtains and had then managed to climb up on to the bed
and was now snuggled down beneath the sheets. She smiled.
'Were you helping me, Neil?' she asked. 'I don't think
I could have done it without you. I knew I could rely on
you. You were always so dependable, dear.'

Well, maybe not always, she amended silently. He had
not been dependable when he had gone rushing away to
look for Leonora, but that was all in the past and she had
never reproached him.

She paused to consider how she felt. Out of breath and
totally exhausted, but she had expected her heart to be
racing and it felt no different. Probably because she had
taken the journey very slowly and sensibly. 'I did, Neil,'
she told him. 'I planned it all and I did it. Poor Marianne
believed my little story and went trotting off to the doctor.
Not that he was there – they never are in an emergency!'
She gave a little laugh to reassure her son that she was not
suffering in any way but simply carrying out what she
thought of as 'the grand design'. 'But she saw the doctor's
wife who was very helpful and looked up my pills in my
notes and counted them out for me. I believe she used to
be a nurse before she married . . . I do hope no one blames
poor Marianne.'

The room was lit by moonlight and she gazed round at
the familiar room with pleasure. As she did so her heart
gave a little jump. 'Too late!' she told it. 'I'm ahead of
you!'

Soon she would be with her son and her husband and all
the unpleasantness would be a thing of the past. She would
not even remember it. Heaven was exactly that – peace and
love.

Georgina closed her eyes. 'Not long, dear,' she told him
and wondered what would happen in the morning when
they found her.

It was seven o'clock next morning before the doctor's wife
remembered to tell her husband about Mrs Matlowe's
sleeping pills and then he swore under his breath, tugged

on his clothes and, ignoring his wife's plea for an explanation, raced out of the house and along the road, round the corner and up to The Poplars, by which time his own sixty-year-old heart was thumping uncomfortably. Muttering yet another curse, he hammered impatiently on the door with the brass knocker and then put his finger on the bell and left it there.

Ida reached the door first and opened it. The doctor gasped, 'Where's Mrs Matlowe? Is she all right? This pill business . . .' He gulped for air. 'It sounds suspicious . . . I don't like the sound of it!'

Ida stammered, 'Where is she? Why, in bed of course. Where else can she be?'

'And is she . . .?' He paused for breath and quickly repeated what his wife had told him. 'Sometimes, when a patient asks for extra pills it can be . . . ominous, if you get my meaning. Do me a favour, will you, and go up to her. I just want to be reassured there is nothing amiss.'

Needing no extra persuading, Ida hurried up the stairs and knocked on her sister's door. When the knock wasn't answered, her own alarm increased and when she saw the empty bed she screamed. The doctor at once hurried up the stairs and for a moment they both stared at the empty bed.

She would have no cause to use the bathroom, thought Ida, because there was a commode next to the bed.

'Where could she have gone?' the doctor asked, his face pale.

'There's another bedroom!' Ida led the way and, quietly opening the door, they gazed at the still form in Neil's bed.

Ida put a hand to her heart. 'Thank the Lord!' she whispered, but the doctor took a few tentative steps into the room. He saw that Georgina Matlowe clutched a bible between her hands.

'Dear God!' he muttered. There was no sign of movement, no rise and fall of the bed clothes. 'I'm very much afraid . . .' Then he stepped forward and gently laid his knuckles against the calm face. He shook his head and took one of her wrists in his fingers and waited for the pulse that did not come. 'Too late!' he said and walked stiffly towards the window where he stood looking down into the garden while he tried to compose himself.

Ida cried, 'Oh no! *Georgina!*' She stood beside her and, snatching up the bible, laid it on the bedside table. Falling to her knees she laid her face against Georgina's hand and began to cry.

The doctor waited until the worst was over but he felt his own despair – the sense of failure he always felt when he lost a patient.

Marianne had been in the kitchen making an early cup of tea for herself before supervising the twins' breakfast but now she arrived on the second landing in time to hear the shocking news. After a moment she said faintly, 'The letter! I wonder . . .'

Ida seized on the words. 'What letter? Marianne, what are you saying?'

The doctor drew a sharp breath. Marianne told them about the letter Georgina had been writing the previous day.

She looked at the doctor. 'Are you thinking it was a suicide note? I don't think so. She said it was her will.'

Ida said, 'Please fetch it at once.' As Marianne made a move towards the door Ida said, 'On second thoughts we had better all go down to the study.' To the doctor she said, 'Do you need or wish to be there?'

'If it is a suicide note then yes, I'm sorry, but I need to report it. A crime will have been committed.'

Minutes later they were all sitting in the study. Ida had read the first few pages aloud and they were all consumed with deep dismay.

Ida's voice faltered. For once she felt completely out of her depth. Turning to Marianne she said, 'I have a bad feeling about this. Do you think Richard Preston should be here?'

Marianne hesitated. Shocked, she was unable to think clearly, and both women glanced at the doctor for help.

The doctor said, 'I think perhaps we should read it to the end before we involve anyone else. You will need to know

exactly what happened to Mrs Matlowe's daughter-in-law
– and it's my job to write the death certificate for Mrs
Matlowe.'

Grateful for his advice Ida rallied. 'Then we'll finish
reading it – although the letter so far fills me with dread.'

By the time she reached the end of Georgina's confession Ida's worst fears had been realized.

She whispered, 'Marianne, will you please telephone
Richard Preston at his hotel and break the news. He will
have to know. And so will Cook and Lorna.'

Marianne stammered, 'But what on earth shall I say to
him? I don't want to be the one to tell him . . .'

Ida was staring at the letter. 'It was an accident,' she said.
'Leonora's death was an accident. It wasn't deliberate. It
wasn't murder! Georgina would never . . . I mean, she was
not a violent person.'

The doctor sighed. 'But she lied to the police at the time
of the disappearance and thus interfered with the investigation. She caused a death, which is manslaughter, and in
her panic, she hid the crime.'

Ida, still dazed by the revelations, shook her head. 'And
made it look like a betrayal on Leonora's part! Oh! Whatever
will Richard say when he knows?'

The doctor glanced at Marianne. 'It may be best to call
him with the news.' To Ida he said, 'If it would help you,
I will stay a little longer. My presence may prove a sobering
influence – to hopefully avoid any unnecessary histrionics.'

Ida agreed gratefully and Marianne went reluctantly
downstairs to the telephone.

She felt a rush of compassion for the young man when
she heard his voice and recalled that he had probably spent
hours at the hospital with Ivy Busby. When she announced
herself she assumed she had called about the hospital patient
and said, 'She's in a very bad way, Marianne. She may not
recover but if she does she will be severely handicapped.
I can imagine her distress – her speech is impaired as well
as her movements. She will be heartbroken to realize that
there is no way she can come back to America with me. I
cannot imagine . . .'

'Richard, I have to stop you.' Marianne's voice shook. 'I have more bad news.'

'More? What has happened?'

'Mrs Matlowe has died of an overdose and has left a . . . a very revealing letter. The doctor is here and we think you should come right away, if you can. The letter concerns your sister.'

There was a long silence.

'Marianne, are you saying that there's a connection between them – between the letter and Leonora?'

'Yes, I suppose I am.' She closed her eyes. 'Richard, please don't ask me for any more details. You will have to read it for yourself.'

'So this is very bad?'

'Yes. Can you come?' When he made no answer she added, 'You came to England to find out what happened to Leonora. Now we know.' She replaced the phone and paused to steady herself before making her way to the kitchen. Marianne said simply that there had been a serious problem and the doctor was in the study with Ida.

'I shall be with the children for the moment,' she told them, 'and I think you should send up their breakfast as usual.'

Twenty minutes later Richard arrived to find that Marianne was with the children and Ida and the doctor were waiting for him in the study. In the meantime Ida had finished rereading the letter and now, without a word, she handed it to Richard.

The doctor was writing out a death certificate when Richard gave a cry of anguish and broke down in tears. Ida, keen to escape the worst of the storm, hurried downstairs and asked Cook to send up a tray of tea for three. 'On second thoughts use the large teapot and send crockery for four. Mr Preston is going to need a cup of tea.'

'Marianne said it was serious,' Cook prompted.

'That was an understatement,' Ida said, her voice hoarse. 'My sister is dead. I can't say more now as the doctor is waiting for me.'

'Dead?' Cook stared at her. 'But I thought . . . that is, we were talking yesterday and reckoned she was on the mend. Being sensible and taking it easy like she was told.'

'It has taken us all by surprise.' Ida turned and made her way back to the study.

In her absence the doctor had turned Georgina on to her back and had drawn up the sheet to cover her face. 'I'll go now,' he said, 'if you'll forgive me for changing my mind. But I have a surgery at eight thirty and must write out the police report on this occurrence before my patients start arriving. The sooner the police decide how they want to treat this revelation, the better it will be for all of you.'

Marianne was waiting for him at the bottom of the stairs.

'Doctor, I do hope you are not blaming your wife in any way for what has happened. She was simply trying to help me with the problem of the pills.'

He patted her arm. 'Thank you for your concern but I'll see to it that she is not held responsible. She acted in good faith.'

Back in the schoolroom with the twins, Marianne cleared away the breakfast things and set them some sums to do. As she turned to go Edie said, 'What's happening, Marianne? Lorna said there's been a disaster.'

Emmie said, 'A disaster is something terrible, isn't it? Like . . . like a house falling down or a flood.'

Faced with two pairs of anxious eyes, Marianne did not want to lie to them. 'Your Aunt Ida is going to tell you all about it very soon,' she told them.

Ida was on her way to the schoolroom as Marianne carried the breakfast tray downstairs and Marianne warned her that the children were full of questions.

'They don't miss much, bless them!' Ida said. 'I asked Richard if he wanted to break the news to them as he is their uncle and I am only a great-aunt. He thinks I will do a better job. He is dreadfully shaken by the letter but he came for the truth and now we have it. Spare him a few comforting words, Marianne. He has an awful lot on his shoulders.'

In the study Richard turned towards her, his face etched with bitterness. 'So it was her! I should have guessed. Neil's wonderful mother! It's a good job he died before the truth came out!'

'I'm so sorry, Richard. I wish things could have turned out differently. I hope we can somehow soften the blow for the children.'

'I want her punished for what she did to Leonora but she has managed to escape the net.' He shrugged. 'Dying peacefully in her sleep. She didn't deserve it. Leonora didn't die peacefully, did she? She was murdered.'

'No! It was an accident, Richard.'

'So she says. I think otherwise!'

Marianne regarded him sadly. She wanted to offer words of comfort but nothing she could say would lessen the agony of mind that now burdened him. It was easier for him to hate than to grieve, she assumed, at least for the present.

'We can't change the past, Richard. Somehow we have to go on. You still have Leonora's beautiful daughters. In the circumstances Ida may agree to let them go to America. The sooner the better. She might come with them – she no longer has to care for her sister. They could have a month or so and then return to start their new school in the autumn.'

He frowned. 'I want to be here for Leonora when they . . . when she is brought up from that damned boat house. To think she has been there all this time and I didn't know!'

'Is that how you want to remember her, Richard? Being dragged to the surface of the water. Do you think she would want you to watch something like that? Why not take the girls away from it all and show them America where their mother was brought up? Where she was happy. Where she and Neil met and fell in love. Show them all the family photographs and the family pets. I think your sister would want you to put Emmie and Edie before anything else.'

Marianne saw that he was reconsidering – or hoped he was. She stepped nearer and put her arms around him. He was shaking and she held him closer.

Suddenly he stepped back a little and looked at her. 'You could come with them, Marianne, instead of Ida.'

She shook her head. 'Ida would be better,' she explained.

'It would be a reconciliation for the two families. Ida was in no way to blame for what happened. She's a good person.'

Downstairs the telephone trilled and Lorna came up to say it was Donald Watson to speak to her. Marianne gave Richard a quick kiss and a smile. She went down to face the start of what she knew would be two weeks or more of hectic activity involving the police, the solicitors and the coroner's court, not forgetting Georgina Matlowe's funeral, which, because of the unusual circumstances, would almost certainly be delayed. She quailed at the thought of it but then told herself firmly that it would, it *must,* eventually come to an end. One day the worst would be over and she had a new life to look forward to.

EPILOGUE

Almost a year to the day later Marianne Watson, busy in the office with the three letters Donald had left her, became aware of a familiar clatter of footsteps on the stairs and paused in her work. There was no knock on the door and before she could call 'Come in!' Emmie and Edie erupted into the room with squeals of excitement. Now nearly nine, they looked very grown up in their school uniforms, complete with hats and blazers. They wore navy blue drill slips over white blouses and the badge on the blazer pockets read Dewsbury Girls' Preparatory.

'How nice to see you both,' Marianne cried, holding out her arms for a joint hug. 'I suppose today was your last day at school.'

'It is,' Emmie informed her, 'but we were allowed to leave an hour early – so here we are! Where's Mr Watson?'

'He's with a client but he'll be back later.' She smiled. She felt the usual tug at the heart as she looked at them. She had grown fond of them but, with things the way they were, she now spent little time with them – although the previous week they had spent a day together at the Henley Royal Regatta. Cook had prepared a delicious picnic and Ida, Marianne and the girls had settled themselves on deck chairs on the riverbank, below the Chinese lanterns, from where they could watch all the river craft with their eager passengers. It was a magical day that Marianne would cherish in her memory.

None of them had understood the technicalities of the various races or the vagaries of winds and currents but the atmosphere had been exciting and the four of them had returned home pleasantly weary.

Emmie said, 'We told our teacher about the regatta and all the races . . .'

'But we couldn't remember who won them but Miss Riley said it didn't matter . . .'

'And we drew some pictures to take to poor Nan, to cheer her up. Aunt Ida says she hasn't long to go so we must be very kind to her.' Briefly Emmie looked suitably chastened but quickly brightened.

Edie lowered her voice. 'We didn't tell Cook about her aspic jelly melting . . .'

'And all the tiny vegetables floating about!' Emmie giggled. 'I liked the strawberries and cream best.'

'I liked the fairy lights on the bridge when it started to get dark. It looked like fairyland.'

Marianne said, 'Your Aunt Ida tells me you are off to America again soon. Won't that be wonderful?'

Edie nodded, 'She is really our great-aunt but if we call her that it makes her feel old.'

Emmie said, 'We shall see our kitten again – the one Grandmother Preston bought for us . . .'

'. . . but he'll be a grown-up cat now,' Edie reminded her, 'because we can only see him once a year in the summer holiday.' To Marianne she said, 'We call him Stripy because he's tabby with lots of nice stripes . . .'

'Like a tiger.'

'And Mr Barnes has given us a photograph of our mother and father in a lovely silver frame and we can keep it!'

Emmie nodded, smiling. 'Mother was very pretty and she is holding us both and smiling at our father. Aunt Ida says she was very happy. They both were.'

'How lovely! Mr Barnes is very kind.'

Emmie nodded then sat down on the client's chair and adopted a serious expression. 'We've come to see you, Marianne, because we want you to investigate something for us.'

'Really? And what is it – this "something"?' Marianne kept her face straight with an effort.

'Something very strange has happened to our roses – the

ones that Grandmother bought for us when we were babies. They've moved.'

Edie nodded earnestly. 'We will pay you out of our pocket money if you take on the case.'

Marianne's heart missed a beat as she was instantly jolted back to a time she would rather forget. For a moment she regretted having explained her new work to the twins in such detail, but they had been intrigued by her move from The Poplars when she ceased to be their governess.

'Well,' she said, playing for time. 'I'll ask Mr Watson if we have time but we are very busy.'

Emmie said, 'The roses have changed places! Aunt Ida thinks we're imagining things but we're not.'

Edie regarded her earnestly. 'We didn't say they could move. They just did. We asked Mr Blunt if he did it but he shook his head and said it was a complete mystery and when he saw what had happened you could have blown him down with a feather!'

Marianne stifled a groan. Some matters were definitely best forgotten, she reflected, but she now had visions of being asked for the result of the 'investigation', as soon as the twins returned from America. Better to nip the idea in the bud now, she decided.

'We'll do our best,' she promised, 'but I have to warn you that some strange things are so very strange that they are never explained. Never. We investigators call those "unsolved cases". They are very special cases. It's like a riddle that can never be solved. Your mystery might be like that.'

Edie looked pleased by the prospect and glanced at her sister. 'A very special case!' she said.

At that moment there were more footsteps and Ida appeared in the doorway. She smiled at Marianne but shooed the twins out of the office. 'We're off tomorrow,' she said. 'Lots of packing to do this evening!'

Marianne said, 'Have a safe journey and give my kind regards to Richard when you see him.'

'I will, Marianne, and we'll see you when we get back.

You and Donald must come to tea with us before the girls start school again.'

Marianne listened to their cheerful chatter as they went downstairs. Ida's life had been transformed and Marianne almost envied her – travelling to and fro across the Atlantic – but then she glanced down at her wedding ring. With a contented sigh, she once more applied herself to the type-writer. She told herself that she was very happy to be where she was and nothing and no one could ever tempt her to be anywhere else.